Death in the Spotlight

Also by Robin Stevens

Murder Is Bad Manners
Poison Is Not Polite
First Class Murder
Jolly Foul Play
Mistletoe and Murder
A Spoonful of Murder

ROBIN STEVENS

Simon & Schuster Books for Young Readers

New York   London   Toronto   Sydney   New Delhi

SIMON & SCHUSTER BOOKS FOR YOUNG READERS
An imprint of Simon & Schuster Children's Publishing Division
1230 Avenue of the Americas, New York, New York 10020
This book is a work of fiction. Any references to historical events, real people,
or real places are used fictitiously. Other names, characters, places, and events
are products of the author's imagination, and any resemblance to actual events
or places or persons, living or dead, is entirely coincidental.
Text © 2018 by Robin Stevens
Originally published in Great Britain in 2018 by Puffin Books
First US edition April 2023
Jacket illustration and design and interior maps © 2023 by Elizabeth Baddeley
All rights reserved, including the right of reproduction in whole or in part in any form.
SIMON & SCHUSTER BOOKS FOR YOUNG READERS
and related marks are trademarks of Simon & Schuster, Inc.
For information about special discounts for bulk purchases, please contact
Simon & Schuster Special Sales at 1-866-506-1949 or business@simonandschuster.com.
The Simon & Schuster Speakers Bureau can bring authors to your live event.
For more information or to book an event, contact the Simon & Schuster Speakers Bureau
at 1-866-248-3049 or visit our website at www.simonspeakers.com.
Interior design by Krista Vossen
The text for this book was set in Goudy Oldstyle.
Manufactured in the United States of America
0323 FFG
2 4 6 8 10 9 7 5 3 1
CIP data for this book is available from the Library of Congress.
ISBN 9781665919371
ISBN 9781665919395 (ebook)

To my father.

Thank you for being so proud of me.

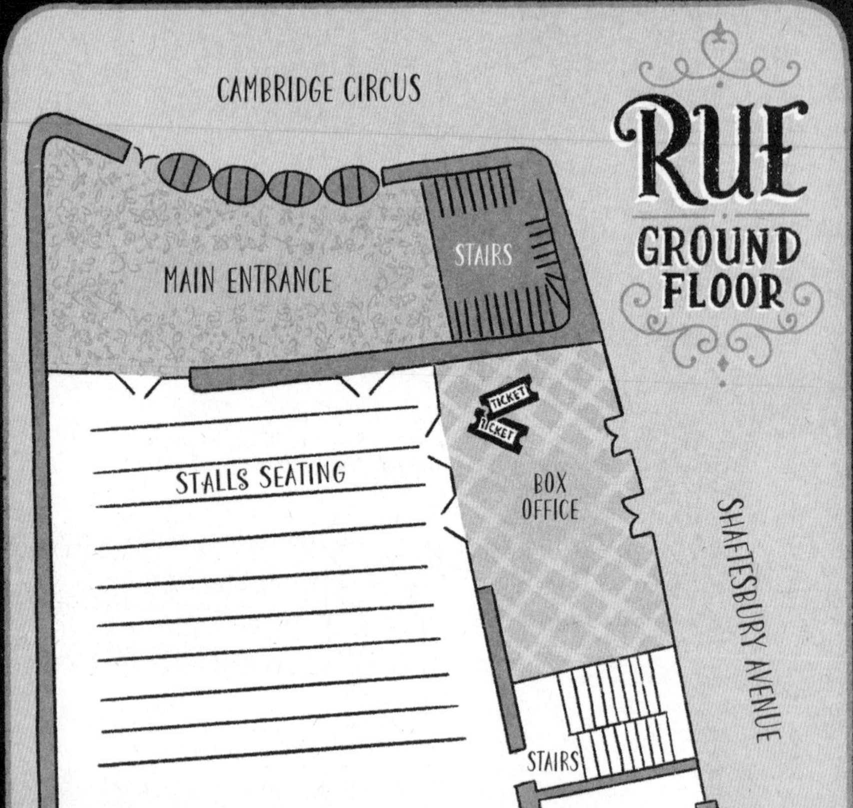
RUE
GROUND FLOOR
CAMBRIDGE CIRCUS
MAIN ENTRANCE
STAIRS
TICKET
TICKET
BOX OFFICE
STALLS SEATING
SHAFTESBURY AVENUE
STAIRS
STEPS
STEPS
ORCHESTRA PIT
PROP ROOM
DOWNSTAGE
PROMPT CORNER
ROSE'S DRESSING ROOM
STAGE LEFT
STAGE
STAGE RIGHT
UPSTAGE
WARDROBE SPACE AND PROPS
BED-ROOM
MAIL ROOM
STAGE DOOR ENTRANCE
JIM'S CUBBY

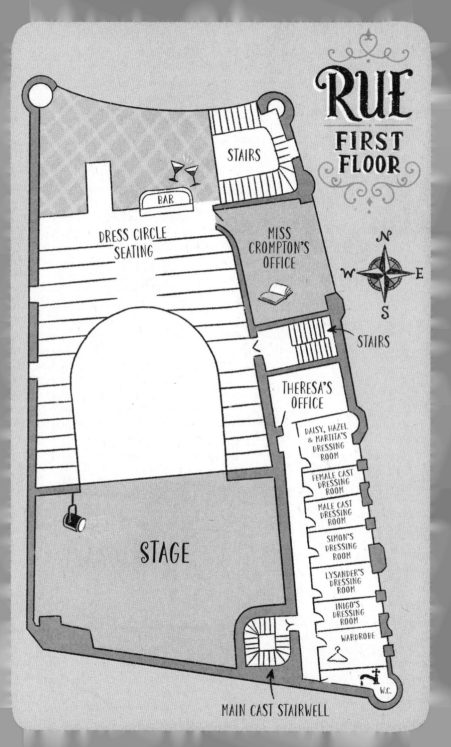

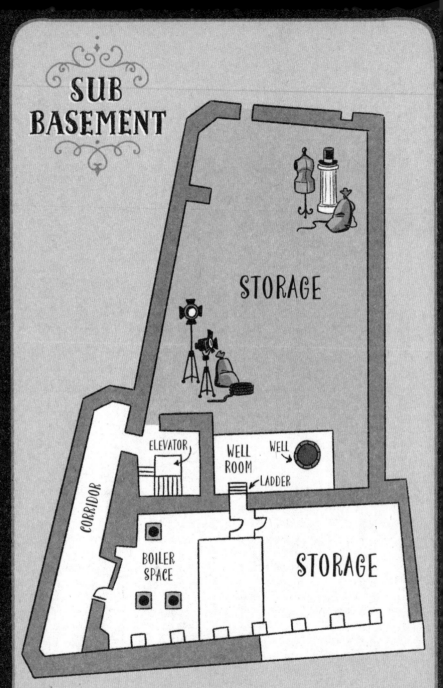

MAP OF LONDON

SOHO

TOTTENHAM COURT ROAD (STATION)

SHAFTESBURY AVENUE

TRAFALGAR SQUARE

RUSSELL SQUARE

WHITEHALL

COVENT GARDEN

HIGH HOLBORN

THEOBALDS ROAD

WESTMINSTER BRIDGE

RIVER THAMES

1. UNCLE FELIX AND AUNT LUCY'S FLAT
2. THE BRITISH MUSEUM
3. FOYLES BOOKSHOP
4. THE RUE THEATRE
5. BIG BEN (THE HOUSES OF PARLIAMENT)
6. MISS CROMPTON'S FLAT
7. CAMBRIDGE CIRCUS

— — —

Death in the Spotlight

Being an account of
The Case of the <u>Romeo and Juliet</u>
Murder,
an investigation by the Wells & Wong
Detective Society.
Written by Hazel Wong
(Detective Society Vice President and
Secretary), age fourteen.
Begun Sunday, May 24, 1936.

CHARACTER LIST

THE RUE THEATRE

Frances Crompton: Owner of the Rue

Theresa Johnson: Stage manager of the Rue

Inigo Leontes: Director at the Rue and actor, playing the role of Friar Lawrence

Rose Tree: Actress, playing the role of Juliet

Lysander Tollington: Actor, playing the role of Romeo

Simon Carver: Actor, playing the role of Mercutio

Martita Torrera: Actress, playing the role of Juliet's Nurse

Daisy Wells: Actress, playing the part of Rosaline and Paris's Page, and president of the Detective Society

Hazel Wong: Actress, playing the role of Potpan, and vice president and secretary of the Detective Society

Annie Joy: Dresser

Jim Cotter: Stage door

UNCLE FELIX'S HOUSEHOLD

Felix Mountfitchet: Daisy's uncle

Lucy Mountfitchet: Daisy's aunt

Bridget O'Connell: Felix and Lucy's maid

Part One
A Tale of More Woe

My name is Hazel Wong, and I am a detective.

When Daisy and I first began investigating, it simply did not seem possible that someone like me *could* detect mysteries. But now I cannot imagine my life without Daisy Wells and the Detective Society, without strange events and awful danger and horrid, heart-pounding surprises. There is always a moment, deep in the midst of a case, when I think that I never want to detect another one. But all the same, if more than a few months go by without a murder, or a theft, or a kidnapping, I begin to feel as though something is missing.

Even by Detective Society standards, though, we are having a most exciting few weeks. We are proper members of a real London theatre company, and thus closer to being grown up than ever before—and, once again, we have found ourselves faced with a ghastly and shocking crime. I do feel almost like one of the heroines of Daisy's mystery novels.

Of course, a book heroine would not have a pimple on her nose, she would not be so fond of cakes (I don't much mind about this difference: in my opinion many book heroines do not eat nearly enough), and she would have no trouble remembering her lines in a play. I have fallen short in all three of these tests, and even Daisy, with her flawless skin and her flair for drama, loves cake. So it is clear that we are real, and really facing our *seventh* murder case. I remember a time when I was surprised we had even got to three.

I ought to explain exactly how we came to be sitting in the dusty, greasepaint-smelling stalls of the Rue Theatre, while a large, blue-hatted policeman stamps about onstage and shouts at us all to *sit tight and not go anywhere.*

Of course, the policeman is here today, and so are we, because of the corpse—which is not a pleasant thing to have to write. Dead bodies are always awful. They are my least favorite part of what Daisy and I do. Daisy is sometimes impatient with me when I say this. But, all the same, I am glad they do upset me. I do not think I would be as good a detective if I stopped caring about the victims. Murder *matters*, and bothering about it helps us solve each case.

But this mystery properly began a few weeks ago, with Daisy's aunt Lucy and uncle Felix. They are the reason why we are at the Rue, and it is funny to think that we were sent here to keep us *out* of detective trouble.

Robin Stevens

"Ooh," Daisy has just hissed under her breath from the seat next to me. "Uncle Felix *will* be annoyed, won't he? We were supposed to be safe from crimes here! Serve him right for treating us like children."

So she is thinking along the same lines as I am, as usual.

While we wait for the policeman to stop marching about and decide what to do next, I will explain all the steps leading up to the moment when the Detective Society came upon their seventh murder mystery.

D aisy and I might look like schoolgirls, but we have not been going to school very much lately. In January, my grandfather, my ah yeh, died. Daisy and I had to leave Deepdean School for Girls (where we are fourth formers), and rush to my home in Hong Kong to mourn him. By the time we came back to England, after all the awful adventures we faced in Hong Kong, it was the beginning of May, and we had missed not just the spring term but the beginning of the summer one too.

I was expecting to be sent straight back to school, but it was decided that we needed a rest after so much upsetting excitement in Hong Kong. We would not go back to Deepdean until the second half of term began, on the first of June.

I thought that we would go to Fallingford, Daisy's house—but it was all shut up, as it usually is these days. Instead, we were sent to London, to stay with Daisy's uncle

Felix and his new wife. We have been told to call the new Mrs. Mountfitchet "Aunt Lucy," and most of the time we remember.

Uncle Felix is just the same as he ever was. He is a fascinating and quite unnerving person, tall and golden like Daisy, and extremely clever too. He has a monocle that he has a habit of screwing into place over his eye and peering at me through, and he has an immensely important and secret job that we are not supposed to know anything about.

This job meant that, during the first week of our stay, he vanished for long stretches of time, returning quite unexpectedly to sweep us all out of the flat and into the glitter of London. He took us for afternoon tea at Brown's, to a magic show and the theatre, and for dinner shockingly late, at eight or nine at night, in restaurants where laughter sparkled off the golden walls, and ladies daringly showed their shoulders in evening gowns. We sipped Robinsons squash from champagne glasses, and I felt quite worldly.

While Uncle Felix was gone, we were left with Aunt Lucy. "I shall be your governess," she told us, mouth set firmly. "I have had practice, after all, and work is . . . quiet at the moment." Aunt Lucy's work is as important as Uncle Felix's, and quite as secret.

I was expecting prim and proper instruction, like porridge for the mind. But I should not have been surprised that the lessons we were given turned out to be, once again, as unusual as Aunt Lucy herself, not like the starchy Deepdean hours of Latin and Deportment and the names of kings.

Just after we arrived, Aunt Lucy found the notebook full of codes I have been practicing (and trying to make Daisy practice), and the next day my desk was filled with more code books than I had ever thought existed.

"Have a look at those," said Aunt Lucy, "and then begin to go through this exercise book. Solve what you can, and bring your work to me this afternoon."

"Dull!" said Daisy, pushing them aside to perch on my desk, but I thought them quite marvelous. I lost myself in them for hours, far past the time I would have been brave enough to be seen studying anything at Deepdean, and only stopped when my brain was humming with numbers and symbols and languages.

Daisy, meanwhile, was given a set of lessons that was quite different. She was taken into another room in the flat, filled with racks and racks of clothes and hats and wigs and drawers full of makeup. After an hour or two, a wrinkly old lady with wispy white curls and a pair of thick spectacles, bent over in a shawl, came shuffling back out, Aunt Lucy following behind her. The old lady stood by my desk, and in a creaky, wobbling voice said, "Hazel Wong! I have a message for you!"

"I know it's you, Daisy," I said to her. "I can see your shoes are the same."

Robin Stevens

"You wouldn't know if you met me on the street!" said the old lady in Daisy's voice. "I do grant you the shoes, though. Bother."

Aunt Lucy smiled at me. "Good eyes, Hazel. You're a natural. More practice needed, Daisy."

Daisy sighed impatiently, but I could see she was thrilled by Aunt Lucy's unusual lessons—particularly because they were secret. There was an unspoken agreement between the three of us that Uncle Felix need not be informed about them. He is a very interesting uncle, but an uncle all the same, and he does not really approve of our detective adventures. Aunt Lucy, we could see, understood that being detectives was not a game to us. It was simply who we were.

Still, it was Uncle Felix who had the final say while we lived with him—and Uncle Felix continued to want us far away from murder or mystery of any kind.

And then George and Alexander came to visit for Daisy's birthday party, during their Exeat weekend. Daisy has written up the case that we solved at the British Museum, so I do not need to mention it here—apart from the fact that it was very exciting, and it made Uncle Felix more worried than ever about us putting ourselves in danger.

And *that* led to the reason why the Rue Theatre was suggested.

III

It was at breakfast on Monday morning, the eleventh of May, that we first heard of it. The maid, Bridget, had just brought in the toast and a pile of cryptic telegrams, neatly decoded in Bridget's clear handwriting. In Uncle Felix and Aunt Lucy's house, everyone seems to have an interesting and secretive life, and Bridget is an interesting and secretive maid who does far more than just the cooking and the cleaning.

Uncle Felix looked up from expertly slicing the bones out of a kipper and spoke to Aunt Lucy.

"I'm glad you're with the girls again this week," he said. "They need a steady influence. The very word 'aunt' sounds sensible. I'm sure you've become more staid since you became one, Lucy dear." He winked at her over his kipper.

"That's nonsense!" said Daisy crossly. "We don't need a steady anything!"

Uncle Felix avoided her glare and Aunt Lucy put down the telegram she had been handed.

"That's a lovely sentiment, but I'm afraid I won't be able to oblige, Felix dear," she said. "Something urgent's come up at work."

"What?" said Uncle Felix sharply. "Nonsense—let me see!"

Wordlessly, Aunt Lucy gave him the telegram and he read it.

"Good grief!" he said. "How inconvenient. You're quite right. You'll be out all week."

"Ooh, what's happened?" asked Daisy. "Is it awful?"

"None of your business, niece," said Uncle Felix. "Lucy, what on earth shall we do? Could Bridget look after them?"

"I'm not a nursemaid, Mr. M.," said Bridget from the doorway. "And you know you asked me to watch those suspicious—"

"Yes, ahem, quite so, I did," said Uncle Felix, frowning her into silence.

"We shall be perfectly all right on our own!" cried Daisy. "We can explore London properly at last. How exciting!"

"You certainly shall NOT!" said Uncle Felix.

Aunt Lucy held up her hand. "Wait," she said. "I've had a thought. Let me make a few telephone calls."

She murmured something to Uncle Felix and then went out into the hall. Twenty minutes later, she was back, looking serene.

"Felix dear, you want the girls to be watched over in an enclosed space, do you not?" she asked.

Uncle Felix nodded.

"And Daisy, you want excitement, don't you?"

"Naturally!" said Daisy.

"And Hazel, you love stories?"

"Yes?" I said cautiously.

"Well then," said Aunt Lucy, "I think I have found the perfect solution for everyone. There's a girl at work whose aunt is Frances Crompton, the owner of the Rue Theatre. Frances is putting on a new production of *Romeo and Juliet*, but with the flu that's going round this spring she keeps on losing actors. All the usual bit-part players have been snapped up by other theatres—they can afford to pay better, and poor Frances is in a bit of a bind financially at the moment. Under the circumstances, I thought she might not mind looking after two temporary cast members—for a small fee, of course. And she agreed."

"Lucy!" said Uncle Felix. "Well, I suppose they'll be looked after there, at least."

Daisy's eyes were widening, and she looked from Aunt Lucy to Uncle Felix and back again. "What—*us?*" she asked. "*Really?*"

"Really, Daisy," said Aunt Lucy. "Have you heard of Frances Crompton?"

Robin Stevens

"Of *course* I have!" gasped Daisy. "Why, she's famous! The Rue Theatre might be going through a difficult time, but it's still quite the most important Shakespearean playhouse in the country!"

"Excellent. So, how would you like to be in its new production?"

"To go on the stage!" cried Daisy rapturously, all her confusion and suspicion forgotten in a moment. "Goodness, how marvelous! Isn't it marvelous, Hazel?"

"Oh," I said, gulping. "Oh, I . . ."

I can't think of anything worse was what I wanted to say, but I bit my tongue. Daisy looked so shiningly excited that I tried to ignore the roaring black gulf that had opened up in my stomach.

"I thought you'd be pleased, Daisy," said Aunt Lucy, smiling. "A bit part in *Romeo and Juliet*!"

"Aunt Lucy, I shall not have a *bit part*," said Daisy scornfully. "I shall be the star."

"Daisy dear, you could not be anything else," said Uncle Felix. "I suppose it is a neat solution for you. But what about Hazel?"

"I shall be all right," I said, swallowing with difficulty.

"I quite agree, Hazel," said Aunt Lucy. "You may not think yourself an actress, but I know better. You've been around Daisy for too long not to be able to pretend."

"Rude!" cried Daisy. "You've only been married to Uncle

Felix for five months and you're already becoming far too much like him."

Uncle Felix laughed, and smiled at me, and Aunt Lucy smiled too. And I wondered, at that moment, whether this was not another of Aunt Lucy's unusual lessons.

I am still not sure. But, whether it was supposed to be or not, that is why Daisy and I joined the Rue Theatre Company.

As Daisy, Bridget, and I stood in front of the Rue
Theatre after lunch the next day, I felt rather
queasy, as though I was still on the boat that had
brought us back from Hong Kong. I had been in agonies
all morning, while Daisy danced about the flat in raptures.
I could hardly bear the thought that I would have to act—
and in front of people!

But I had to admit that the theatre itself was a glori-
ously impressive place. The Rue is set to one side of
a roundabout near Leicester Square, and it is a red-
and-white-brick cliff of a building, studded with shiny windows. It looks rather like a castle, and it even has four slender turrets shooting up the front of it like battlements. The
noise of battle surrounds it too, for the roundabout in front
sends up constant noise, all the howls of brakes and horns
and shouts that are the sounds of London in a hurry.

London ought not to feel so different from Hong Kong,

but it does. Although it is spring here, just as it was in Hong Kong, in London that means sun mixed up with chilly, windswept days, rushing gray skies, and pattering rain, with only a few small, sad flowers drooping in pots on window-sills.

I miss Hong Kong's generous heat, its wide, bright skies and blooming jungle. I even miss its spiders. And I miss the feeling of being at home. In Hong Kong I could breathe out, but now that we are back in England I have to go back to being wary. It's as though being in Hong Kong removed a layer of my skin, and now I have to grow it all over again.

But, all the same, I am not quite as different in London as I am at Deepdean—or rather, there are more people here who are different like me. I have seen several faces on buses and on the London Underground just like our friend George, and even (my heart jumps with excitement every time) a few faces like mine.

As I was thinking all this, Bridget ushered us through the main doors of the Rue, and we found ourselves in a hallway that swept upward in gold and black and red. It was empty, and there was a wonderful hush as the doors swung shut behind us and cut off the noise from outside. Light glittered from chandeliers and shone darkly off marble, and the very air smelled warm and rich. At the sight of all that magnificence, Daisy expanded, eyes shining in the lights. It was so beautiful, so magical. I found myself smiling.

Robin Stevens

"Now, remember what your aunt said," Bridget told us firmly, her wide, freckled face and dark eyes frowning. "Be on your best behavior or, despite everything, Miss Crompton will send you straight back home. Is that clear?"

Bridget is very no-nonsense. She says this is because she grew up in Dublin.

"Crystal," said Daisy, rolling her eyes.

"*Best* behavior, Daisy," said Bridget, swatting at Daisy's shoulder. "You shan't get anything past me."

She winked at us both in a way that was clearly a warning, just as someone came down the stairs toward us.

This person was wearing a shapeless brown dress, and she moved heavily, thumping her feet down on each step and squeezing the gold railing so hard I thought she might leave dents in the metal. She was old, even older than most of our teachers at Deepdean, and her hair was gray and close-cropped. She was built as solidly as her footsteps, and the round glasses that sat on her nose looked tiny on her large face.

"What are you three doing here?" she barked at us. "We're closed, you know!"

"Good afternoon!" said Daisy, bobbing a curtsy. "You're Miss Crompton, of course—I've seen your picture. We've come to be in your play."

"Good afternoon," said Bridget, standing up straight. "I'm Bridget O'Connell. I believe you spoke to Mrs. M. on the telephone about these two girls?"

"Yes, all right, very good, but why are you *here*? This is the public entrance. Theresa—that's my stage manager—left it unlocked in error. My actors go through the stage door at the back, no exceptions. Do you think you are more important than them?"

My heart sank. Miss Crompton did not seem very friendly.

Daisy blinked. "We made a mistake," she said, squaring her shoulders and standing as upright as she could next to Bridget. "It won't happen again."

Miss Crompton narrowed her eyes. "It certainly won't," she said. "I was just coming to lock up—this entrance won't be in use until opening night itself. All right, girls, follow me, if you please. Your aunt has arranged that you are to be in my play, no matter how dreadful you are, but, all the same, I'm curious to see what you're made of."

I had been to plays before, and sat in the nice dusty darkness of the stalls, but I had never been on a stage. I had not realized how very big a theatre is, the way the circles of seats rise up in front of you like mountains, the way the lights get in your eyes and the greasepaint smell gets in your nose, the way your legs go wobbly and you want to sink through the floorboards and never be seen again. That afternoon, standing on the vast, empty stage alone, even my breath seemed to echo around me.

"State your name!" boomed Miss Crompton from somewhere in the stalls.

"Er," I said stupidly. "Um . . ."

"Does not know her own name," said Miss Crompton. "Excellent. Begin your recitation, if you please."

Daisy and I had discussed this, just in case we were asked to audition. I had spent the previous afternoon learning a very sensible speech by Juliet's Nurse. But when I opened my mouth I froze. The words slipped out of my mind, and all I could think of was part of "Ode to a Nightingale."

"Thou wast not born for death, immortal bird!" I gabbled.

It was such a schoolgirl thing to recite, a poem that everyone learns when they are little shrimps.

"Perhaps the self-same song that found a path
Through the sad heart of Ruth when, sick for home,
She stood in tears amid the alien corn . . ."

Then, of course, I realized why I had chosen it: I have often felt like Ruth in that poem, and I did at that very moment. I staggered on to the end, melting under the lights and frying with dreadful shame, for I had let out more of myself than I had meant. Then I stopped and there was only a ringing silence. I felt as though every empty chair was staring at me.

"Unique," said Miss Crompton's voice from the stalls. I knew she did not mean it kindly. "Off the stage, if you please. Next!"

I scrambled down the little set of steps to the right of the stage as quickly as if it had tipped me off. I sank down into a plush seat next to Bridget, who was making deft squiggling notes in a small code book, just as Daisy came waltzing on.

Safe in the stalls, I suddenly felt the dazzling excitement of the theatre again. The golden arch over the stage shone like a promise and the velvety darkness of the wings was heavy with the most thrilling mystery. In the middle of it all, Daisy seemed to glow. She stood with her hands clasped and her feet positioned as though she was about to do ballet, and she was beaming.

"Good afternoon!" she trilled. "I am the *Honorable* Daisy Wells. May I begin?"

"You may," said Miss Crompton—and did I imagine it, or was there a chuckle in her voice?

Daisy threw herself into a kneeling position and reached forward. Her face changed to an anguished mask.

"*What's here?*" she cried. "*A cup, closed in my true love's hand? Poison, I see, hath been his timeless end . . . I will kiss thy lips!*"

She leaned forward and made a very small motion with her lips, as though she was being forced to kiss her great-aunt Eustacia at Christmas. I tried not to giggle. Daisy and romance do not get on.

"*O happy dagger!*" screamed Daisy, leaping upright and waving her fist in the air. "*This is thy sheath; there rust, and let me die!*"

Robin Stevens

She plunged her hand into her stomach and doubled over, gasping. She slowly crumpled to the ground, making small whimpering noises, twitched twice, and then lay still.

I waited. Bridget turned a page in her notebook and sighed to herself. At last Daisy rolled over and opened her eyes.

"I'm all right really," she said to Miss Crompton.

"I had guessed as much," said Miss Crompton. "Well, well. That was wonderfully tasteless. You clearly have no formal training and a very active imagination, but I commend your enthusiasm."

"Thank you," said Daisy, curtsying. "Who will I be playing?"

Miss Crompton sighed. "Since you are joining the Rue out of necessity, and at the request of your aunt, I shall make the most of the situation. You will be playing two small roles: Paris's Page and also Rosaline. The second is a wordless and usually unseen part, of course, but she will be a vision in this production. And both have great potential for drama."

"Hmm," said Daisy. "I accept. What about Hazel? After all, I can't possibly act without her."

"Miss Wong, are you *sure* you would like a part?" asked Miss Crompton. Without stopping her scribbling, Bridget turned to stare at me, lips pursed. I wanted to sink down into my seat, but then I saw Daisy up on the stage. Her arms were folded and she was trying to look commanding, but she only succeeded in looking at me rather pleadingly.

Daisy had traveled halfway across the world for me, I thought. To me, stepping onto a stage felt almost as enormous a journey. But I decided that I could do it, and I would, for her.

So I swallowed down the rushing terror in my throat and said, "Yes. Please."

Robin Stevens

R eally!" said Daisy later. "Isn't this wonderfully exciting? Miss Crompton has made the Rue famous. Her run of *Hamlet* with Archibald Duke lasted almost three months, and Hilda Dove says she owes her career to her!"

"Who *are* these people?" I asked. "Is Hilda Dove her real name? How do you *know* all this, Daisy?"

"Hilda Dove wasn't *born* Hilda Dove, of course. Most actors choose better names when they go on the stage—who'd go and see a leading lady called Bertha Jones? And I know because of Bertie," said Daisy, waving her hand airily. "He's quite obsessed, and I steal his theatre magazines. After all, you never know what knowledge may turn out to be useful—and so it has proved."

"But you never bother to learn codes!" I protested.

"That is information *you* are taking care of," said Daisy. "If I spent time learning it too, I would simply be wasting the space in my brain. Anyway, Hazel, that's why I know all about Miss Crompton and the Rue. She's quite brilliant—she bought it up twenty years ago when it was failing and she's absolutely made it *the* place to see Shakespeare. She's worked with Inigo Leontes and Linda Torrence—and now she'll be working with Daisy Wells! And Hazel Wong, of course. Really, though, I do think she could have found you a better part than the silly servant *Potpan!*"

"It's all right!" I said. "You know I'm not an actress, Daisy. I don't mind at all."

But, although I couldn't say so to Daisy, I *did*. Potpan, my part, was one of the Capulets' servants, at the Capulet mansion during the scenes at the party where Romeo and Juliet first met. It was a tiny role—but not quite as tiny as I had hoped. For I had discovered that it *had lines*.

"'We cannot be here and there too . . . ,'" said Daisy, grinning, as though she had read my mind. "I should think even you would be able to manage that. Oh, this really is amusing. Just wait until I tell George—"

"*If you tell George or Alexander anything about this, I will never speak to you again*," I said breathlessly.

The thought of Alexander finding out that I had been forced to pretend to be a boy called Potpan made me feel shaky and rather ill. Of course, one of Daisy's parts was a boy part too, but I knew that Daisy would look simply wonderful as Paris's Page in leggings and a jerkin, not boy-like at all.

I told myself, for the tenth time, that Daisy needed this. In Hong Kong, although she tried to deny it, her world had been overturned. In Hong Kong, I had been the important one. I had been *famous*, and I knew it had taken everything in her to bear it. The Daisy of two years ago could not have managed it. So I owed it to her to prove that I could be a true friend too—even if it meant that I had to spend the next few weeks pretending to be Potpan while Daisy was the beautiful Rosaline, who glided across the stage like a jewel. Rosaline, I thought, would have been an Honorable if she was English. It was very clear from the parts we had been given which one of us was the president of the Detective Society and which was her secretary.

"All *right*!" said Daisy, putting up her hands in mock horror. "I won't tell anyone! Detective Society honor. But, really, it's not as though I have it any better. I have to learn plenty of lines for the Page, and I have to be ogled by a horrid old man when I'm Rosaline."

"Romeo isn't old, is he?" I asked.

"He could be," said Daisy darkly. "We'll meet the rest of the company tomorrow."

When we came back to the Rue the next day, Bridget escorted us through the stage door, as directed. This was a little black door set into a red-brick wall at the back of the theatre, almost hidden until you went looking for it.

It was like stepping into the Secret Garden, only far more unnerving.

Daisy pushed the door open, and we found ourselves in a warm, wood-paneled little space where an old man was sitting in a cubbyhole to the right of us, just the way the porter had at Maudlin College last winter. He had flyaway white hair and a scrubby little beard that looked as though he hadn't trimmed it for several days.

"Hello," he said, training his beady blue eyes on us. "Who might you be?"

"We're *company members*," said Daisy, drawing herself up. "I'm *Rosaline*, and also Paris's Page. And who might *you* be, if you please?"

"I'm Jim Cotter," said the old man, narrowing his eyes at Daisy. "I'm stage door. I'm always here, night and day, and if you want to get into the Rue, you've got to go by me and sign my book. I live here, I sleep here and I've got eyes in the back of my head. Sign in here, if *you* please."

Daisy wrote her name in flowing letters and then handed the pen to Bridget.

"Daisy Wells and Hazel Wong," said Jim, his gaze flicking between us. "All right. You're in . . ." He glanced down at a clipboard in front of him. "Dressing room seven. Up those steps on your left and then up the stairs by the elevator. Don't use it, mind—it hasn't worked all month and there isn't the money for the repairs at present. You'll see a whole

26   *Robin Stevens*

line of dressing rooms on your right. Won't be hard for you to find yours. Off you go, and don't mess about."

"Thank you," I whispered.

I was suddenly overcome with awkwardness. Jim was so businesslike, and I realized that being part of the Rue was going to be quite grown up, in rather an intimidating way. Daisy had turned fifteen in April, but my birthday was not until the summer, and at that moment the difference felt enormous.

Daisy strutted past Jim as though she was walking into the most marvelous party, and I scuttled after her.

We pattered up some steps, and then turned left into a twisting flight of stone stairs. They stretched away both above and below us, wrapped round a narrow elevator. Up and up we went, and came out on a low, narrow, gaslit corridor with lots of doors opening to the right of us. My heart lifted a little, for this reminded me rather of the smaller Deepdean corridors, dark and full of bits of old furniture.

Dressing Room 7 turned out to be almost at the end of the row. It was very small, and lit inside with a gas jet that sputtered, and it had a funny smell, strong and rather like paint. There were two mirrors surrounded by flaring gas-lamps, and a rack for costumes. But makeup was scattered in front of one of the mirrors, and there were several dark robes hanging on the rack. It looked as though someone was already using this room, and they had just gone out for a moment.

The feeling of not belonging came back to me, stronger than ever, and I stepped backward into Bridget, who grumbled and pushed me forward again.

"I think this room already belongs to someone, Daisy," I whispered nervously. "There must have been a mistake. What's that smell?"

"Oh, that's the stuff you use to get off greasepaint," said Daisy knowledgeably. "It smells horribly strong, doesn't it? And don't be silly—we won't be sharing. This must all be left over from the last production. I think it was *Measure for Measure*. No, we'll have our own dressing room, I'm sure of it.

"Now, Hazel, I have to tell you something *important*. I looked at that sign-in sheet and I believe I've seen who's playing Juliet. *Rose Tree!* Not her real name, of course, a rather silly stage one—but she's famous! She only left RADA last year, but all London's going wild for her already. Bertie went to see her in *Happy Families* at the Lyric, and he raved about her in a letter. Ooh, and she's got a fascinating past too. She lost her parents when she was only thirteen! Fancy, what bliss."

"Daisy!" I said.

The dressing-room door had swung shut behind us, but at that moment it creaked open again. I glanced into the mirror in front of us and saw a young woman reflected in its frame. She was almost as tall as Daisy, with dark brown hair swept back off her face and large brown eyes, and she looked hardly grown up at all. In fact, I realized, she looked

Robin Stevens

only old enough to be at university, perhaps even a little younger than Bertie. She had a wide mouth that pursed up as she caught sight of us, and dramatic dark eyebrows.

"What are you doing in my dressing room?" she asked. Her accent was subtle, not quite English, and I couldn't place it.

"I beg your pardon! This is *our* dressing room!" cried Daisy, spinning round to face her and gasping in shock. "Dressing room seven. We were told so by Jim."

"Frances! Now there are *children* in my dressing room!" the girl shouted, leaning out into the corridor. "Frances! Frances! This is *too much*!"

I could feel myself gaping. Daisy was frozen with indignation, and tinges of pink had appeared high up on her cheeks. She does not like to be called a child.

I heard voices, and then the girl shoved back into our dressing room, followed by Miss Crompton.

"Look! They say this is their dressing room!" she cried, waving at us furiously.

"Well, it is. I put them here, Martita darling," said Miss Crompton. "They're the newest members of the company, and they need a dressing room. They also need someone to help them adjust to the theatre, and I thought you could do that."

"But they're children! They have a *nurse*!" shouted Martita, pointing her finger at Bridget.

"I'm *not* a nurse," said Bridget coolly. "I am a maid, and I am completing the task I have been given by my employer, which is to bring the girls to the theatre and ensure they are safe. Now that I have done so, I'll be off to my real job. I'll come to collect them at seven this evening."

"Thank you, Bridget. Now, Martita, don't be rude," said Miss Crompton as Bridget left with a nod to both of us. "I'm asking you to do this, and you shall do it."

"*This is Rose's fault*," hissed Martita furiously, and she actually stamped her foot. "She takes my part, she takes my dressing room, and now I have to *look after children!*"

"I am not discussing this anymore," said Miss Crompton firmly, as though Martita was no older than us. "Anyway, it will help with your part. You will be a lovely Nurse, darling, and Rose will be a lovely Juliet. Inigo and I agree that making the Nurse and Juliet the same age is a very powerful class statement. Now, I'd better introduce you all. Daisy, Hazel, this is Martita Torrera."

"It's a stage name," said Martita sulkily, folding her arms. "Not real. I'm actually Portuguese, not Spanish."

"Yes, darling, because no one wants to see an actress called plain old Marta Pao. That's show business—you know that. Everyone knows where Spain is and, besides, when we put you in heels you have the build to be a Spanish beauty."

Martita rolled her eyes and made a face.

"Now, all of you, rehearsal begins in ten minutes. I expect

you to be there. Daisy, Hazel, we'll be on book for the next three days, so there's still time for the blocking of your roles and for you to learn the ropes—but I expect you to be off book by the end of this week."

She backed out of the room and closed the door behind her. We were left alone with Martita.

"What's off book?" I whispered to Daisy.

"*Really!*" huffed Martita.

She turned to look at us, her arms still crossed. I wondered if she was upset about being reminded that she was having to pretend to be from a different country. People sometimes ask me if I am Japanese and it makes me furious.

"Don't you know *anything* about *anything*? Haven't you ever been in a play before?"

"No," I said weakly. "No, we've—we don't—"

I had to breathe very deeply and remind myself that I was being brave.

"How old *are* you?" asked Martita. There was suddenly a rather kinder expression on her face.

"*I'm* fifteen," said Daisy. "I've been fifteen for ages, and Hazel's fifteen awfully soon, aren't you, Hazel? And we *do* know about the theatre, I promise we do. You'll see—we'll be absolutely excellent!"

And she stared at Martita, the flush of color in her cheeks deepening.

Martita led the way out of our dressing room to the stage for rehearsal. I expected Daisy to whisper to me about how rude she had been, but she kept her mouth shut, and only gazed thoughtfully at the back of Martita's head. I didn't mind that Daisy was quiet—I felt wobbly all over with nerves, washed again and again with utter terror.

We threaded our way through the wings, and then I was stepping into the spotlight again.

But it turned out to be not quite as dreadful an experience as the audition, for this time the stage was filled with talking, laughing, shouting people, and crowded together they reminded me of something.

For a while, I could not think what it was—but then I realized. The people on this stage might all be grown-ups (or at least older than us), but the way they were chattering and clustering together was exactly like a group of

Deepdean pupils at the beginning of a new term. They had already made their alliances like the second form had when I first arrived at Deepdean. At the Rue, Daisy and I were the new girls.

I breathed a sigh of relief. This was all right. I knew how to wait and watch until I understood the situation—and it helped that each of these people looked as though they expected to be the center of attention. Their clothes were so gorgeous it took me a few moments to notice the patches on their knees and the rips at their hems, the places where things had been twice mended with slightly different threads. The men all wore jewel-bright cravats, and looked (I was reminded of Bertie and Harold at Cambridge) rather long-haired and terribly aesthetic, and all the women were wearing a fearful lot of makeup.

Martita looked back at us once more—and then she let out a sigh and rolled her eyes.

"Oh, come on," she said. "I suppose I have to introduce you to the company. Remember I don't want to be doing this at *all*!"

But, despite those words, her expression was kind—as was her offer to show us about. I wondered whether Martita might be the sort of person, like our friend Lavinia, whose bark was worse than her bite.

She dragged us across the stage to where a short, stocky, dark-skinned man was standing. He had a broad, smiling face and short dark hair, and he wore a shirt with brightly colored braces. He looked very young for a grown-up too, only a few years older than Martita. When he saw her, he held out his arms to her. She put hers round him and kissed his cheek.

"Simon!" she cried.

I thought that they might perhaps be in love, and I saw from Daisy's scowl and narrowed eyes that she did too, but then they began to chatter away to each other about people I didn't know, leaning their heads together just like our schoolmates Kitty and Beanie, and I realized that they were simply very good friends. If Martita had chosen this friendly looking person as her ally, then she really might be quite kind.

"Daisy, Hazel, this is Simon Carver," said Martita, turning back to us at last. "We were in *Measure for Measure* together in our last run. Simon, these girls are apparently part of the cast now. They've been given to me to look after."

"Oh, hey, poor you," Simon said to us with an American accent that gave me a start, for it was rather similar to Alexander's. "Martita is a horrible person." But he winked and grinned, and Martita thumped him on the shoulder, looking furious and fond at the same time.

"I'm kidding, obviously. Martita is amazing and we're the best of friends—the two of us have got to stick together among all these English people."

Robin Stevens

"We do," said Martita, the corners of her mouth quirking up. "But it's dreadful, Simon. It *is*! Rose has taken the good dressing room and now I'm sharing with these two."

"So? They seem great! Rose does have a lot to answer for, though," said Simon, his face falling. "I've got to tell you what she—"

"Martita!" called out another male voice. "My darling!"

Martita's blooming smile shut off like a light, and I saw her draw into herself as she turned to the speaker.

This man was tall and slender, with pale skin and rather long brown hair flopping about his temples. He had his arms out to hug her, and Martita stepped into the hug—but there was something about her movements that told me she did not really want to be hugged at all.

"Hello, Lysander," she said.

Simon stepped backward, frowning.

"Aren't you going to introduce me to these two?" asked Lysander, gesturing at Daisy and me.

"Girls," said Martita, "this is Lysander Tollington. He's playing Romeo."

"I *am* Romeo," said Lysander, stroking back his hair and smiling at the two of us with all his teeth. They were very white and even, but somehow it wasn't a nice smile. "And you are . . . ?"

"The Honorable Daisy Wells," said Daisy. "And this is Hazel Wong."

"Ah, an aristocrat," said Lysander. "Sent by your papa, were you?"

"My uncle, *if* you must know," said Daisy. "And what's wrong with that?"

"Nothing, apart from the fact that you didn't need to show any talent to get a part," said Lysander, sneering. "The English class system is ridiculous."

Daisy was still gasping with rage at this cutting but not entirely untrue statement when Miss Crompton came striding onto the stage. She was wearing the same square brown dress as yesterday, and no makeup at all, but everyone hushed and turned to her as though she had a crown on her head. Next to her hurried a small woman with light-brown skin carrying a clipboard, her thick graying hair twisted up into a complicated braid.

This, I thought, must be Theresa—the stage manager Miss Crompton had mentioned.

Behind them both walked a man who made me wonder whether *Romeo and Juliet* had already begun, for he looked like a character in a play. He was old, and his skin was very dark and slightly freckled. He had a halo of close-cropped white hair and he was wearing a long purple cape. He held his arms half crossed in front of him so that the material billowed down around his body and swept away behind him.

"That's Inigo Leontes!" hissed Daisy like a prompter in my ear. "He's a terribly famous tragic actor! He's played

Robin Stevens

Othello, of course, and Macbeth and Hamlet, all at the Rue, and now he's Miss Crompton's director, and the principal investor too. He's put lots of his own money into the Rue, so really it's almost as much his as Miss Crompton's."

"Good afternoon, cast!" boomed Inigo, flinging his arms out wide. "And to our two new members: welcome to our theatre and our play!" He gave a deep, dramatic bow to me and Daisy.

"My theatre, Inigo darling," said Miss Crompton, patting his shoulder. "Mine and Theresa's. Your play."

"Of course!" cried Inigo, not ruffled at all. "For the benefit of the new arrivals: this theatre, of course, *belongs* to Frances. But the production is mine. I am bringing the Bard's great romance, *Romeo and Juliet,* to life at the Rue in only two weeks. I have a vision!"

"You certainly do," said Miss Crompton. "And I agree with you on it." She frowned. "Actors have got in the habit of *declaiming* Shakespeare as though they're speaking nonsense poetry and not simply talking to one another. We won't have any of that in *this* production."

"INDEED!" thundered Inigo. Miss Crompton blinked at him, and he coughed and said, "Indeed. This play will be realistic. It will be immediate. It will be GENIUS!"

There was a commotion at the side of the stage. Inigo paused, and then one more person burst out of the darkness into the glare of the lights. She was young, probably

Simon's age, and her face was beautifully painted; she had red lips and dark, long-lashed eyes. She was quite an ordinary height and size, with long blond hair, but there was something about the way she moved that made it impossible to look away from her. She was like a magnet, and she made me gasp. She walked to the middle of the stage and shrugged her shoulders.

"I'm *here*, darlings," she said.

"Hello, Rose dear," said Miss Crompton. "Thank you for joining us." She smiled, and I felt rather surprised. Miss Crompton had not shown herself to be someone happy with lateness.

"*Darling* Frances!" said Rose, turning her hypnotic gaze on Miss Crompton like a beam of light.

"Rose, this is the *third* time this *week*," rumbled Inigo.

Rose narrowed her pretty eyes at him a little and pouted. "I was *busy*," she said. "I'm here now, aren't I? What does it matter?"

"Perhaps she got lost in *all the space in her dressing room, which is next to the stage*," said Martita quite clearly.

Miss Crompton swung her head round. I saw Martita's chin go up. Her cheeks flushed and her eyes glittered. And, from the middle of the stage, Rose glared straight back at her.

"Now that Miss Tree is *here*," Inigo went on, ignoring Martita's sharp words, "I can introduce our two new

Robin Stevens

company members. Miss Daisy Wells will be making her debut as Paris's Page and as the figure of Rosaline at the Capulet party, and her friend Miss Hazel Wong is playing the small but crucial role of Potpan."

There was a roll of laughter and I flinched. Daisy bowed.

"Girls, let me introduce the company to you. Our Romeo is Mr. Lysander Tollington." Inigo waved toward Lysander, who bowed ironically. "And Juliet's Nurse—a young woman in this production—will be played by Miss Martita Torrera. As well as directing, I will play Juliet's confessor, Friar Lawrence, and Romeo's bosom friend Mercutio will be played by Mr. Simon Carver." He gestured at Simon, and as he did so an odd, disappointed expression flashed across his face.

He pointed out the actors who would be playing the Montagues and the Capulets, Paris, the apothecary—and at last he introduced Rose. As he did so, it was as though a bright light had been thrown on her. It was clear that she was the star.

"Hazel, Daisy," said Inigo, "this tardy female is our Juliet, Miss Rose Tree. She comes to us fresh from her triumph in *Happy Families* last month at the Lyric, and this will be her first Shakespeare."

I glanced around and saw that everyone was staring at Rose. Miss Crompton looked amused and fond, Lysander looked—the polite word, I suppose, is romantic—Inigo looked annoyed, and both Simon and Martita looked furious. Rose, meanwhile, stared straight out into the empty auditorium, posing for them with a little smirk on her face—and I wondered then whether all was well at the Rue Theatre.

T he actor playing Romeo was a horror, wasn't he?"
said Daisy to me that evening.

"Don't be awful, Daisy!" I said, although privately I agreed with her. Lysander had made me uncomfortable. He stood too close to people and stared at them for too long, and there was an angry energy to him that I did not like.

"He was, though," said Daisy. "He's a nasty man. You'll see."

"Well, at least you're only in two scenes with him," I said. "And it's all just acting, anyway."

"*Life* is acting," said Daisy. "That doesn't mean you aren't allowed to complain when you have to act with someone dreadful."

I thought to myself that, if life was acting, it was a pity that I was no good at acting at all.

Mercifully, I was only required for one speaking scene,

and a few more as a silent, lurking part of the crowd, and so most of the time, I quickly realized over the next few days, I could simply wander around the Rue Theatre with Daisy.

Once we were through the stage door and past Jim and his book, and Bridget had waved us off each morning and gone to run her mysterious errands for Uncle Felix and Aunt Lucy, we were swallowed up in the strange world of the Rue. It became all-consuming, and I almost forgot, for the time I was there, that the rest of London existed.

I discovered that what a theatre had been in my head—the red seats, the golden arch like a picture frame, the stage itself—is only a little slice of the *real* theatre. A theatre stretches out in all directions beyond what the audience can see—back, up, and down—and, although it seems so simple and glossy, it is really made up of endless secret places. Even the stage is not one single space but levels that can be hidden or revealed like peeling an onion.

The top of the gold proscenium arch, which hides the curtains, is not really the top of the theatre. Instead, you can stand in the middle of the stage and tip your head back and look up and up and up into the flies, hanging with lights and pulleys and ladders. It's like staring up into the sky and seeing another world suspended above you. The stagehands all run and jump about on the ladders in a way that, quite frankly, makes me feel sick, although Daisy sighs longingly as she watches them.

Robin Stevens

Below the stage is the under-stage area and basement, and below that, after another turn of the stairs, are the service rooms: the generator room, the cellar, and the old dark room that holds a well—a real one, we learned from Jim, that drops down into London's water table.

I got a creepy feeling when I found out about it. I wondered what else might be far beneath the Rue's floor and it made me feel wriggly, just as I do when I stare down into the sea and imagine all the creatures swimming about in it, too far down for me to see.

Everything in a theatre is backward and oddly skewed, like a mirror version of life. There's no left or right, but only stage left and stage right, upstage and downstage, prompt side and opposite prompt. The prompt box is in the corner at stage right (the other side to most theatres, for the Rue is built oddly to block off the noise from the street outside), and that is where the stage manager, Theresa, usually sat during rehearsals, clutching a copy of the play to her chest and hissing at the players whenever they forgot a line.

Often Miss Crompton came to stand next to her, one hand on her shoulder, watching the play. When Theresa wasn't acting as prompt, she was dashing about the theatre making telephone calls and ticking things off on her clipboard and arranging for the rips in the heavy velvet stage curtains to be mended.

Theresa and Miss Crompton, I realized, managed all the

guts and muscles and blood of the theatre, while Inigo only hovered beatifically out in the stalls and on the stage itself, directing rehearsals in a most godlike way. But with every day he became more and more like the Old Testament God rather than the gentle New Testament one, for rehearsals were not going particularly well.

Partly this was my fault. The first few days of our rehearsals at the Rue reminded me of what I already knew: that, although I have been getting better and better at being myself, even the thought of pretending to be someone else still sends me into hot and cold horrors. As Potpan, I forgot how to move my hands and feet. I forgot what to do with my face, and how to open my mouth and allow words out.

"Good grief, girl, SPEAK!" Inigo shouted at me again and again. "It's a few simple lines! You know how to speak, don't you?"

"Um," I said.

"See here!" cried Inigo, and he came up onto the stage, his cloak billowing, and spoke the lines for me, leaving me feeling even worse, and more confused, than I had before.

"It really is doable, my dear child," said Miss Crompton after I had staggered offstage, face blazing. "Imagine you're speaking to a friend. Do you have any boy friends?"

Of course, at that question I utterly lost my breath and my voice and simply gaped at her.

"Heavens, you do need coaching. Martita, help her," said Miss Crompton, giving me a firm but not unkind pat on the shoulder.

Martita rolled her eyes and puffed out her cheeks—but later, in the dressing room, she sat down with me for nearly twenty minutes and worked me through the lines again and again, until I almost did not feel ashamed to hear myself saying them.

"There!" said Martita at last. "There's hope for everyone, even the idiots."

She said it as rudely as she could, but I had learned by then that the rudeness was only for show. Her actions were kind, and that was what mattered. Beneath her snappy exterior, Martita was hiding fierce goodness and warmth. She was willing to help people she liked, no matter what it cost her.

"She really is nice, isn't she?" I asked Daisy.

"Humph!" said Daisy, sticking out her bottom lip. "I suppose so."

"Don't you like her?" I said, surprised, for I had seen Martita patiently working with Daisy on her graveyard scene, showing her how to project her voice into the depths of the stalls.

Robin Stevens

"She's all right," said Daisy, wrinkling her nose, her cheeks a little red. "I suppose. She's not *bad*."

But there was a larger problem than my nerves: Rose and Inigo could not seem to get on.

After everyone had gone off book (which means they had learned their lines), and after the company had spent a day pacing around the stage and mumbling alarmingly at the floor (which was apparently not a mistake, but the blocking that Miss Crompton had mentioned), they all began to look up and speak their parts wonderfully.

The very best of them—and even I saw it—was Rose. She was a beautiful actress. As Juliet, she made herself seem younger, more hesitant, but with a bold, funny spark in her that I could not help liking. I even believed that she adored Lysander's rather aggressive Romeo.

She would not stay quiet when she disagreed with Inigo's direction, though, and their discussions usually ended with Rose speaking to Miss Crompton and setting off an argument between her and Inigo. Miss Crompton bristled and glared, Inigo became more and more Old Testament, and Rose pouted and took refuge in Wardrobe with Annie, the dresser, who had become her fast friend.

Wardrobe itself was part of our warren of pocket-small, gas-jet-heated dressing rooms on the first floor, and it was where Annie worked. She was a young, talkative woman who was as dramatic as the clothes she hemmed and darned and tacked together. She had a wildly curly fair head of hair always tied about with bright-colored scarves. Her necklaces and bracelets glittered and clicked and her outfits shone in shades of red and purple and green.

"Inigo's a stupid old man," I heard Rose say to Annie one morning as she was being fitted for her day dress. "Just because he used to be a big star—now he's an old has-been. He can't stand to see me succeed! I hate him!"

Annie made a soothing, mouth-full-of-pins murmur in reply. And I thought to myself rather uncomfortably that, although I knew that everyone at the Rue was a good actor, I was not sure whether they were all good people.

Robin Stevens

It wasn't just Inigo who didn't get on with Rose. Martita and Simon were also cold to her, snubbing her and leaving her out of conversations, and pointedly refusing to run through lines with her offstage. At first, I thought this was rather cruel of them—and rather odd, when Simon was so friendly to everyone else, and even Martita was secretly kind. They were such friends too, that it seemed almost like bullying to refuse to let Rose in.

"I feel quite sorry for Rose!" I said to Daisy. "I know she can be a bit rude sometimes, but it's not her who's causing problems. It's Inigo and Martita and Simon who are being awful."

"You *would* say that," said Daisy, wrinkling her nose. "Because you think that, deep down, everyone is as good-hearted as you are. Only they're not. Rose certainly isn't. Everyone's upset with her because she's upset them. She might be nice to the people she thinks will help her, like

Miss Crompton and Annie and Lysander, but underneath she's not nice at all. *Watch* her, Hazel!"

I folded my arms. "I think you're wrong!" I said. "You'll see."

During our next rehearsal, I watched Rose with an indignant fire in my chest. Daisy always thought the worst of people and it really wasn't fair.

We were working on the first act, and it was time for Daisy's scene as Rosaline. She had to drift across the stage at the opening of the Capulets' party, looking beautiful, just before Romeo saw Juliet for the first time. I stood watching, and Rose came to stand next to me.

"Daisy is so lovely, isn't she, darling?" she said, leaning against me with her arm about my shoulder. I was still learning the way actors called each other "darling," no matter how they really felt about each other. It seemed a very odd habit.

"She is," I said.

I'm used to Daisy's beauty by now, and find it—not *boring*, not at all—simply normal.

"Do you think that tiara is a little much, though?" asked Rose thoughtfully. "I'm sure it's not, but—"

"Oh, perhaps it is," I said, staring. Daisy was piled high with paste gems, to make her look truly jewel-like.

"Daisy," I said, when she came over to me. "What if you took off the tiara? I think it would make your hair stand out more."

"Hmm," said Daisy. "I suppose I . . ." She paused and glared at me. "Was that your idea?" she asked.

"Yes!" I said. "Wait, no. Rose was just—"

"ROSE!" hissed Daisy. "There, do you see?"

"She was being nice!" I cried.

"She was NOT!" said Daisy. "Think about it. Rose tells you that I'm wearing too much jewelry. She knows you'll tell me, and she knows I listen to you far more closely than I do to anyone else. I'm more likely to take off the tiara if *you* tell me to, and if I take off the tiara I'll look less glamorous. Which means that *she'll* look better when she comes on."

"Daisy, that's ridiculous," I protested. "No one is *really* that cunning."

"I am," said Daisy. "It's not so difficult. You just need to know people. You need to be able to tell what makes them tick. I'm good at it and so, it seems, is Rose. Well, I won't give her what she wants—see what she does then!"

I had a sinking feeling in my stomach. Daisy was being ridiculous. Except . . .

The next time she stepped out onto the stage, Daisy was still wearing the tiara. She gleamed like a star.

"Darling Frances," I heard Rose say coaxingly. "Don't you think that tiara's a little too much? It's Juliet who shines like a rich jewel, not Rosaline."

"Rose darling," said Miss Crompton, "it's quite all right.

You look simply divine. But—Annie my love, could you look at taking a few brilliants off Daisy's crown?"

Annie hurried over, her bracelets jingling and her curly hair wild, and poked at Daisy's headdress while Rose cooed happily and Daisy scowled.

I thought guiltily about what Daisy had said—and I knew that, as usual, she was right.

Robin Stevens

After that, it was as though someone had snapped their fingers and woken me up. I did not like being awake, not at all, but I couldn't help seeing what I did. All Rose's kindnesses left a bitter aftertaste.

I had thought Rose was being polite in the face of Martita's scorn, but I realized that she never managed to have even a single conversation with Martita without mentioning *dressing rooms*. She was nicest to Miss Crompton when Martita was about, and, whenever Miss Crompton said something kind about Rose in return, Rose made sure that Martita heard. I saw the pain in Martita's eyes, and I understood that she was cut deeply by the fact that Miss Crompton was taking Rose's side over hers.

Rose was charming to Simon, but it was utterly hollow. "How lucky you are, to die so early as Mercutio!" she told him. "Lysander and I have to keep on acting for *hours* after you."

"Mercutio's a great part," Simon said coldly.

"It *is*," said Rose. "Especially for *you*. I mean—the way you look. The opportunities are so *limited* apart from trage-dies and bit parts, aren't they? I can't imagine you playing a romantic character. You just don't have the—*features* for it. You're a wonderful Mercutio, though!"

I saw Simon's hands clench. I suddenly felt rather sick. I understood what Rose was really trying to say, and it made me see that all Simon and Martita's coolness toward Rose was entirely justified.

Rose was utterly flirtatious with Lysander, whispering and canoodling with him in dark corners, but she was smug about receiving letters from other admirers too, and this made Lysander horribly jealous. Once I heard him shout at her and shake his fist in a most threatening way. Lysander was as sharp and angry as Rose was cunning and manipula-tive, and I realized that their romance was as empty offstage as it was true in the play. Lysander, I had learned from read-ing some of the magazines Daisy lent me, was truly famous, and so it was a clever move to charm him—but not at all an honest one.

Rose was only really friendly with chatty Annie in Wardrobe—and so Annie spent hours pinning and tucking Rose's outfits, and, even barefoot in her white balcony-scene nightie, Rose looked a vision. Martita, meanwhile, grum-bled about Rose and made bored faces during her fittings, and the Nurse costumes Annie turned out for her looked dull and boxy, more nunlike than anything else.

"It's a joke," she said to us, staring into the mirror in our dressing room. "I could be sixty!"

"You don't look sixty," I said encouragingly. "She doesn't, does she, Daisy?"

"Um," said Daisy, staring at her hands. "No, I suppose not."

Daisy was still unaccountably quiet around Martita. If it had been anyone else, I would have thought she was shy—but I knew that the Honorable Daisy Wells does not believe in shyness. I was rather confused, but also highly amused, for it was so odd watching Daisy at a loss for words. Once, when Martita spoke to her unexpectedly kindly, I even saw Daisy stammer as she replied, a blush creeping across her face.

"You're quite right, I look seventy," said Martita gloomily. "It's all Rose's fault. I didn't come to England to be a character actress!"

"Why *did* you come to England?" I asked. I was curious about this. Martita's accent marked her out from the rest of the company—she was like me, a girl from another country trying desperately to find her place in England.

"I came to be a star, of course," said Martita. "And Portugal isn't such a good place at the moment. Have you heard about it?"

I made a polite noise. Sometimes I forget how much Deepdean protects us from the rest of the world. We had seen a glimpse of what was going on in Europe on the Orient Express last summer, but since then I had not had time to think much about anything besides murder and my family in Hong Kong.

"There is a very unpleasant man in power," Martita said matter-of-factly. "People are attacked if they do not agree with him. But really I left last year because my parents would not let me stay with them any longer. We had . . . an argument. And so in the middle of the night I dressed as a servant girl, got on a horse, and rode away from my town, all the way through the country to the seaside.

"When I got there, I commandeered a ship, and I made it sail all the way to England, and when I arrived I stole another horse and rode it all the way to London. I had always wanted to become an actress, you see, and I knew London was the best place to do it. When I got here, I was utterly destitute. I tried to get jobs, but I didn't manage it.

"I was living on the streets when Frances found me. She can behave rudely, but inside she is the kindest woman in the world. She took me in and let me stay with her and Theresa, and I have been acting at the Rue for almost a year. Frances has been better to me than my own mother, and I . . ." She hesitated. Now I understood why Martita always looked so sad when Miss Crompton preferred Rose to her.

Robin Stevens

"I'm sorry," I said, for I really was. I liked Martita more and more. However . . . "Is—is that story all true?" It sounded like something from a rather silly adventure novel.

Martita paused, and then she winked at me. "The last part is," she said. "And some of the rest. I'll leave it up to you to guess which. Actresses are supposed to invent their lives, aren't they? Now, will one of you put this horrid cloak thing on me properly? I can't seem to do it up."

"You shouldn't have said that to her!" cried Daisy as soon as Martita had left the dressing room. "Anyway, how could you know it wasn't all true? Think of all the fantastical things that have happened to us!"

"She didn't commandeer a ship, Daisy."

"She might have!" snapped Daisy with a blush.

"You just like the idea of Martita as a pirate queen," I said, smiling.

"Be quiet!" cried Daisy, folding her arms, and I could not make her say anything more about it.

XI

And then, on Monday, when Daisy and I had been members of the Rue for just under a week, a great bunch of hothouse flowers arrived for Rose. They were huge deep blooms the color of the Rue's seats and quite as plush-looking. The card with them only said:

To the Star

Rose was absolutely delighted with them, and paraded them around the Rue. Miss Crompton smiled, Martita rolled her eyes, Simon shrugged, Inigo sniffed, Lysander glared, and Annie treated everyone who came into Wardrobe to a long description of all the roses in her mother's garden. (Annie spoke almost constantly, a cloud of chatter that enveloped anyone who went near her.)

Theresa trimmed the flowers and put them in a vase, and that seemed to be the end of that.

That afternoon, though, I came upon Lysander in the under-stage corridors. He was talking to Rose in a low, angry voice and pressing her up against a rack of heavy costumes.

"Who sent you those roses?" he was asking. "Where are they from? *I* didn't send them. Who else do you have on the hook?"

"Lysander, stop it!" cried Rose, struggling away from him. "I'm sure they're just from one of my admirers. You know, all those silly stage-door Johnnies who wait for me outside the theatre. Get off! You're hurting me!"

"Good," said Lysander roughly, seizing her wrists. "*You're* hurting *me*. I thought you cared most about me, but if I find out there's someone else . . ."

"There isn't," said Rose, a note of panic in her voice. "Lysander, they're just from a fan—and I can't help it if I have fans, now!"

Lysander sneered, and then he dropped her hands and stepped away. Rose was left panting, glaring after him with an expression that was half rage and half fear.

And then came the second bunch of roses.

They were there when we arrived at the Rue on Tuesday morning, and the first we heard about them was Rose's shouts from her dressing room. The whole company converged on her (Daisy, of course, in the lead) and found her room filled with the scent of roses. Some of their petals had fluttered to the floor, and I thought for one horrid moment that their red splashes were blood.

"Whatever is it, Rose dear?" asked Miss Crompton, while Theresa knelt down and began to tidy up efficiently. Martita, behind her, snorted and turned away.

"Someone's THREATENING ME!" cried Rose. Her face was pink with anger. She had something in her hands, a square of white card, and she thrust it at Miss Crompton.

"Ooh, let me see," said Daisy, nosily contriving to pop her head over Miss Crompton's shoulder. I stood on tiptoe to get a look, and at last I saw too.

ROSES ARE RED

VIOLETS ARE BLUE

YOU OUGHT TO BEHAVE

I'M COMING FOR YOU.

Daisy read it out loud. There was a silence, and then Simon laughed. We all looked at him, and I felt the hair on my arms prickle.

"What?" he asked, raising his eyebrows at us all. "It's a joke, right? I mean, it's not real. No one does that for *real*!"

"Of course it's real!" snapped Rose. "How dare you! I bet *you're* the one behind it. You're trying to frighten me off, all because *I'm* the star and *you're* not."

"Rose!" said Theresa. "Calm down, my girl."

Robin Stevens

"I shall deal with this," said Miss Crompton firmly to the company. "Theresa, stay with me. The rest of you, go. Inigo, begin the rehearsal, if you please—a scene that Juliet doesn't appear in."

We all scurried back out into the corridor. I felt oddly ashamed, as though I'd seen something I was not supposed to. Daisy, though, was pinching me repeatedly.

"Ow!" I said. "Stop it! I know, I know."

"I should hope you do!" hissed Daisy. "I knew it was only a matter of time before we discovered a mystery at the Rue! Hazel—we are back on a case again!"

XII

B ut our efforts to discover who was behind Rose's bouquet did not come to much. Jim at the stage door told us that the flowers had been brought by a Covent Garden delivery boy, and when we went to Covent Garden (Daisy had a sudden and desperate desire to buy Aunt Lucy flowers on Wednesday morning) we found that the order had been placed by an anonymous child with a scrap of paper and a ten-shilling note.

"Blast," said Daisy. "They must have been paid to do it. But by who? It's not as though we can narrow down Rose's enemies, either! Anyone at the Rue might want to upset her."

"Not Miss Crompton!" I argued.

"Even her," said Daisy. "She's being nice to Rose because she's the star, but Rose's complaining is beginning to wear thin. Just you wait and see."

. . .

That day, the tension at the Rue could be cut with a knife. The spring flu had knocked out the actors playing Benvolio and Peter, and so Miss Crompton ordered everyone to take on a second understudy role. Martita continued to snub Rose constantly, Simon and Rose clearly could not stand each other—and I kept on seeing Inigo and Simon speaking together in hushed tones, breaking off whenever they saw someone coming by. They seemed as thick as thieves. Lysander was also continuing to be very cold with Rose, all his flirting frozen into bitterness.

The threats to Rose kept on coming that week. That morning there was a single rose, its petals cut in half, and a slash in one of Juliet's ballgown costumes, right across her heart. On Thursday there was a single peacock feather, terribly unlucky in a theatre, sitting on her dressing table.

Rose was absolutely furious about it all, and Daisy and I were bewildered. There was only one thing we knew: these latest efforts could only have come from *within* the theatre. Jim kept rigid watch on the stage-door entrance, and front of house was locked up tight (Daisy checked). There was simply no way in, and no possibility that anyone not part of the company could have had the opportunity to leave these things for Rose.

And then, on Thursday afternoon, Theresa fainted clean away in the middle of a rehearsal, and had to be rushed off to the hospital by the actor playing Tybalt. She had the flu, and she was prescribed bed rest.

"Ah, poor Theresa!" cried Simon when we were all told that she would not be coming back that day.

"The problem is, she's been worked too hard," said Lysander, scowling. "She ought to be part of a union!"

"We all work too hard, Mr. Tollington," said Miss Crompton. "And we are all part of the same union."

"The workers ought to rise up," said Lysander, his face flushing. "That's what this country needs. A revolution!"

"If there was one, wouldn't your parents be in trouble?" asked Rose. "Your father's an admiral, isn't he? Didn't he put you through acting school?"

I remembered how Lysander had accused Daisy of only getting her part because she was a member of the aristocracy. I glanced at Daisy now, and saw her watching Lysander with interest. Rose had spoken as though the thought had only just occurred to her, quite innocently, but Lysander's face flamed furious red.

"At least *my* parents are alive!" he growled.

Rose hissed.

"Do be quiet, all of you," said Miss Crompton, frowning. "I need to think. With Theresa ill, there's going to be a lot of extra work to do."

"Don't worry, Miss C., it'll be okay," said Simon in his warm, kind voice. "We'll all pull our weight."

Robin Stevens

"That's good of you, Simon darling," said Miss Crompton. "But I was in fact wondering whether Martita could help me while Theresa is away. She knows the theatre well, and she has seen us both work."

Martita flushed, and looked pleased and upset at the same time. I thought I understood why. To be singled out by Miss Crompton showed how much she trusted Martita; but the work she would have to do was hardly glamorous. "Oh," she said, her brows drawing together, "I—I— Oh, all right."

But I reeled from the poisonous look that Rose gave her. The hatred, I realized, truly was on both sides.

Over the next few days, Martita spun around the Rue Theatre, ordering sets to be moved, asking for costume changes, coaching actors through their lines and speaking her own in double time. Her Nurse was young and beautiful but overworked, pretending with a cross voice and a friendly wink at the audience to be bowed down with cares that made her older than her years. I saw Martita whirling in and out of the stage door, fetching and carrying, staggering under the weight of enormous boxes of old programs and posters, fabric and sandwiches, and grumbling cheerfully about it. I thought that in some respects at least, real life imitated the play.

The others helped, in their way—or rather, Simon

good-naturedly fetched and carried whenever Martita asked, Lysander declaimed about cooperation in villages in Russia and then did nothing at all, and Rose only helped when people were looking at her.

Much to my surprise, Daisy, the girl who never does a thing she does not think important, was more useful than all the rest of them. After the third time I found her dragging a heavy crate through the Rue's corridors on Friday afternoon, I had to say something.

"Daisy," I said. "Do you think Martita's the one who's been threatening Rose? Is that why you're following her like this, to watch her?"

"Oh," said Daisy, straightening up abruptly, her face quite red with effort. "Yes, that's exactly it. I'm watching Martita in case she's the person behind those threats. If you could just help me get this to Miss C.'s office, I will tell you more about my plans presently."

We passed Martita in the corridor as we shoved the crate along. I stared at her to see if she looked in any way guilty, but all I saw was a person who was harassed and annoyed. Her cheeks were flushed and her thick dark hair was escaping from its pins.

"I'm off to collect another delivery from the printer's," she said breathlessly. "Posters. I'll be gone for twenty minutes. Daisy, make sure everything's ready for Act One, Scene Five, will you?"

Robin Stevens

"Yes, Martita," said Daisy briskly. "Of course I will."

"I don't believe you about Martita," I said once she had gone. "You aren't just pretending to help. You really want to!"

"Of course I don't! You should know perfectly well by now, *Hazel*, that I am *acting*, and, as I tell you *repeatedly*, you need to practice it."

"Nonsense!" I said. The way Daisy spoke—the pink in her cheeks and the gleam in her eyes—gave away the lie behind what she was saying. "You've been behaving so oddly around Martita, ever since we met her. I think you—"

"*If you say another word, I shall scream*," snarled Daisy. "I don't want to talk about it, Hazel. I don't! Leave it, will you?"

"All right!" I snapped back. "But—you're being horrid!"

The contents of the crate were bundles and bundles of programs, and we piled them up in the corner of Miss Crompton's chaotic office, next to groaning heaps of old play scripts, dead flowers in chipped vases, loose pens leaking ink across screeds of paper, and several three-legged chairs. We did it crossly, catching each other's eyes and glaring.

"Oh, I wish something else would happen soon!" said Daisy at last. "Everyone's so on edge!"

What neither of us knew was that it was already happening.

Martita came hurrying back from the printer's with a thick tube of posters under her arm, sealed up with the printer's mark.

"Here," she said to a passing stagehand. "Put these up outside, will you? I must get onstage."

The stagehand nodded and took the roll—but ten minutes later he was back. He hovered downstage, beside Theresa's empty prompt corner, a puzzled expression on his face.

The company was rehearsing Act One, Scene Five. Romeo and Juliet had just touched hands at the party for the first time, and now Juliet was learning from her Nurse that Romeo was really the son of her family's enemies. Daisy and I, our cues done, sat at the edge of the stage, watching. Martita was mid-line when she saw the stagehand.

"*The only son of your great enemy*— What is it? What do you want?" she called, spinning round and putting her hands on her hips.

"Not again!" cried Inigo from his seat in the stalls. "This is too distracting. Frances, I need Miss Torrera to focus on her role! She really can't be the stage manager as well as the Nurse. Stop, stop!"

Rose sighed and threw up her arms. "*I* haven't gone wrong once!" she complained. "It's *always* Martita."

"What is it?" Martita asked the stagehand again.

"It's the posters," he replied apologetically. "You're sure that they were the right ones to be pasted up on the side of the theatre?"

"Yes, I'm sure! Haven't you put them up yet?"

"I think you ought to come and look at them," said the stagehand. He seemed nervous now. "It's not right, it really isn't."

"Has something been misspelled?!" called Miss Crompton, striding up the aisle between the stalls. "All right, show us what the trouble is."

Miss Crompton, Inigo, and Martita hurried away after him, and there was a lull, while onstage Rose stretched and hummed and muttered her next lines to herself. She was quite alone in the spotlight, but she moved as though she knew she was being watched, tilting her head upward and shaking back her hair. I looked around and saw Simon standing in the wings, stage left, his arms folded, waiting for his next scene at the beginning of Act Two. Lysander had just come offstage and was half hidden behind a flat, and Annie had come down from Wardrobe with a bundle of Act Two costumes and was hovering upstage.

A shrill whistle cut through the air. I was startled, heart beating, and looked upward automatically. Daisy, next to me, tensed like a cat. It is very unlucky to whistle onstage, for someone up in the flies might hear it and mistake it for the cue to lower a sandbag or piece of scenery.

"Who did that?" cried Rose. "Who was it? You idiots, that's dangerous!"

"Hey, it wasn't me!" Simon said, shaking his head. Lysander crossed his arms and Annie shrugged, her hands draped in deep swags of material.

Then Miss Crompton came storming back through the stage door. I had almost forgotten those posters. I assumed, rather vaguely, that the lettering must be blurry, or had perhaps been printed back to front. But I was clearly wrong. Miss Crompton's face was gray with fury.

"Come outside at once, all of you!" she cried. "I have been forgiving of whichever one of you has been playing these pranks on Rose up to now, but this is too much. Come outside—perhaps seeing it will make the culprit own up!"

We all glanced at each other in confusion, and then rushed off the stage, through the corridor, past Jim (who shouted in annoyance that we had not signed his book), and out into the brisk spring evening air.

Robin Stevens

London as the sun is going down is lovely. All its bright signs are flickering on and the lights on omnibuses and motor cars are glowing. That day the sky was still blue and white high above the tops of the buildings, but down where we were the air was dim and dark.

We turned left out of the stage door, onto the quick-moving street, and Miss Crompton led us all to the place where a chain of round lights like crystal balls lit up the Rue's outside wall, covered in posters. There was the whole history of the Rue in peeling paper—fading and half-covered advertisements for a hundred closed plays. And there, at the very top of them, where the new playbills for *Romeo and Juliet* should have been, was a row of simple black-and-white posters that gave me chills as I read them. They each said the same thing:

DING DONG BELL
ROSE'S IN THE WELL
WHO PUT HER IN?
ONLY TIME WILL TELL . . .

Below the words was a crude sketch of a well, with a pair of feet wearing little slippers poking out of it.

I felt Daisy give a little shiver of excitement beside me. "*Watson!*" she breathed.

And then Rose screamed. It was an unearthly sound,

threading itself demonically above the noise of car horns and tires.

"WHO DID THIS?"

Everyone froze in place, staring at her like a tableau.

"WHO?" Rose screamed again. She was crying, I saw—really crying. I didn't blame her. Coming after all the other threats and that whistle, this must have felt like the final straw. I had a pang of sympathy for her once again.

"Rose darling, stay calm," said Miss Crompton. "It'll be all right. We'll get to the bottom of it."

"THEY ALL HATE ME!" shouted Rose, her voice cracking.

"I'm sure they don't," said Miss Crompton. Her voice was soothing, a teacher talking to a sobbing shrimp. Then she turned on the rest of the company. "If the culprit does not reveal themselves, I shall dock the pay of everyone here," she said. "Own up immediately!"

But everyone was silent.

"We shall get to the bottom of this!" declared Inigo.

"And we shall have the posters taken down immediately," said Miss Crompton.

"Now, now, we mustn't be hasty," said Inigo, drawing himself up and shaking out his cloak. "We will have new ones made, of course, at the printer's expense, for this is clearly their fault . . . but do we really need to remove these straight away?"

Robin Stevens

His eyes met Miss Crompton's, and a flicker of understanding passed between them.

"Well . . . ," said Miss Crompton slowly. "Well now. Let me think."

"Of course you have to remove them!" cried Rose, pointing at the posters. "You can't possibly leave them up. I am being threatened! Someone did this to ME!"

An expression crossed Inigo's face. It was almost— delight? But then it was gone, replaced by magnificent concern.

"They did indeed!" he cried. "And it is dreadful, Rose. Of course it is! But you must have heard that there is no such thing as bad publicity? These playbills are intriguing. Perhaps they may draw more of an audience."

"Hmmm," said Miss Crompton. "I believe I know someone at the *Evening Standard* who may be able to run a piece. I can call him—would Monday suit for interviews, do you think?"

"This is impossible!" cried Rose. "You can't be serious, Frances! I'm the star! Does no one care that I'm being threatened?"

But, although the company seemed fascinated by the posters, no one seemed to care much about Rose herself. The actors who played Lord and Lady Montague whispered excitedly. Simon was grinning, while Martita flicked back her hair and smirked. Lysander leaned forward and muttered something in Rose's ear that sounded very much like, "Getting your comeuppance at last, eh?" At this, Rose gave an angry shriek.

Only Annie looked troubled. She turned to me and Daisy and said, rather unhappily, "They all do seem to hate her, don't they?"

"That's because she isn't very nice," said Daisy. "I don't blame them!"

"Oh!" said Annie. "I suppose she isn't. She always seems to appreciate *me*, though. Do you really think she's so unpleasant?"

She was staring at Rose as if she was seeing her for the first time. And, as I looked around at the company, I had a thought that worries me even more now. Everyone knew how to play a part. How could I be sure which of their emotions were real, and which were for their audience?

There on the street, staring at those horridly creepy posters, I knew that the mystery at the Rue Theatre had taken a new and darker turn.

Part Two
The Place Death

s Rose burst into angry sobs once again, it was the stagehand who spoke. "It wasn't my fault," he insisted, holding his hands up. "Just so long as everyone knows that. I don't want to get into any trouble for this. Just doing my job. It was *her* who told me to put the posters up!" he added, pointing to Martita.

"Ah!" cried Rose, whirling round to face Martita. "Then it's YOU who's behind this! It must be! You've been jealous of me ever since I got the part of Juliet, Martita. Admit it!"

Suddenly everyone was shouting, and I felt I was drowning in the chaos.

"But I wasn't the one who ordered the posters. And I never even opened the parcel!" cried Martita. "I went to get them from the printer and I gave them straight to you. I never knew what was on them!"

"That's true!" Daisy whispered. "I saw the seal!"

I had too, but all the same I knew that we were in a

theatre, where nothing could be counted on to be what it seemed.

"We have to check, Daisy," I whispered back. "We can't just take Martita's word for it."

"All right," said Daisy. "The thing to do is telephone the printer. I can do it, but I shall need you to distract Miss C."

"How?" I asked, panicked.

"Hazel, honestly! I won't even answer that question. Just trust yourself!"

By this time, several passers-by were pausing on the street outside the Rue to look curiously at our group, and at the furious figure of Rose.

Inigo seemed to come to a decision. "Enough of this! Everyone, BACK INSIDE IMMEDIATELY!" he bellowed, flapping his arms like a multicolored bird.

In the chaos, while everyone was piling back into the Rue, I stopped Miss Crompton next to Jim's signing-in book.

"I'm—I'm frightened," I said to her. I realized as I said it that I was, rather. Those posters were going round and round in my head, horribly.

"Now, come along," said Miss Crompton sensibly. "Buck up, dear child. There's nothing to be afraid of at all, just some silly person playing pranks. Actors do this to each other all the time—needle each other, try to upset each other. It's part of stage life, not frightening at all, only

Robin Stevens

annoying. At least, if we manage to get some press out of this, it'll be all to the good in the end."

"*Can* you get publicity from this?" I asked.

"Of course we can," said Miss Crompton. "You mustn't look so shocked—it's show business. We all care for each other deeply, but the play's the thing."

"THE PLAY'S THE THING!" bellowed Inigo, catching her words as he came striding up to us. "WHEREIN I'LL CATCH THE CONSCIENCE OF THE KING!"

"Wrong play, darling," said Miss Crompton. "Now, if you'll excuse me, Hazel, I must go and telephone—"

"No!" I cried. "I—I— Can't you wait? I feel faint—"

And, to my great embarrassment, I could think of nothing to do but sway forward and nearly fall into Miss Crompton's bosom.

Inigo caught me, and I was fanned and patted and talked to like a baby—which ought to have been infuriating, but was in fact quite gratifying. I had faked a faint, just like Daisy! Perhaps I wasn't such a bad actress after all.

"Goodness!" cried Daisy's voice from somewhere above me, a few moments later. "Hazel, you poor thing!" She knelt over me, her knee pressing on my hand.

"Ow!" I hissed at her.

"Excellent work, Watson!" she whispered back. "I have the information we need! Now, pretend to be better. There's somewhere we need to go."

I sat up and blinked, and told everyone that I was feeling so much better, thank you—no, really I was.

"I shall take her somewhere to sit quietly," said Daisy, and pulled me toward the stairs—but, instead of going upward to our dressing room, she dragged me down, through several twists of the staircase, to the underbelly of the theatre.

As we descended, Daisy whispered encouragingly to me.

"See? Of course you can act, Hazel. You can do anything you put your mind to. And anyway, acting is all about belief. *Believe* you are a character and you will be. So. I went to Miss C.'s office to find the number for the printer, and then telephoned them to ask about the order. The printer told me that Theresa had ordered the correct posters for *Romeo and Juliet* a few days ago, but then there was a call yesterday afternoon from someone who said they were Martita, changing the order to the posters we all saw. Martita came in today, Friday, to collect them, paid, and rushed out again without opening the parcel."

"That doesn't prove anything!" I said.

"Of course it does!" said Daisy. "Why would Martita call up and give her own name if she was behind it? No, someone *pretended* to be Martita on that second telephone call! As you know, it's terribly hard to hear anything properly on the telephone—all you have to go on most of the time is the name the other person gives. We're surrounded by actors, too—anyone at the Rue might have faked it, even one of the men. The person at the printer's *thought* it was a woman they spoke to, but they weren't terribly sure. Honestly, the general public are *so* unobservant."

"I still think it's most likely to be Martita!" I said.

"It's *least* likely to be her!" said Daisy swiftly. "She's not stupid, Hazel. She was the one who collected the posters, so the obvious culprit. None of the other threats can be traced back to anyone, so why is this one different?"

"She might have made a mistake!" I said. Daisy sighed.

"I shan't keep trying to convince you," she said. "But you'll see. I do not suspect Martita. Now, haven't you guessed where we're going yet? We're off to observe the scene of the crime!"

"But there isn't a scene of the crime!" I protested.

"That is simply not true," said Daisy, raising an eyebrow at me. "The posters were very clear: someone is plotting to hurt Rose, and the plot will involve a well. And, as we know perfectly . . . *well*, there's one at the bottom of this theatre. We must assume that this well is therefore important, and we would be remiss if we didn't pay it a visit. Don't you see? It might not be the scene of the crime *yet*, but everything tells us it will be, soon enough! Oh, Hazel, this is why I'm still the president of the Detective Society, despite all that business in Hong Kong."

Daisy really *is* still quite cross about Hong Kong.

Of course, as soon as she mentioned the well, I realized

she was correct. I felt rather foolish not to have thought of it. Perhaps I am still not as good a detective as Daisy. Perhaps . . .

But then I remembered that Daisy and I are a brilliant detective double act because we notice different things. There are many things I have seen that Daisy never could have—it's no good either of us trying to measure up to each other.

And I knew that I needed Daisy at that moment. We had come out into the low dark under-corridors of the Rue, stuffy and hot as I breathed in. Around us were the enormous hulking shapes of the theatre's boilers and generators, spiderwebbed and casting jumpy shadows behind shadows as we turned the pocket flashlights we always carry on them. I reached out and seized Daisy's hand.

"It's all right, Hazel," she murmured. "You know perfectly well that I shall kill anyone who tries to hurt either of us."

I felt comforted.

At last we came to the dark doorway that led down into the well room. We had to turn, one by one, and climb down a short ladder into the room itself. The rusting iron of it scratched my hands and left them stinging, and as I climbed I could feel the quiet space of the room at my back. It seemed to be waiting for me.

When we were both down, Daisy and I turned and played our flashlights around the crumbling stone walls of the room. There was nothing on them but a few unlit candles in sconces. Everything smelled of damp, and the walls breathed cold. I shuddered. On the floor we saw a few smudged footprints, and discarded cigarette butts that showed that people had been here—but we couldn't tell who. And there was the covered well itself sitting in the middle of the room, dark and low down like something crouching.

Of course, Daisy went scampering up to the very lip of the well and pushed aside its wooden cover to peer down. She leaned out over it and I had to bite my tongue to stop myself calling out to her to be careful.

"Nothing in here," said Daisy, her voice booming out hollowly. "Apart from— Oh look, some cigarette butts floating in the water—"

"Come away!" I said at last, because she was leaning farther and farther down. "I don't want to have to get you out!"

"It would be terribly difficult," agreed Daisy, mercifully leaning back again and sitting down on the chilly stone floor. "In fact, I think that if I did fall in you would be unlikely to get me out alive again. It's very narrow—I should be stuck!"

"Daisy!" I cried. "Stand up and let's go. I don't want to be here any longer. There's nothing to see."

"Suit yourself," said Daisy, rolling her eyes. "I like it here.

It really would make the perfect place to commit a murder, wouldn't it?"

"NO!" I said. "I hope we never come here again."

But, as it turned out, Daisy was quite right. And we *did* come back, just a few days later.

Robin Stevens

I almost don't want to get to what happened, because I am still reeling from what Daisy and I saw—what we found—but of course I know I must. I have to get past the part where the murder is real and let it become a problem to be solved. When I write things down, they become mine, my puzzle, like something Aunt Lucy might set me to work on; not horror but logic. Daisy made me the Detective Society secretary because she thought it was not as important as being president, but she didn't realize then that writing something down makes you the most import-ant person in the story.

She has discovered it by now, but I am still the person who writes all our murder cases. Now that I have started, not even Daisy could make me stop.

The most bothersome thing (as Daisy would say) is that for once we were not on the spot during the crucial time. We had left the Rue Theatre last night—Saturday—as had most of the rest of the cast. Which means that for this murder case, although we know much more background than the policeman who has been called in, we have to rely on the word of all our suspects. And all our suspects are people who invent themselves for a living.

First I will note down everything we *did* see at the Rue yesterday. We were there all afternoon, for Daisy and I are both in the first act. The actor playing Benvolio was still ill, and so Theresa (who was back at the Rue) came and stood on the stage, reading lines, for Romeo and Mercutio to speak their parts at. Simon went leaping around her like a demon, reciting Mercutio's wild speech about the fairy queen Mab, and something about that contrast gave the rehearsal a disjointed, creepy feeling.

The whole theatre seemed to be at odds with itself. There was a feverish atmosphere seeping into every corner of the Rue, as though the whole cast was sickening for something. I didn't even have to mention it to Daisy—we both knew that something was brewing.

Theresa did not look at all well. Her skin had a yellowish tone to it, and she swayed about, glassy-eyed, but refused to go home.

"I'm quite all right," she said, waving us all away. "Don't you worry about me."

Inigo was directing the rehearsal like a particularly

Robin Stevens

angry deity, Rose and Martita were sniping at each other furiously—Rose was still loudly convinced that Martita was behind the posters—and Rose and Lysander seemed to have had yet another argument. They said all their lines about falling in love beautifully, but they clasped hands as though they wanted to do violence to each other.

Then, when Rose went to change her clothes before the second act (it was part of Inigo's vision that actors should rehearse in their costumes in the last few weeks of rehearsal, to help them inhabit their parts), she cut her foot on a bit of broken glass on her dressing-room floor.

We all heard her scream. I had a moment of feeling quite calm, as though I'd been waiting for rain and at last it had begun to pour.

But, when we ran into the dressing room, we found Rose perfectly all right, and only bleeding from a long, deep cut on her right heel. Annie rushed to get the medical kit from Wardrobe, dabbed Rose's foot with brown iodine, and wrapped it tightly in soft white gauze.

After that, Rose limped about, shooting furious glares at everyone out of the corner of her eyes.

"It was you who left that glass lying around, I know it was," I heard her hiss at Lysander.

"Of course it wasn't me, you madwoman!" cried Lysander. "You're quite desperately unhinged, I tell you. No one left anything in your room."

"*Poor Rose*," murmured Simon. His words were kind, but somehow I didn't think he sounded kind at all. He was watching Rose with a small smile that was quite unlike his usual friendly grin.

Later that day, Martita was having trouble with her Nurse costume, so Annie came into our dressing room and deftly pinned it and sewed it up, talking in a cheerful stream that I caught and lost and caught again. Daisy was reading *Enter a Murderer*, and I was trying to do the crossword, but mostly doodling in the margins.

"What a lovely figure you have," Annie said to Martita. "I have to watch mine, you know. With all these stories in the papers, it's so terribly hard to know what to eat. Do you take vitamins, Martita?"

"Vitamins are an English piece of nonsense," said Martita coolly.

"Well, I'm sure you don't need to bother. You'd look lovely in a bathing costume. I never bathe anymore now that I know how dangerous it can be, but I had a lovely costume from Woolworths when I was a girl and I used to go to the seaside with my family. Yellow and blue it was—it always made me think of the sea, and how my brother and I used to bury our feet in the sand. Feet are a funny thing, aren't they? So ugly, really, mine especially. Poor Rose, cutting her foot!"

Robin Stevens

"Feet are very funny," said Martita, and I could tell she was trying not to laugh. Annie's needle flashed in her left hand and the gas jets popped and glowed. It was all rather soothing, and I breathed it in. I was finding it difficult to concentrate. I was thinking about Rose, and about the posters, and the hothouse blooms with their strange notes.

Annie went on, talking about feet and sand and swimming and mothers and fathers and families and babies and birthmarks and bathing costumes again.

"I liked it so much, I almost didn't want to get it wet. That's why I was there in the first place. My parents told me how silly it was, not wanting to get a bathing costume wet! I am so lucky to have them. My parents, I mean," said Annie, in one of the odd leaps she was prone to.

"Oh really? I think parents are a tragedy," said Daisy, looking up from her book. I could feel my heart racing. Somehow the conversation had ended up in a place that Daisy and I usually avoid more than anything. "Families are simply dreadful."

"Oh!" said Annie, looking rather upset. "Mine are a wonderful support. My mother—"

"Most parents *are* dreadful people," said Martita. "Mine are quite awful. They hate me."

Annie dropped her needle with a little gasp.

"What are you all talking about?" asked Rose, sticking her head round the open door. Something about her expression made me wonder how long she'd been standing outside.

"Nothing, Rose darling," said Annie quickly.

"We're talking about how awful parents are. Did you hate your parents too?" asked Martita, laughing.

Annie breathed in sharply. Rose stepped backward out of sight and slammed the door.

"You shouldn't have said that!" whispered Annie. "*You know!*"

Martita shrugged. "She's said worse to me and Simon before," she said. "And anyway—families *can* be horrible. Even the families you make yourself—they betray you. Sometimes you have to protect yourself."

I saw her hands in the mirror clench together. I knew she was thinking of Miss Crompton, and I suddenly got rather a chill.

Robin Stevens

III

That evening the company would be rehearsing Act Two. The cast who wouldn't be needed were given the rest of the night off—those of them who hadn't already gone home ill. I waved goodbye to them and went to sit at the side of the stage with Daisy as Simon, Lysander, Rose, and Martita readied themselves to go onstage. Bridget would be on her way to collect us soon, but Daisy and I both wanted to watch Rose for as long as we could.

Scene One begins with Romeo pining after Juliet, and Mercutio and Benvolio joking together about Rosaline. Theresa put Simon and Lysander into their positions, fed Lysander his first line, and then fainted dead away stage left.

Lysander stepped backward with his hands up defensively, but Simon caught her as she fell.

He lowered her to the shining boards of the stage and knelt beside her as we all rushed over.

"Hey there," he said quietly. "Theresa, hey, wake up."

Theresa sat up with a gasp, and then began to cough. Her skin had gone waxy and she was shivering all over.

"I'm quite all right," she gasped. "Oh, let me be, Simon my boy—stop bothering me!"

"ENOUGH!" shouted Miss Crompton. She was standing above Theresa, fists on her hips and feet apart. "Theresa my love, I cannot work with you if you die. You must go home at once—there's simply nothing else for it. Martita—no, you're on soon, aren't you, dear? All right—Daisy, Hazel. Your maid is coming to collect you in a few minutes, anyway. Take Theresa to the stage door, ring for a doctor, and have Jim wait with her for a taxi home. I know perfectly well that Theresa will try to get away if she's not stopped."

"I won't!" said Theresa weakly. "Don't be silly, Frankie."

"My dear idiot," snapped Miss Crompton, "GO HOME."

We had learned by now that, when Miss Crompton spoke like that, it was best to obey. So we half walked, half carried Theresa to the stage-door entrance. When we got there, Bridget was already waiting for us. She put down her notebook, took one look at Theresa, and refused to leave her. Instead, she hailed a taxi, and we all sat quietly in it as it wound its way through London and over the great rushing river to Lambeth.

I had perhaps not really understood, or thought about, the fact that Miss Crompton and Theresa lived together until we arrived at their flat. I saw that although it was handsome and well-appointed, with walls covered in actors' glossy signed photographs, it had only two bedrooms. One of them was filled with Martita's untidy things (for she really did live with them) and the other was as clean and staid as Miss Crompton and Theresa, a double bed at its center.

I noticed it, and noticed Daisy and Bridget noticing it too. Daisy started, folded her arms in embarrassment, and stepped out into the corridor as quickly as she could. I was rather embarrassed too, for it was all very grown up, like properly imagining Uncle Felix and Aunt Lucy being married.

Sometimes I have considered being old, twenty-five, and allowed to live on my own with anyone I like, without a matron telling me to eat vegetables and go to bed on time. I cannot really imagine my father approving of it, and so the vision dies, but all the same . . .

Bridget pursed her lips a little, and then sighed as she led Theresa, shivering and pale in the face, to bed.

"I'm all right!" said Theresa. "Don't you worry about me."

"Nonsense," said Bridget as she tucked her in efficiently. "Don't be a martyr. Daisy, telephone the doctor, if you please."

I felt sorry for Theresa. She looked so small and weak lying in bed, not like a grown-up at all.

Daisy went to the telephone and I peeked in at Martita's room. Things were dropped carelessly about on the floor, and there was an explosion of makeup scattered across the dressing table. But I also saw something that gave me pause. There was a half-packed bag on the floor. I remembered what Martita had said about even the families you choose betraying you. Could Martita be planning to *leave* Miss Crompton's house and the Rue?

This felt significant, and I went to tell Daisy. She had hung up the telephone and was hovering in the hallway beside it, her mouth covered with her handkerchief. "Breathe through your nose, Hazel!" she whispered. "Detectives must not get ill!"

"I think Martita's packing up!" I whispered. "I think she's *leaving*, Daisy!"

"Where would she go?" asked Daisy, and I saw the wrinkle appear at the top of her nose above the handkerchief. "No, she can't. That's idiotic of her!"

"Don't get upset!" I said. "She's been awfully hurt by Rose, Daisy, you know that."

"I know!" cried Daisy loudly, and then lowered her voice. "It's just that—Martita—she *can't* leave the Rue, that's all. She has nowhere else to go!"

I stared at her, and under my gaze Daisy flushed and lowered her eyes.

"Daisy—" I began.

Robin Stevens

"Daisy!" called Bridget from the bedroom. "Will you telephone your uncle and explain why we're late?"

Daisy snatched up the telephone again as though it was a life raft, and she was drowning in the sea. I sighed.

The operator put her through to Uncle Felix's flat, and I could hear his low, ironic, rather blurry voice at the other end of the line. I understood what Daisy meant about telephones. I could hear Uncle Felix's tone, but not much of his accent itself. It would be easy to pretend to be someone else on the telephone, and of course Daisy has done so many times.

Daisy gestured to me and I crowded next to her with my ear pressed to the receiver.

"Hello, Uncle Felix," I said.

"Hazel, Daisy, what mischief have you got yourselves into now?" asked Uncle Felix, half amused and half concerned.

"No mischief!" cried Daisy. "Really, Uncle F. We're helping a poor woman from the Rue who's ill with the flu, and Bridget is with us. It was her idea!"

"Hmm," said Uncle Felix. "Why do I never want to trust you, dear niece?"

"I don't know!" said Daisy. "I am utterly trustworthy! It's your own suspicious mind. Anyway, we're in Lambeth now, but we'll be home as soon as *ever* we can, when the doctor arrives. We haven't got into any trouble at all!"

"I find that hard to believe, Daisy," said Uncle Felix—but

I thought he was smiling at the other end of the line. "All right. Come home soon, and don't get mixed up in any crimes on the way!"

Which, as Daisy points out now, was a deeply ironic thing for him to say.

Robin Stevens

The first hint we had that something truly dreadful had happened at the Rue was when we arrived at the stage-door entrance on Sunday morning. Jim was sitting at his desk, looking quite haggard with worry.

"What's up, Jim?" asked Daisy curiously.

"It's happened at last," he said to Daisy. "My mind's begun to go. I always hoped I'd be spared, but that's the way of life. The rot sets in. Might as well retire now and book my space in the graveyard."

"Are you dying?" I asked, alarmed.

"Might as well be," said Jim. "What use is a doorman who can't watch the door? I swear I never left my post last night until the theatre was locked up and I went to bed, not once, but—although I never saw her go—she went. It's witchcraft."

"*Who* went?" asked Daisy. "What's happened?"

"Rose Tree left halfway through rehearsal last night,

according to the signature in my book," said Jim bitterly. "And she's not come back in this morning. Miss Crompton says she must be ill, same as half the cast. But—it's all wrong!"

"Goodness me!" said Daisy. "How very . . . interesting. Hazel, come along!"

But when we rushed into our dressing room, both dying to discuss Rose's mysterious disappearance, Martita was already there, painting her eyes on in the mirror as the gas jets sputtered and flickered.

"I suppose you've heard that Rose hasn't bothered to turn up today," said Martita, looking at us in her reflection. "Good riddance! I hope she never comes back."

"Why don't you think she'll come back?" I asked. "Isn't she just ill?"

"Who knows!" said Martita. "I don't much care."

"Will you play Juliet today, since she's not here?" I asked. I was looking at Martita and wondering. I knew Martita wasn't lying when she said that she hoped Rose would never come back. But surely Rose could not really have *gone*?

"I suppose I will," said Martita, and she smiled thoughtfully at herself in the mirror. "If I have time. Theresa's still ill, so I've got to fetch and carry for Frances today as well as speak the Nurse's lines. The way this production is going, I shall end up playing the Nurse and Juliet in the same scene. Avant-garde as anything!"

Robin Stevens

"We can help you!" said Daisy. "I—I could play the Nurse, if you'd like."

"Or we could look for Rose," I said.

"Don't be stupid," said Martita. "Don't bother. She'll be off somewhere, sharpening her claws, waiting for the perfect moment to come back and ruin our lives. She knows how to make her entrances and exits, does Rose Tree."

I told myself she was right. Rose must be somewhere in the swirl and bustle of London. But then why were the hairs on my arms prickling?

"What happened last night?" Daisy asked. "When did Rose leave?"

Martita sighed.

"She was being a diva as usual," she said, turning round from the mirror. She had not quite finished doing her right eye, and the effect was rather alarming. "Moping about on her cut foot when I know she was faking. I saw her walk on it perfectly easily in the corridor, but when she came out on the stage she behaved as though she'd never walk again. She made the balcony scene impossible—Lysander was stuck clinging to the trellis, looking as though he wanted to murder her, and I could have hit her myself.

"Then she decided her costume wasn't right, and I had to call Annie out of Wardrobe to fix it. Not right! A thread was loose on the bodice, that was all. We had to wait while Annie fiddled with it and talked us to death. I didn't see what happened after that—as soon as I was backstage I had to run about helping Frances. Everything ran as normal until after our break at the beginning of Scene Five, when Rose came onstage still wearing her nightdress costume from Scene Two and marched straight back off again. She was in a rage about something. I went to her dressing room after her, to persuade her on, but she wouldn't come. She was in a fury about *something*. She shrieked at me to leave her alone, so I did.

"Twenty minutes or so later I went back in to get her, but by then she wasn't there. We had to pause the rehearsal while we all searched, and then Frances went and looked at Jim's signing-out book and found Rose's name written in it. She'd just gone home without telling anyone! So of course rehearsal was over for the night, and we all went home as well. I tell you, she's playing with us. She'll come back."

I wanted to believe it was as simple as that, but the detective side of me did not. When I looked at Daisy, I knew that she didn't either.

Rose had gone, but no one had seen her leave. Jim never missed anything, but he had missed her. She had cut her foot yesterday afternoon, and blamed Lysander for leaving glass on her dressing-room floor. The people who had been left in the theatre when we took Theresa home were Inigo, Miss Crompton, Lysander, Simon, Martita, Annie, and Jim, and, of those, at least four of them disliked Rose. And someone had been threatening her . . .

Robin Stevens

There was a knock on our dressing-room door. It was Miss Crompton, and her face was drawn and solemn.

"Martita," she said. "I've just been on the telephone to Rose's boardinghouse. She hasn't been back since she left to come to the Rue on Saturday morning."

The hairs on the back on my neck stood up. So Rose had definitely not gone home last night. Where could she be?

Daisy's hand closed around my wrist in an iron grip, and she hissed into my ear. "Hazel! Come with me. I've had an idea. It is a very terrible one, and I hardly want it to be correct, but—come on!"

She dragged me through the corridors of the Rue, down and down and down the stairs into the dark, quiet set of under-rooms, the last of which was the well room.

"They looked for her last night!" I protested. "She can't still be in the theatre!"

"They looked for her," said Daisy grimly. "Which probably just means *called* for her in each room, assuming she could respond. They were looking for a live woman who could speak to them. But what if they were looking for the wrong thing?"

I shuddered. I have never wanted Daisy to be incorrect so desperately.

The door to the well room was shut, and the room was dark and quiet when we pushed it open. We had to climb down the little ladder to the stone floor, which was rough and uneven under my feet. The room smelled stale, a little of cigarettes, a little of greasepaint and cold cream, a little of cold stone and a little of iron.

"Daisy!" I said. We swung our flashlights around, and saw that the dirt on the floor had been disturbed and kicked up since we had last visited. There was one print clearly visible in the dust—a bare foot with something blurring the middle of it. Something like a bandage.

"*Draw that*," snapped Daisy, all business. She swung her flashlight back to the little exit ladder, and we both saw a white thread that had become caught on one of the rungs. Daisy pulled out her handkerchief and stepped toward it.

"Daisy!" I hissed. "Leave it! It might be important."

"That's why I want to take it!" protested Daisy, but she stepped back empty-handed. We did not even need to mention that the police would be called.

Only then did we turn to the closed well.

"I don't want to look," I whispered.

"Nonsense," said Daisy. "On three. One—two—three—"

We pushed off the cover and swung our flashlights down into it—and saw what we knew we would.

My breath was loud in my ears and the hand that held my flashlight trembled. Far below a pale shape was caught half in and half out of the dark, glistening water. I could see the sodden hem of a white gown, and two feet sticking up, the right one bound with gauze. It looked like the posters come to life—but this was no joke. I felt very ill.

"It's Rose," I gasped. "Daisy, we've found her!"

I stepped away, and crouched down with my head pressed against my knees in their scratchy woollen tights, but Daisy didn't move.

"That," she said, "is quite horrid."

"Daisy, stop looking!" I whispered.

"Don't be silly!" said Daisy. "She's dead—she doesn't care."

But I found that I cared for her. I felt hot and itchy, as though there were spiderwebs all over me. I hate corpses.

Daisy paced about the well slowly, shining her flashlight across the floor. Once she knelt, and quickly stood up again. I sat with my arms wrapped round my legs and watched her. Daisy has no problem with crime scenes at all—in fact, she relishes them. I sometimes worry about that.

She turned and paced her way back across the floor, stepping carefully round the footprint and the scuff marks. "You *have* sketched this, haven't you, Hazel?" she asked.

I got out my notebook and drew—one version of the whole room, with the well and the print marked, including the location of the white thread, and one close-up version of the bare footprint, its measurements taken with string. I would have done it earlier, but the body had distracted me. I was on edge, my head aching and my skin prickling.

Daisy stood over me and sighed.

"Don't, Daisy!" I said. "Don't say it! You know I don't like this part!"

"I have said, time and time again, that you must develop a thicker skin . . ." Daisy began. I glared up at her in the glow of our flashlights, and she paused and then went on. "But I do know that you are *trying*. Now, what have we learned here?"

"Rose fell down the well," I said faintly. "She's stuck upside down."

"All true, Watson, but that's not all. Rose *might* have overbalanced and tipped in on her own—were it not for the fact that the well cover had been carefully put back on afterward. That, combined with this pattern of scuff marks, tells us a different story."

"Rose was here with someone else," I said slowly. "These marks—they might be from a fight. And then . . . Rose didn't fall into the well. She was *pushed*."

I imagined the scene, and it made me feel iller than ever. "Ugh!" I cried. "This is awful, Daisy! It's a murder!"

"Murder is always awful," snapped Daisy, "which is why we must detect it. Now, what happened next? The murderer stayed for long enough to cover the well, hiding the body from last night's quick search, but not long enough to notice the footprint on the floor or the white thread on the ladder. Why?"

"Perhaps they didn't have a flashlight?" I suggested. "Or they had a candle that went out?"

"Don't be silly, Hazel. There's no wax on the floor," said Daisy briskly. "No, they must have had a flashlight, and they must have been forced to leave before they had finished tidying the scene."

"What if they were running for their cue?" I asked. I said it simply because I had got so used to the Rue that my life seemed measured out in lines and scenes now, instead of the Deepdean bell. But Daisy started and clapped me on the back.

"Oh, excellent, Watson!" she cried. "Of course! Rose

must have died sometime during last night's rehearsal. Front of house is all locked up until opening night, and the only other way in or out is through the stage door—but Jim would have noticed if someone else had come in off the street. That means that the only suspects we have for this crime are the people who were still in the Rue last night. Now, we just need to discover the last moment Rose was seen alive! Oh, if only we'd been here last night!

"Well, Hazel, I think there's only one thing we can do now. We must make the discovery known to the rest of the company, and there is a neat way to do this *and* test the sound qualities of this room. We have been professional actresses for nearly two weeks. Now is the time to use all that Martita has taught you about projecting your voice, so I hope you've been listening to her. On three again, Watson. One, two, THREE!"

Truly, I thought that I had not learned much about projecting anything. Martita had despaired of me only the day before in the kindest way possible, not even shouting, and it made me despair of myself too. When I am onstage, I have barely learned to stop looking down at my feet. But, all the same, the shriek that came out of my mouth made me jump. I suppose it was the pent-up horror of being in *another* dark room with *another* dead body, as though my real life is the same nasty dream I must keep living.

No one answered.

We waited thirty seconds by our wristwatches and then screamed again, even louder. Daisy's scream was so piercing that I had to cover my ears.

"Good heavens," she said, out of breath. "This room really is blocked off from the rest of the theatre. An ideal place to murder someone! Make a note of that. All right, this time

I shall climb the ladder and open the door first. Remember, Hazel, when everyone else comes running, you are a very frightened little girl who has just seen something absolutely dreadful. If you can manage it, cry."

"I *know*, Daisy!" I said.

"I'm only saying it because I am convinced that you can do it," said Daisy. "I believe in you, dear Watson."

She winked at me, rubbed a little dust into her cheek and rumpled her hair, then scaled the iron rungs of the ladder and threw the heavy door open, letting out another piercing scream.

"HELP!" she shrilled. "OH, HELP, SOMEBODY, HELP!"

"HELP!" I echoed, following her up and out of the well room. I felt foolish. I knew that anyone would take one look at me and know that I was acting. But my foot caught on the top step of the ladder and I thumped to the ground, tears starting in my eyes. I bit my cheek and by the time I was on my feet again I hardly needed to act.

This time the company heard us. People began to pelt down the stairs.

Miss Crompton arrived first, brandishing her keys and a flashlight. She is always very well prepared. Inigo, cloak flapping, was just behind her.

"Whatever is it?" Miss Crompton cried. "Daisy, Hazel, what is all this?"

Robin Stevens

"Body!" I gasped. "We've found Rose's body in the well!"

Daisy very subtly shoved me aside and took center stage in the dusty, tightly packed little corridor, just as Simon and Martita arrived. Lysander was behind them with most of the rest of the cast, and Annie and the stagehands brought up the rear. The corridor was now as crowded as a train carriage, and I had an odd, whole-body memory of that evening on the Orient Express, although the Rue's basement was as different from the gorgeous Orient Express as anywhere could be.

"ROSE IS DEAD!" screamed Daisy. "She's in the well, just like the posters said! Oh, it's too horrid! I can't bear it!"

"WHAT? Don't toy with us!" roared Inigo, throwing his hands in the air.

"I'm not lying!" said Daisy, slightly too annoyed for the part she was playing. "It's absolutely true—you can see for yourself! We pushed open the cover and there she was!"

"That's a joke, right?" asked Simon. He reached for Martita's hand, but she flinched away. She was standing still, her lips pulled tightly together and her eyes narrowed as she watched Daisy. She looked . . . guarded, as though she didn't want to give anything of herself away.

Annie threw her hands over her face in horror, and Lysander's mouth gaped, his lips opening and closing silently.

Miss Crompton simply pushed us all aside, her face set, and strode toward the well room.

"LIGHTS!" she shouted briskly, and there was a scramble as everyone hunted for more flashlights and candles and then piled inside behind her.

"Watch the crime scene!" cried Daisy. "Er—I mean—do be careful!"

With light and shadow dashing about across its walls, the well room looked eerier than ever, as though it was full of ghosts. I shivered and drew close to Daisy, who put her arm round me tightly. I knew that she was still just acting, but all the same it was comforting.

Miss Crompton, clutching her own flashlight in her hand, moved toward the well.

"This had the cover on when you found it?" she asked.

Daisy and I nodded. Miss Crompton stood by the edge of the well and peered down into its depths. Everyone was deadly silent.

When she stepped backward and turned round, her face was very drawn. She suddenly seemed much older.

"It's true," she said in a voice so quiet it was almost a whisper. "She's there."

There was uproar. Annie screamed, and so did Lysander.

"WE MUST LIFT HER OUT!" Inigo was bellowing.

"No! We have to telephone the police!" cried Miss Crompton.

Martita turned and walked toward the well. She had a

flashlight too, and she shone it down into the far water.

And then she said something that made my skin crawl.

"Methinks I see thee, now thou art so low,
As one dead in the bottom of a tomb.
Either my eyesight fails, or thou lookest pale."

It was only Juliet's speech to Romeo in Act Three, Scene Five, which I had heard a hundred times by now—but I had never heard it spoken like this.

And I suddenly felt uncomfortably suspicious of Martita.

And so here we are, scribbling in the stalls (or at least I am scribbling; Daisy is stewing about ruined crime scenes and idiotic clodhoppers), while the policeman who was called by Miss Crompton stamps about the Rue and destroys the scene of the crime even further. He is not being careful at all, and it makes me feel sweaty with annoyance.

Daisy has just looked over at what I was writing and said, "Heavens, Hazel, I'm rubbing off on you! You never used to be so cynical about the police!"

This is not fair. I am not cynical about the good ones. I was not safe enough to feel cynical about Detective Leung during our case in Hong Kong. But blue-coated English bobbies, who have seen fewer dead bodies than Daisy and me, I have learned to be suspicious of. It is simply not wise to assume that grown-ups are any better at solving murders than we are.

· · ·

When the policeman, PC Jellicoe, first arrived, he went trudging into the well room as though he was expecting to find nothing more down the well than a white sheet. He came out very pale. Then he went barging back into Miss Crompton's office to telephone for more police, a whole crew to pull out the body, and cornered Miss Crompton to ask her what had happened.

"I simply have no idea," said Miss Crompton forcefully while we all stood about and Daisy and I did our best not to look as though we were taking in every word she said. "It was a perfectly ordinary evening. We were working through Act Two. We lost Peter and Benvolio—"

PC Jellicoe looked concerned, and Miss Crompton said quickly, "Not dead! Merely ill. There's something going around. My stage manager, Theresa Johnson, was sent home in the early evening with it. These two girls, the ones who found Rose, they and their maid took her, and they spent the evening in Miss Johnson's flat."

Daisy and I both heard that—she was making us Theresa's alibi, and conveniently not mentioning that Theresa's flat was her flat too, all in one breath. It was very neatly done.

"Everyone had to pull together and they did. There's no argument in my company," said Miss Crompton firmly, and I wondered if she knew the same Rue Theatre that I did.

"Rose was perhaps a little giddy—there's a reporter coming on Monday to talk to her and the rest of the cast about, well, about press for the production. She dropped a glass in her dressing room and stepped on it—she really wasn't focused. But I calmed her down, and we proceeded in quite an ordinary way until after the break, when she refused to come out onstage for Scene Five. I sent Martita Torrera to her dressing room to get her, but she was unsuccessful. Inigo decided to wait to summon her again, but, when Martita went in again later, Rose had gone. We all looked, but we were searching for"—here Miss Crompton's gaze faltered—"a live woman. We never thought to open the cover and look down the well. If it wasn't for the girls, who knows when she might have been discovered?"

I wondered a little about this story. Miss Crompton was making it sound as though Rose was responsible for smashing the glass, but I did not think that was true. Was she being truthful about everything else?

"And what were you two doing in that room?" PC Jellicoe asked me and Daisy.

I froze. Only the most improbable answers came into my mind. But Daisy, of course, did not turn a hair.

"We were playing hide-and-seek!" she said. "I came in and found Hazel, and then we both noticed that the well's cover was a little loose, and we moved it and looked in, and then— Oh! It was TOO dreadful!"

I breathed again.

"Hide-and-seek," said PC Jellicoe slowly, writing it down

in his small notebook as though it was not a ridiculous lie. "This is all very useful. Now, you sit tight. I need to make a map of the scene—need to get it in my head before the super comes."

"Super?" asked Miss Crompton. Her voice was a little sharp. "Can't you clear this up on your own?"

"Not on your life," said the policeman. "I've had my orders. The station's sending someone. He should be here shortly."

Daisy and I, sitting with the rest of the cast in the stalls, are both rather worried about this mysterious super. What if he is a bad policeman? What if he is a good one? We have clues. We saw the crime scene. We are at the beginning of our investigation. But what if this detective swoops in and takes it away from us, and then comes to all the wrong conclusions? What if he sends us home? We ought to have telephoned Uncle Felix, after all. . . .

The door of the auditorium has just banged open and a man has come striding in, his greatcoat swirling around him. He has swept off his hat and is holding it in his hand. His nose is long, and he has a crinkled face and thick dark hair that is slicked back on his head.

I reached for Daisy's hand and squeezed it as hard as I could. My heart is doing strange things in my chest and my head is whirling.

This policeman is not just anyone.

He is Inspector Priestley.

Part Three

They Will Murder Thee

I nspector Priestley strode onto the stage and turned round to stare out into the stalls.

"Who is in charge here?" he asked.

"I am!" cried Inigo, stepping forward. "I am the director!"

"This is *my* theatre," said Miss Crompton, drawing herself up. "And so I am in charge, Inigo darling. I am Frances Crompton. And who might you be?"

"Inspector Priestley, madam," said the Inspector, bowing politely. "I have been called in to investigate this case."

"What are we going to do?" I whispered to Daisy in panic. What if Inspector Priestley told the whole of the Rue that we were not just company members but detectives? What if he told Uncle Felix that we were mixed up in another murder case? "Daisy!"

"Shh, quiet!" Daisy whispered back. "I'm thinking. And *don't* tell me to think more quickly!"

I bit back my intended reply.

The Inspector turned round to face the stalls and nodded at us all. I told myself that, in the glare of the stage lights, he could not make us out, but all the same his dark eyes swept across us and I swore I saw them flicker and pause on my face.

"I must ask all of you here not to leave this theatre!" he called out. "Stay where you are. I will be interviewing each of the people who were here last night in turn."

"Is that really necessary?" asked Miss Crompton. She looked uncomfortable.

"You yourself told my officer that the body was covered over, which rules out an accidental fall. I'm afraid that in these circumstances a proper investigation is necessary. Now, would you be able to tell me the best place to hold my interviews? Do you have somewhere we could use?"

"I suppose you may use my office on the first floor," said Miss Crompton, folding her arms. "The bar can serve as a waiting area. But you must understand that rehearsal will have to continue this morning. We are of course terribly sad about poor Rose, but the show must go on. We open in just a few days, after all."

I watched Miss Crompton carefully. She had seemed truly upset when we found Rose's body in the well— but now, just like yesterday when the posters were discovered, she seemed to be thinking only of the theatre, and

Robin Stevens

of how this might affect business. Was it just because she had to put aside her grief and think of the play? Or . . . was Daisy right? Had she liked Rose only because she was the star? I remembered how fond she had seemed of Rose, that first day Daisy and I arrived at the Rue. All that fondness seemed to have vanished now.

"We certainly do," agreed Inigo. "I don't suppose you know when journalists will be allowed into the theatre?"

"*Journalists?*" asked Inspector Priestley.

"There is no such thing as bad publicity, Inspector," said Inigo. "The thing has occurred. We may as well turn it to our advantage!"

I remembered what he had said yesterday and shivered a little. Was there anything Inigo would not do for publicity? Might he even . . . murder for it?

"An interesting attitude," said Inspector Priestley. "But I'm afraid I don't work with journalists, unlike some other police officers. You will have to wait until I am done, sir. Now." He turned his gaze on Martita. "I have seen from the program my officer gave me that you are the understudy Juliet."

"What of it?" asked Martita, folding her arms to match Miss Crompton. The whole Rue Theatre seemed against Inspector Priestley.

"Merely asking," said the Inspector mildly. "We shall discuss it later. Miss Crompton, may I be taken to your office?"

"Daisy! Hazel!" called Miss Crompton. "Come here! You can show the Inspector to the office and fetch him whatever he needs. Inspector, these are the girls who found poor Rose."

Of course, she had no idea that we meant anything to the Inspector at all, and we could not refuse her request without explaining ourselves. Daisy and I looked at each other. We would have to go through with it.

As we walked down through the stalls, past frightened, angry cast members muttering to each other, I felt dizzy and unreal. I wished like anything that we were wearing some of Daisy's disguises. I imagined the Inspector staring at us and not remembering us—but, of course, that was merely a fantasy. Although I was in my doublet and Daisy was in her gown, we were quite obviously Daisy Wells and Hazel Wong, two Deepdean schoolgirls with a reputation for being found near dead bodies.

Up the steps onto the stage we went, and then we were in the dazzle of the stage lights, and the darker glare of the Inspector. I saw him start just a little, and I knew he had recognized us. I cringed. Daisy, of course, simply stuck her chin out and marched over to shake his hand.

"I am Daisy Wells and *this* is my friend Hazel Wong," she said firmly. "We are delighted to meet you for the very first time, because we have never been involved in anything like this before."

I could see the corners of Inspector Priestley's mouth crinkling, and knew in a glorious rush that we had nothing to fear from him. He would keep our secret from both Uncle Felix and the rest of the Rue. We could not have our suspects knowing that we were practiced detectives, not when a murder had just occurred that any one of the company might have been part of.

"Good morning, ladies," said the Inspector. "How wonderful to meet you."

"Yes, it *is*," said Daisy and she took his hand forcefully. "Now, if you'll just come this way immediately, Hazel and I will guide you to your interview room. . . ."

Inspector Priestley allowed himself to be dragged offstage right into the stuffy darkness of the wings. It was only as we turned into the stairwell that led up to Miss Crompton's office that the Inspector spoke.

"And what," he said, very softly, so softly that anyone listening would not be able to hear, "is the Detective Society doing at another murder scene?"

"Do you know," said Daisy brightly, "that was *just* what Hazel and I were asking ourselves when you arrived. We didn't witness the murder, *most* annoyingly, but luckily we are part of the company—"

"Madam Super," said Inspector Priestley, "you are trying

to chatter me into forgetting my question, and it will not work. Miss Wong?"

I gulped. "Daisy's uncle and aunt sent us, to keep us out of trouble," I said as we walked up the stairs to the office. "We haven't called them yet. We *can't* let them know. We aren't supposed to be detecting anything . . ."

"Anyway, what are *you* doing here?" Daisy butted in. "This isn't Gloucestershire."

"I've been promoted," said Inspector Priestley. "The Fallingford case got me noticed."

"I'm glad it helped *you*," hissed Daisy. "Why, of all the—"

"But we *are* part of this case," I said, as quickly as I could. "We found the body, and we've been part of the cast for almost two weeks. We know the Rue inside out."

"What Hazel is trying to say is that on this occasion we are willing to let you help us solve the case," said Daisy. "And *don't* just say no like a grown-up. You've seen us solve three cases—and we've solved three more without you there."

The Inspector's forehead wrinkled.

"Please," I said. "Let us help you. I promise we'll be good!"

"You know we're good detectives. You gave us *badges*!" said Daisy, her voice trembling with outrage as we pushed open the door into Miss Crompton's chaotic office.

"*Let me speak*, Miss Wells. You are not part of the police so you cannot officially be part of this case. However, I will not stop you detecting. I will turn a blind eye and a deaf ear to anything you do that is not obviously dangerous or criminal, and in turn you will make sure that what you are doing does not reach the ears of my higher-ups. Do you understand?"

"Yes!" I said gratefully.

"Why?" asked Daisy suspiciously.

"Because last time I met you, you saved a little girl's life, and you deserve a reward greater than badges for that," said Inspector Priestley. "That is all the reasoning I will give, Miss Wells. Do not look a gift horse in the mouth. If you please, will you ask all the relevant members of the company to come to the waiting area, and then bring the young woman who is now playing Juliet to be my first witness? Miss Wong, I am going to turn round, and I expect you to be gone before I turn back. *Where* you go is your own business."

The Inspector turned away to face the wall of the office (rather marked and stained) and cleared his throat. For a moment I could not think what he meant, and then I understood. He was suggesting I hide so I could listen in to the suspects' statements.

I panicked. It was like a deadly serious version of What's the Time, Mr. Wolf?, a game that always frightens me anyway. I glanced around the room. It was awfully full of rubbish, but all the same there did not seem much to hide

Robin Stevens

behind apart from chairs and piles of papers. And then I caught sight of a little wardrobe just next to the door. It was half open, and I could see that there was a small space beneath Miss Crompton's hanging coats. I am short still (I am beginning to think I will always be short), and I knew that, although Daisy could never twist herself into that space anymore, I could. So I crept in, and crouched down, knees to my chest. I pulled the door almost closed behind me just as the Inspector turned round.

He looked about the room, then smiled and took off his greatcoat. He settled himself in Miss Crompton's big leather chair, behind her desk, and laid out his notebook carefully before him. I could see a sliver of the Inspector and more of the empty seat in front of him. I breathed in mothballed dust as I pulled out my casebook and pencil and balanced them on my knees, inches from my face. I was glad all over again that I had learned shorthand from Alexander.

That made me think of the Junior Pinkertons, of course. Half-term was here, and I knew George and Alexander were planning to spend the week in London. I had been quite horrified at the idea that they might ask to come to the Rue, for I had not wanted them to see the difference between my performance and Daisy's—but now I realized that they might be able to help us solve this mystery.

I was so much in a dream that I almost missed the door opening beside me and Daisy coming in with Martita.

Why am I the first person to be interviewed?" asked Martita crossly, before she had even sat down.

"I should think it was obvious, Miss Torrera," said the Inspector. "I have asked you to speak to me first because you are Juliet, now that Rose Tree is dead. You obviously gain from her death, and that makes me interested in you. Thank you, Miss Wells. You may go now."

Daisy curtsied and turned to leave. But she glanced back at Martita as she went, and for a moment her face suddenly slipped out of its polite mask and into an expression of terrible concern. Then she scowled and narrowed her eyes, turning back into my don't-care best friend as though nothing had happened. I held my breath. It felt as though I had seen something important even before the interviews had begun.

The door closed behind her and I turned my eyes back to Martita and the Inspector.

"Now, Miss Torrera, you are Spanish?"

"Portuguese," said Martita, bristling. "My name is invented, like everything at this theatre. Frances didn't think my real name was dramatic enough for the audience. Apparently, Spanish girls are more alluring."

She curled her lip as she said it, and I felt for her. At the Rue, no one is really themselves, and I saw again that Martita was not happy playing that part.

"Now, on to the matter of your role. Now that Rose Tree is dead—"

"I will be given the part," said Martita, tossing back her hair. "But I didn't kill her for it."

"We shall see," said the Inspector very calmly. "Now, tell me, if you please, about last night. What did you see? What did you do? I'm not trying to trick you. I simply want to know what happened."

Martita told the Inspector what she had told us about the night before, almost to the word. At least, I thought, her story was consistent—or was that a mark against her? Was it odd that she'd already chosen what she wanted to say? Rose had stormed off at the beginning of Scene Five, Martita had gone after her, and Rose had shouted at her from her dressing room to go away. Martita had decided to leave her alone for a time. When she went back, Rose was gone.

"How long?" pressed the Inspector.

"How should I know? Half past nine, I think—yes, I remember seeing the clock on the stage door when I went to ask Jim if he had seen Rose. That was at twenty-five to ten, so I must have gone to look for her at half past nine. And I left her for the first time at about five minutes past nine."

We could check this, I knew. And, if it was true, that meant we could already narrow down the crucial time to twenty-five minutes.

"How did you feel about Rose, Miss Torrera?"

"I hated her, of course," said Martita. "I don't need to lie. I wanted to play Juliet, and Frances—Miss Crompton— told me I would, until Rose auditioned. She's more famous than I am after *Happy Families* was a success and so she'll bring in better publicity, and Frances needs that. *Measure for Measure* closed after two weeks. But Rose never missed an opportunity to rub it in, as slyly as she could, that she was the star and I was not. She might have been charming on the surface, but she was a witch of a woman and I'm glad she's dead. But, as I said, I didn't murder her. If I had, I would have done much worse to her than tip her down a well. Although it's . . . poetic justice, isn't it? To really throw her down a well, after those posters?"

"Which posters do you mean?" asked Inspector Priestley, a cat that sees a mouse. My heart thumped at the memory.

"Don't you know?" asked Martita, raising her eyebrows. "I

Robin Stevens

thought you were in charge of this case. Someone had been sending Rose threats. First roses, with horrid notes; then peacock feathers—that's a theatre superstition, Inspector: they're supposed to be bad luck—and finally they ordered obscene posters that bragged about Rose being thrown down a well. And now she *has* been!"

"Well, now I know," said the Inspector. "Thank you, Miss Torrera, you may go."

As Martita stood up to leave, I thought she looked rather uncomfortable, despite her bold bluster. I found myself feeling nervous. I was willing Martita to . . . to stop being so much like herself. She was such a forceful person, all teeth and claws, in spite of her hidden kindness—and I knew the Inspector well enough to realize that he was not impressed by her rudeness.

"I must ask that you have your fingerprints taken by my colleague," said Inspector Priestley, "and hand over the costume you were wearing last night. Off you go—and remember, you may not leave this theatre."

"I promise," said Martita, and her light, quick steps passed me.

"Ahem," said Daisy's voice, very loud behind me. She was still acting the part of Efficient Police Secretary. "Inspector, I have Mr. Carver to see you."

"Thank you, Miss Wells," said Inspector Priestley, and I could see him trying not to smile.

Simon came forward into the room. His tread was heavier than Martita's, solid and steady, and he took his seat with a reassuring thump, stretching out easily.

"Good afternoon, sir," he said cheerfully. "How can I be of service?" He was so *very* cheerful that I was instantly suspicious. Why was he not more upset?

"You can begin by telling me what happened last night, Mr. Carver," said the Inspector.

"Of course, sir. I play the part of Mercutio, so I was here until—well, until the rehearsal ended, I guess. I'm on in Scene One, and then Scene Four."

"How long was rehearsal to continue?"

"Until the end of Act Two, sir," said Simon. "But Scene Four was my final appearance."

"Then why did you stay?" It was a clever question and I was impressed.

"Oh, well—because Mr. Leontes is on again in Scene Six. I love watching him. He's incredible, a real inspiration to me. I'm here because of him. I—I wouldn't be an actor without him. He brought me into this company, sponsored me when I first came over from the States. I can show you my papers if you want, by the way. They're all in order.

"Anyway, I went to see Jim at the stage door after my part in Scene One was over so I could have a smoke. Then I came back into the stalls to watch Mr. Leontes in Scene Three, before I went on again for Scene Four. Mr. Leontes

Robin Stevens

and I spoke together in the stalls during our break. That's where we were when the break ended and Rose got upset. She marched off the stage and later we heard . . ." He paused.

"Heard what?" asked Inspector Priestley. "And when was this?"

"It must have been just after nine. And, well, we heard Rose yelling at Martita," said Simon reluctantly. "So loud we heard her from onstage. She was saying something about Martita hurting her, but I know that's just Rose exaggerating."

My skin prickled.

"Hurting her?" asked the Inspector.

"Look—I don't—I don't think it meant anything. Rose was always saying mean stuff, to me and to everyone else. She was a nasty, angry person. Mr. Leontes and I went backstage to check up on her, and saw Martita running out of Rose's dressing room, really upset. Martita's a great girl. We got to be friends during *Measure for Measure*. Man, it's a pity how she's been—"

Simon stopped speaking again.

"How she's been what?" asked Inspector Priestley.

"It's nothing, sir," said Simon. He still sounded so cheerful, I thought, though I knew he must be nervous. Simon was a friendly person, but hearing him now I suddenly wondered if there was a hollow space behind that cheerfulness. Was it real, or was it just a panicked show?

"She wanted to be given Juliet, I know, though Rose won the part. I get it—I would've liked to be Romeo, but things don't work out sometimes."

"But instead you were cast as Mercutio?" said Inspector Priestley. "Why?"

"You'd have to ask Frances about that, sir," said Simon. "Since you can't ask Rose."

There was something in his tone that made me grip my pencil tighter.

"Why would Rose have had anything to do with you being cast as Mercutio, Mr. Carver?" asked the Inspector. "Surely that isn't the decision of another actor or actress."

"If you'd known Rose, you wouldn't ask that," Simon told him. "I won't say anything more about it."

It was as though an iron curtain had come down. He would only say that he had gone back to his own dressing room after seeing Martita, and that's where he was when he heard the hunt for Rose begin, just after nine thirty. So, I thought, looking back at my notes from Martita's interview, he had been alone during those twenty minutes.

"I think that's everything, Mr. Carver," the Inspector said at last. "One final question: did you like Rose Tree?"

"With all due respect, that's not the right question, sir," said Simon.

"And what might the right question be, Mr. Carver?"

Simon got up. "Did Rose Tree like me?" he said. "Or

Robin Stevens

to be more accurate—did Rose Tree like the color of my skin?"

And he strode to the doorway.

"See my officer to have your fingerprints taken and your costume examined!" the Inspector called after him.

"Well," he said into the silence. I peeped through the gap in the wardrobe doors and saw him staring into space, looking very thoughtful. I was thoughtful too. Simon did not have an alibi. And, from what he had said, it seemed as though he might have had a real reason to resent Rose Tree.

Daisy was back, a minute later, with Inigo Leontes, and his presence made the office space feel suddenly very small and very dingy.

"Inspector!" he bellowed, striding through the door as though he was the general in a battle scene. "I am here to answer your questions!"

"Very good, Mr. Leontes," said the Inspector. "Please do take a seat."

"I prefer," said Inigo, throwing out his arm and billowing his cloak, "to stand."

"By all means," said Inspector Priestley. "If you could begin with an account of your movements yesterday evening."

But it took Inigo a while to get to the murder. He could not stop talking about the Rue and its successes. In a way, I thought, that was rather like a magician doing a trick, making you watch the bright thing in his right hand so you will not see the truly important thing in his left.

"This theatre is a wonderful place!" he cried. "Frances—Miss Crompton—has nurtured it to become the *only* place to see Shakespeare. She raised *me* up as a younger actor when other theatres would only use me to shock audiences with the color of my skin, and now I repay her by directing her wonderful productions. We collaborated on *Measure for Measure* only this spring, in which I introduced London to my protégé, Simon Carver—"

"But *Measure for Measure* closed after only a few weeks, did it not?" asked the Inspector.

Inigo opened his mouth silently, as though he had been given the wrong cue and couldn't think what line he should say in response.

The Inspector continued. "Of course, the Rue is important to you and Miss Crompton. But I gather that you may not be in easy financial circumstances currently. Now that a woman has been killed, will you not have to close this production too?"

"I hope not," said Inigo, his tone almost sulky. "You will have to speak to Miss Crompton about that."

"Mr. Leontes, things do not look well for your cast members," the Inspector went on. "As far as I can make out, the only suspects seem to be the people I have gathered in the bar area. The Rue operates a strict signing in and out policy, so we can be certain of who was in the theatre at the time of Rose Tree's disappearance."

"Such a dreadful thought!" cried Inigo. He put his palm to his forehead, and I saw that he once again knew his part. "But it is true. Doorman Jim is ever-watchful. I must assure you, though, good sir, that although I was present, I myself am in no way involved. As I play Friar Lawrence in this production, as well as directing, I was onstage for Act Two, Scene Three. After the end of my scene, I went back into the stalls. Young Simon came to sit near me during our break, after his part in Scene Four was over, and we spoke for several minutes about his performance, and how it might be improved.

"Rose then came onstage for Scene Five, still in her balcony-scene nightdress, announced that she wouldn't perform anymore that evening, and flounced away again. Martita was sent after her. We—that is, Miss Crompton, Simon, and myself—all heard the beginning of their altercation, and Miss Tree's scream, and hurried backstage just in time to see Martita running away from the room in some distress. She told us all that it was best to leave Rose alone for the present. I felt it was prudent to follow her advice. Simon and Lysander—who had also come back down from his dressing room to listen in to the argument—returned upstairs, and I went back onto the stage with Frances."

The Inspector's pencil was shooting across his notebook, and so was mine.

"And what happened next?" he asked.

Robin Stevens

"Next? Frances and I discussed some ideas we had for set design," said Inigo. "Then I went to stand at the stage door and speak to Jim, and Frances went to the ladies' room, I believe. So, you see, the last I heard from her, Rose Tree was alive and screaming."

"And what was she screaming?" asked the Inspector.

"Oh, something theatrical—what was it? Yes, I have it. *You will murder me,* I believe. Misspoken, of course; the true line is: *they will murder thee.*"

My heart jumped. Why had Martita and Simon not said this? And *was* it just a line from *Romeo and Juliet* or something more sinister?

"Did you like Rose Tree?" asked Inspector Priestley.

"Certainly not," said Inigo. "My vision was for her to play Juliet opposite Simon as Romeo, but she put an end to that. Said she wouldn't kiss him because—well, because of the color of his skin. Said we couldn't make her. Since that was true, and since she is already the talk of London while he's still finding his feet, we had no choice. Simon became Mercutio and Rose got a fair Romeo, not a Black one. The West End must wait a little longer to fall in love with a Black man, it seems, although I am proof that they will pay to watch one act out a tragedy. But that is a minor disappointment, Inspector!"

"Interesting," said Inspector Priestley. "Now, if you could speak to my colleague about having your fingerprints taken and your costume looked at, I think that will be all. I can hear Miss Wells at the door with my next subject."

"Thank you, Inspector," said Inigo magnificently. "I trust you will find me innocent as soon as possible."

But I saw that his hands trembled a little as he said it.

Robin Stevens

Next was Lysander, and he was in a dreadful funk.

"I don't see why this is necessary," he muttered, shuffling down in his seat and crossing his arms.

"Mr. Tollington, a woman is dead," said the Inspector. "Does that not matter to you?"

"Millions die every day from government neglect," said Lysander, beginning his favorite topic. "Do you see anyone caring about them?"

"I see a great many people caring about them, and I also see that you are trying to change the subject. Now, you are the son of Admiral Manfred Tollington, are you not?"

"No!" said Lysander. "Yes."

"Indeed," said Inspector Priestley mildly. "Raised at Parkview Hall near Rochester, schooled at Eton and RADA."

"So?" muttered Lysander, sinking even lower down in his chair. I almost laughed. Lysander spent so much time railing against the wealthy and entitled, pretending he had to scrimp and save, but all the time he was really just like Daisy.

"I am simply trying to understand you. Now, what were your movements last night?"

"I don't remember," muttered Lysander. "I was onstage! I'm Romeo—I'm on for all the scenes we were rehearsing."

"But I heard you left the stage after Scene Four, during the break."

"No!" said Lysander. "I tell you—I was onstage until Martita came to tell us that Rose wasn't in her dressing room."

"*Were* you?" murmured Inspector Priestley. "Mr. Leontes tells me that he saw you come down from your dressing room during the altercation between Martita and Rose Tree, and that you followed Simon Carver back upstairs to the dressing rooms after it was over. So you must have gone upstairs after the end of Scene Four. Mr. Leontes remained onstage with Miss Crompton, but you were not there."

"All right, I suppose I was. I needed some time on my own," said Lysander, getting crosser and crosser. "I went back upstairs after the row too, but I was at the stage door smoking when Martita began to shout that Rose had disappeared. Really, this play is cursed. You've heard about those threats against Rose? Whoever was behind them sent her absolutely mad. She was behaving like a nightmare, and

Robin Stevens

she made sure we were all as unhappy as possible as well."

"So, you didn't like Rose Tree?" asked Inspector Priestley.

"Wait! I—look, Rose annoyed me. But—we were very close. Artistic temperaments, you understand? We argued, but it spurred on our acting. Romeo and Juliet have a fiery relationship and life imitated art. Rose was . . . well, she was a beauty."

I thought back to the arguments I'd seen between Rose and Lysander, how cruel he had been to her, and how furious she had seemed. And I was sure that Lysander was not telling the whole truth.

"See here, I didn't kill her!" he cried. "I wouldn't! I have no reason to. I loved her, I tell you. You can—you can put that in your pipe and smoke it!"

"I'm more of a cigarettes man, I'm afraid," said the Inspector. "What do you smoke, Mr. Tollington?"

"Roll-ups," said Lysander. "That's what we all smoke here. Anything else would be bourgeois. Can I go?"

"You may," said the Inspector.

Lysander leaped up and dashed out of the office as though he was being chased.

Inspector Priestley leaned back in his chair and stared upward. "What is that quote?" he said, seemingly to himself. "Oh yes . . . *the gentleman doth protest too much, methinks.* Not quite the right play, but it will do."

There was a knock on the door, and Jellicoe, the police officer who had arrived at the Rue first, stepped into the room. As I looked at his blue-coated back from my hiding place, he appeared very tall indeed, and almost imposing.

"Coroner's here, sir," he said. "Wants to have a word. Do you have a moment?"

"Yes, all right, Jellicoe," said Inspector Priestley. "Tell the other witnesses that they'll have to wait a little longer. I think it'll be good for them."

"Yes, sir," said Jellicoe, sounding rather pleased. "They're all stewing, sir. I keep on stepping out, just as you suggested, and every time I come back I hear another little tidbit."

"Excellent, Jellicoe. Well, lead on."

They left the room together, and the door closed with a thump.

Only a breath later it opened again.

"Hazel!" hissed Daisy's voice into the silence. "Hazel, where are you— Oh! Hello."

I had unfolded myself with difficulty from the wardrobe and was crawling out of it. I did not do it in a particularly ladylike manner, and I thumped onto the carpet, red-faced and panting.

"Hello," I said. "I've got a fearful lot of information, Daisy!"

"Oh, so have I!" cried Daisy. "Inspector Priestley is a genius. He's got them all crammed together in the bar, and they keep on accusing each other. Martita's blaming Lysander for all the horrid threats, Simon thinks it's Miss Crompton's fault, Miss Crompton and Inigo have been whispering together furiously about alibis, and Annie is sitting in the corner, talking everyone's ear off about all the murders she's ever read about in the newspapers. But they're all quite clear about timings. Rose and Martita had their argument at about five past nine, and then Martita looked in on Rose's dressing room just before half past, and found that she'd gone. We know the murder must have happened sometime in between!"

"I know!" I said. "And no one has an alibi for that time yet. Lysander and Simon were both alone in their dressing rooms, Martita was running around the Rue, and, even though Miss Crompton and Inigo were onstage together for a while, they left before Martita raised the alarm. Inigo says he went to visit Jim at the stage door, and I think Miss Crompton was in the loo—but they were alone! Any of them might have done it!"

"Timings are going to be exceedingly important in this case," said Daisy, nodding. "We must re-create the crime at the earliest opportunity. And I wonder what the— Oh, quick! I can hear them coming back! Those clodhopping shoes . . . back in the wardrobe, Watson!"

I scrambled back inside. Daisy closed the door after me and slipped out of the room. A minute later, the office door opened.

"Thank you, sir," the Inspector was saying. They both stepped past my hiding place, and I could see that the coroner was short and old. He looked rather like Daisy's family doctor, Dr. Cooper. "You are sure of that?"

"Yes, absolutely. The lady has been in the water for approximately half a day," he was saying in a clipped, official voice to Inspector Priestley. "She has washerwoman's skin, and, since she was stuck facedown, lividity has caused the face and neck to have pronounced purple discoloration and swelling. It is impossible to tell much else from the body, I'm afraid."

"Did she drown?" asked the Inspector. "Or was she already dead when she entered the water?"

"No way to know for certain. I should say that violence was a possibility, but because of the way she was found, even an autopsy is not likely to tell us much. The only thing I did note was a deep cut to her right foot, which also seems to have occurred close to the time of death, though clearly before it, as it had been tended to and bound."

I thought again of the footprint on the floor, and Rose falling down the well, and I felt myself trembling.

"Thank you, sir," said the Inspector. "Please do let me know any further results as soon as you have them. I will carry on here."

The coroner nodded briskly and turned to go.

"And please ask that blond child hovering unsubtly outside to send in the next witness!" called the Inspector after him.

W hat a terrible tragedy!" Annie gasped, almost as soon as Daisy brought her in. She was draped in bangles that jangled distractingly, her face was painted dramatically and framed by her wildly curly blond hair. "And to think, just yesterday she was alive. It's dreadful. It makes me fear for my life. How common *is* murder? How many cases have you solved, Inspector? I remember I heard once about a woman who—"

"Murder is, happily, not common at all," said the Inspector, cutting her off. "Now, Annie Joy, you are the dresser on this production. I understand that you move between companies for each new production. Before the Rue, you were at—"

"Oh yes, the Criterion in February and the Apollo for Christmas. I do get about, but thankfully there's always so much demand—"

"Very good," said the Inspector, still sharp. "Now, what happened last night?"

"WELL!" said Annie. "We've begun to rehearse with costumes, you see, so I stayed late in case there should be issues, and of course there were. Lysander needed his doublet fixed, and I had to come out onstage to fix Rose's nightie for Scene Two, and then Martita complained about her robe, and then I was in Wardrobe on the first floor, sewing Rose's ballgown which isn't needed in Act Two, and working on the Apothecary's velvet hat, and then I looked in on Rose in her dressing room to make sure my stitching was holding and—"

"That was when?" asked the Inspector.

"Oh, the middle of Scene Three, I think. And then—"

"And how did Rose seem?"

"Oh, ordinary. She was kind to me—she praised my work. It's dreadful to think she's dead now, after all that; it's so hard to understand. There she was, talking to me quite as usual, and then, only a few hours later—she was gone! You never think that death will really happen; it seems like something in a play."

"So Rose was kind to you?"

"Oh yes, always," said Annie, nodding her head firmly, so that her curls bounced. "She was a lovely lady, so talented. I asked her how she got her skin so clear and she said lemon juice, which is interesting because I myself have tried that remedy and it only makes my cheeks—"

"Did you hear any altercations? Shouting, perhaps?"

"Oh no, I don't think so— Wait, perhaps I did! It was later in the evening, after the break. Rose and Martita were arguing, but I didn't go out to listen. It happened so often that I thought the best thing to do was ignore it."

"Where were you when you heard it?"

"In Wardrobe, surely— No, wait, I don't think I was. I was powdering my nose in the—you know—loo. I heard it above the noise of the running tap. Then I went to smoke by the stage door and I was back in Wardrobe when Martita came in to say that Rose was missing."

"Do you smoke often?" asked the Inspector.

"Oh, not regularly," said Annie. "Sometimes I cadge one off the others—it doesn't do to keep cigarettes around the costumes, you know. Why, once I had an actress put down a lit match near some lace and the whole thing went up like a—"

"*Thank* you, Miss Joy, you may go now," said Inspector Priestley.

Jim was next, in a very odd mood. He came limping in—he had an old war injury that made him walk with a hopping, almost sideways gait—and sat down in the chair with a triumphant *thump*.

Robin Stevens

"I knew it!" he said, again and again. "I told them—I told them nothing gets past me. I would have seen her! But they didn't believe me. Now they see!"

"They do indeed," said the Inspector. "So, what did you see last night?"

"The Act One cast signed themselves out as usual," said Jim. "Then came Theresa Johnson with Miss Wells and Miss Wong and their maid. Anyway, so they go, leaving Miss Crompton, Mr. Leontes, and the rest of the Act Two cast—apart from the actors playing Peter and Benvolio, who have the flu. Simon came out to see me, and Lysander and Annie came to cadge cigarettes from me—Lysander was smoking outside when Martita came to look for Rose. Miss Crompton discourages smoking in the theatre. She's worried that the whole place might go up if someone's careless, so the company either comes to stand at the stage door or goes down into the well room."

"What about Martita?" asked Inspector Priestley. "Did she come past?"

"Oh, she was rushing about. She came by several times—asked me to find some keys for her and so on. Then Mr. Leontes came to talk to me—he was still with me when the alarm was raised, as it happens. He's a gentleman, he is. The tales he can tell about the theatre! We had a nice chat about old times. He and I worked together many years ago on a production of *Hamlet*. You should have seen him holding Yorick's skull!"

I know it is all just part of a play, but the image of Inigo digging up graves and staring at bones made me feel rather wobbly.

"So—everyone except Miss Crompton stopped by to speak to you," said Inspector Priestley, writing.

"That's correct," said Jim. "Everyone except Miss Crompton—and Rose Tree. Of course, I saw them all again at the end of the night, after Rose had been discovered missing and they'd given up the search, but I never saw her. And now we know why! I thought I was losing my mind. Couldn't get to sleep last night! But I was right. I never did see her, and now no one will ever see her again."

And Jim sat back in his chair, arms folded, looking strangely pleased.

"She wasn't a good person," he went on. "I see people every day, but they don't see *me*. These actors and actresses and famous folk—they don't think I matter! But I'm always there at the door, and I see what people are really like. Rose thought I wasn't important, and serve her right. She's got what she deserved."

And, with that, he got up and walked away, leaving me feeling distinctly chilly.

Robin Stevens

There was only one suspect left to interview. It was odd to be suspicious of Miss Crompton, but Daisy and I have learned from our investigations that no one should be left out of consideration. Even the unlikeliest person may have committed the crime, and so it would be wrong to discount anyone until it is certain that they couldn't have done it.

Miss Crompton came in with her arms crossed and her chin jutting out. Even the close-cropped curls of her hair looked belligerent.

"So, you have interrogated *my* cast," she said. "What are your conclusions?"

"I can't tell you that yet, I'm afraid, madam," said Inspector Priestley. "I can only ask you to account for your movements last night, and tell me the nature of your relationship with the deceased."

It was funny to listen to Inspector Priestley's manner

change as he spoke to different people. He was as much of a chameleon as Daisy, I thought—able to tell everyone what they wanted to hear.

"Rose Tree was a clever girl," said Miss Crompton. "We got along very well, and I cast her as my Juliet. She could be overly dramatic, and she certainly rubbed some of the company up the wrong way, but that is the nature of theatrical temperaments. She was a born star, an actress in her soul, and people like that don't always form close alliances. She and Martita are really so similar. Both have lost their parents one way or another, and have been forced to struggle to find their way onto the stage. Perhaps that's why they fought. You will have heard about their argument last night? I know it sounds terrible, but I can assure you that there is nothing sinister to it. Just two girls letting out their temper on each other."

She raised her chin and glared at the Inspector.

"If that argument was harmless, who else might have had a grudge against Rose?" asked Inspector Priestley.

"Please do not ask me that," snapped Miss Crompton. "I will not give up a single member of my company. They are *mine*, you understand? This is my theatre and they are all my family. Everyone is welcome here, no matter who they are. The world can be cruel to those who are different, and the Rue is our refuge from that."

The Inspector shrugged. "That is a wonderful sentiment,

but I'm afraid that one of your family is guilty of a terrible crime. Now, where were you yesterday evening?"

"Onstage with Inigo, watching him direct," said Miss Crompton.

"I understand Miss Johnson had been taken ill, and Miss Torrera was filling in for her. Surely you helped Miss Torrera with the stage-manager duties?"

"From time to time. But I *was* onstage when Martita and Rose had their argument, and I remained there with Inigo until just before Rose was discovered to be missing. I am not stupid, Inspector. I know these are the crucial times. I was with Inigo, then I went to powder my nose in the ladies'. I was only gone for two or three minutes, and when I came back Martita told me that Rose was missing."

So Miss Crompton, like Inigo, admitted that there was a brief time in which she had been alone. How long, I wondered, would it have taken to actually kill Rose?

"Inspector," Miss Crompton went on, "is this really murder?"

"There's no doubt about it, madam."

"Murder!" muttered Miss Crompton. I was expecting to hear her sound sorrowful, hurt, horrified. But instead she sounded . . . thoughtful, almost calculating. "Will—will the papers hear of it?"

"What *is* the Rue's obsession with newspapers?" asked the Inspector.

"Inspector, in our business, there truly is no such thing as bad publicity. I am sure Inigo has tried to be coy about it, but I don't see the point. A dead body in our well sells tickets. Everyone loves a crime, and murder is the best sort. I am sorry that Rose is dead—I felt for her, and she played Juliet beautifully. But her death will guarantee us a month of full houses, if not two, and the Rue is badly in need of full houses. I must think of my theatre and I *will*."

And, with that, she stood up and strode out of the room. My head was in a whirl. Had Miss Crompton just given herself, and Inigo, the perfect motive to commit the crime? It was almost too horrid.

I sighed uncomfortably, and Inspector Priestley sighed too.

"That's everyone," he said thoughtfully. "One of them *must* have done it. But who?"

Robin Stevens

The Inspector stepped out of the office into the dusty corridor, and a careful thirty seconds later I followed him. I had no sooner walked through the doorway and turned toward the stairs than a slim hand shot out of a little alcove to my right and dragged me into it.

I found myself squashed up next to Daisy in the heavy darkness.

"Ow!" I said. "Daisy!"

I was rather worried that bits of us were sticking out of the alcove. We are not quite as small as we used to be, especially not Daisy, and it is rather harder for us to hide.

"How do you know it's me?" said Daisy in a muffled voice. "It might be anyone. It might be the killer!"

"Don't be silly," I said uncomfortably. "I *know* you. If it were anyone else, I'd scream."

"But what if I was wearing a costume? What if I was in disguise?"

"I'd still know your hands," I said. "I'd know you anywhere."

"Ugh," said Daisy, and I could tell that she was wrinkling up her nose at me in the dark. "You're such a—Hazel." But her voice was pleased. "Now, Watson, this case is becoming extremely exciting! All our suspects are behaving terribly oddly. I can't tell who is acting and who is not, but I am *certain* that something is rotten in the Rue Theatre. This murder must be connected to the threats against Rose, don't you think?"

"Oh, I agree!" I said eagerly. "We can't rule any of them out yet—although, if it is true that Inigo and Miss Crompton didn't leave the stage until just before Martita raised the alarm, then they are less likely to be guilty, aren't they?"

"Perhaps," said Daisy. "Or perhaps not. We must work out timings before we're absolutely sure. All we know is that Rose must have been killed *after* her argument with Martita and *before* Martita realized she was missing."

"Daisy," I said uncomfortably, "we do keep coming back to Martita, don't we? She was the last person to see—"

"Hazel, DO you know, I think we ought to go and have a Detective Society meeting at once! The bar is empty now that everyone's been interviewed. We can hide there and talk without anyone hearing!"

And I thought to myself that we might have traveled

Robin Stevens

halfway across the world and faced things so terrible that I hardly like to remember them. We might have grown, and changed—even Daisy—but we would always be the same people underneath.

We found ourselves a little nest behind the bar, in the glitter and shine of the front-of-house foyer that was so different from the dark, hot, stripped-down backstage area, to hold our meeting. Our backs were to the wall and we kept our voices low. We could not be taken by surprise.

D etective Society meeting," said Daisy briskly.
"Present: Daisy Wells and Hazel Wong, president
and vice president of the Detective Society. The
case: the *Romeo and Juliet* murder, or the Murder in the Rue
Theatre. Oh, fancy, Hazel, that sounds like the title of that
old story. Remember?"

Daisy makes me read plenty of detective stories, and I
knew the one she was talking about.

"The one by Poe, with the silly ending?" I asked.

"It's not silly!" said Daisy. "At least, it may *seem* silly, but
surely you know by now that most of the silliest things are
true? Fiction is when everything is utterly believable."

"Daisy, there is absolutely no way that—" I began. "Never
mind. *The Romeo and Juliet Murder*. That's the better name.
Victim: Rose Tree. Time of death . . ."

". . . last night, after the beginning of Act Two,
Scene Five," said Daisy, nodding. "Our first task is to

understand what time that really was. In light of what the suspects are all saying—that she was last seen and heard at five past nine, and discovered missing just before half past—I have been considering what we know about rehearsal times for *Romeo and Juliet*.

"So. We left the theatre with Theresa and Bridget at six minutes to seven, and the second-act rehearsal had just begun. Act Two, Scene One would have been over quickly, since Benvolio wasn't there. Then Act Two, Scene Two is a very long one—it's the balcony scene, and that takes ages to get right. So they wouldn't have moved on to Scene Three for more than an hour. Scene Three is shorter—say forty minutes—and Scene Four is shorter again, about twenty minutes to rehearse. Then they took a short break. Which means that Scene Five can't possibly have started before nine p.m. That fits with the evidence that Martita argued with Rose at about five past nine and found her missing just before nine thirty. So I think we can conclude that Rose really *was* murdered between nine oh six and nine thirty p.m."

I wrote that down, nodding. Daisy was right.

"Now, the murder weapon was . . ."

"The well," I said, shuddering. "Oh, that's horrid. The murderer got her into the well room and shoved her down it."

"Yes, indeed," said Daisy. "But there I think is our first truly interesting point. HOW did the murderer get Rose to that room? They must have told her some sort of lie, since Rose wasn't the sort of person to simply trot after someone else without an explanation, and there are several flights of stairs and some very dark corridors between her dressing room and the well room.

"Of course, she may have been dragged there against her will, but that would have been very risky for the murderer—anyone might have heard her yelling. And, for the same reason, I think it's unlikely she was killed *before* she got to the well room—what if someone saw the murderer carrying her there? No, I think Rose walked into that room of her own accord, and very much alive."

"The murderer might have gone down there with her to smoke?" I suggested. "That's what Jim said happened sometimes. Or—or to talk about something secret, or to . . ."

"Or to canoodle!" said Daisy. "That's a distinct possibility. Good. Now, we've begun to consider *when* and *how*. Next is *who*. Who are our suspects?"

"Simon," I said, counting on my fingers, "Martita, Inigo, Lysander, Annie, Miss Crompton, and Jim. We're off the list."

"Indeed we are," said Daisy. "And so is Theresa. She was ill in bed—she certainly couldn't have crept back to the Rue and murdered Rose later that night. Can we rule out any of those seven now that we have heard the interviews? What else do we know about the crime?"

Robin Stevens

"Well, everyone thought Rose had left the theatre last night because her name was in the sign-out book," I said. "Oh, Daisy, I know!"

I told her what I had heard Jim say—in fact, I told her all the information I had overheard during the second part of the Inspector's interviews.

"Well, that is interesting," said Daisy. "If Jim's telling the truth, it follows that the only person with *no* opportunity to fudge Rose's name on the sign-out sheet is Miss Crompton, because she was the only person who didn't visit his cubby-hole. So, if she is the murderer, then she can't have done it on her own. Ooh, what if she worked *with* someone? What if she worked with Inigo?"

"They did give each other alibis for most of the time!" I said thoughtfully. "I don't know! What if we can rule *Jim* out, though? There were people coming and going past his cubbyhole all evening, and not one of them mentioned that he *wasn't* at his station."

Daisy, though, shook her head. "No, Hazel, that's hardly rigorous of you," she said. "Remember that everyone lies, Hazel, everyone. They lie for stupid reasons—Jim may not want to mention that he went to the loo, for example—but they do lie. You must stop being so credulous. Why, after what happened in Hong Kong—"

I cut her off. I still don't like to think of it—or rather, when Daisy mentions it, I realize that it is always sitting at the back of my mind, waiting for me to turn and notice it.

"But, if we can't trust Jim, we shouldn't trust anyone else, either!" I protested. "Not even Martita."

"I can when her evidence agrees with my own calculations," said Daisy shortly. "And it does."

I almost opened my mouth and said the thing then—but I did not want to be the one to bring it up, not after the way Daisy had shouted at me last time I tried to mention it.

"All right," I said. "Let's make a suspect list."

SUSPECT LIST

1. Miss Crompton. MOTIVE: She was Rose's greatest ally at the Rue Theatre and seems sad that she is dead—but she has also been honest about the fact that Rose's death will be good for business, and will help the Rue's money troubles. She clearly cares most about the Rue, and about her company—might she have been willing to hurt one member of it to help everyone else? OPPORTUNITY: She seems to have an alibi from 9 p.m. until just before Rose was discovered missing at 9:30 p.m.—she was onstage with Inigo—but she did also go to the loo for a few minutes. Could this be enough time for her to have gone to the well room with Rose and killed her there? NOTES: She did not visit Jim at the

---

Robin Stevens

stage door until after Rose's disappearance that evening, meaning that she had no clear opportunity to forge Rose's name in the book. But could she be working with someone else—like Inigo?

2. Simon. MOTIVE: He does not like Rose. He hinted, and Inigo confirmed, that he was supposed to play Romeo until Rose objected to the color of his skin. Was he angry enough with her to do something terrible? OPPORTUNITY: He was with Inigo when they overheard the argument between Martita and Rose, but afterward left him and went upstairs to his own dressing room until the alarm was raised at 9:30. Could he have left it to murder Rose? NOTES: Visited Jim's cubbyhole and so could have forged Rose's name in the book.

3. Annie (Wardrobe). MOTIVE: No clear motive. Rose was friendly with her—but she did seem to be uncomfortable with Rose's behavior toward other members of the company. OPPORTUNITY: She was in the loo on the first floor when Martita and Rose had their argument, but was then alone in Wardrobe at the crucial time. She has no alibi! NOTES: Visited Jim's cubbyhole and so could have forged Rose's name in the book.

4. Inigo. MOTIVE: He disliked Rose intensely and says that she is the reason why Simon was not able to play Romeo. He also wants to use her death as publicity. OPPORTUNITY: He was with Simon and Miss Crompton when they heard the argument between Rose and Martita, and he says that after this he went back onstage to talk to Miss Crompton until he left to see Jim just before the alarm was raised by Martita at 9:30. If this is true, then he may not have had time—unless he was working with Miss Crompton. NOTES: Visited Jim's cubbyhole and so could have forged Rose's name in the book.

5. Lysander. MOTIVE: He had been flirting with Rose, but Daisy and Hazel noticed that they had been arguing more and more lately. He is a very threatening person, and he was angry with Rose. OPPORTUNITY: He was in his dressing room, alone, during the time Rose must have been murdered—he does not have an alibi! NOTES: Was at Jim's cubbyhole when the alarm was raised, and so could have forged Rose's name in the book.

6. Jim (stage door). MOTIVE: He did not like Rose, and resented her being part of the Rue. But did he feel strongly enough about her to murder her?

OPPORTUNITY: He says he was at his post all evening. Is this true?

7. Martita. MOTIVE: She hated the fact that Rose was playing Juliet. She felt that the part should have been hers, and was jealous that Rose was allowed to be the star. OPPORTUNITY: She left the stage when Rose refused to come on to rehearse Scene Five. Inigo, Simon, Miss Crompton, Lysander, and Annie all say that they heard her arguing with Rose in Rose's dressing room at about 9:05. We do not know where she went after that. Could she have murdered Rose before she raised the alarm at 9:30? NOTES: Visited Jim's cubbyhole and so could have forged Rose's name in the book.

PLAN OF ACTION

1. Check Jim's stage-door book and ascertain whether Jim can be trusted.

2. Look at timings and decide which of our suspects had enough opportunity to commit the crime.

3. Go back to the scene of the crime and reenact the murder.

4. Visit Rose's dressing room and look for clues.

5. Talk to suspects—decide if any of them could be working together.

Robin Stevens

We did the Detective Society handshake and went down the main stairs together, Daisy moving as though a crowd was watching her. I nudged her. "We're not onstage!" I said.

"The world is a stage, Hazel Wong," said Daisy, grinning at me.

And then we both saw Inspector Priestley at the bottom of the stairs. He was talking to Jellicoe, and we heard what he was saying.

". . . main suspect. Watch her especially. She doesn't seem dangerous, but you never know what she may do. Do you understand?"

"Yes, sir," said Jellicoe. "I'll watch Miss Torrera."

Daisy came to a sudden stop. Her hand shot out and she gripped my wrist so tightly that I could feel it go numb.

The Inspector turned and saw us.

"Ah, Miss Wells, Miss Wong," he said.

"We heard what you just said," Daisy told him. "We heard!"

"Indeed," said the Inspector. "Do you have something to say to me, Madam Super?"

There was the shadow of a smile on his face and his forehead crinkled just as I remembered from our previous cases. It really was true, I thought nonsensically. Some things about people never change.

"I—I—I should say I do!" said Daisy jerkily. "I— What do you mean, talking about Martita like that? Anyone in the Rue might have committed the crime."

"But surely you see that she is the most likely suspect? The threats—the posters—and now the murder. I would be remiss if I did not consider her as such."

"Don't— You—you have no right!" gasped Daisy. "She didn't do it!"

I put my hand over hers to calm her down, but she shook it off.

"Miss Wells, Martita has a motive, she has means, and she has opportunity. You know that."

"How—how DARE YOU!" cried Daisy. "Hazel, come with me! I shall not stand to be here a moment longer!"

She had still not let go of my wrist and it hurt terribly. Now, she dragged me forward—and I had to follow. I needed to half gallop to keep up with her long, furious strides. She towed me into the theatre, halfway into the quiet stalls, and then she stopped and turned to look at me. I saw her face in the reflected glow from the bright and busy stage, rehearsal in full swing, and I saw the absolute despair on it.

"Daisy!" I said. "What's up? *Tell* me!"

Daisy went absolutely pale. "It's nothing, Hazel," she said unsteadily. "Or rather—it is true that I'm concerned. Martita is a friend of the Detective Society, and I'm quite certain she is being wrongly accused."

I stared at her.

"I—" said Daisy. "I— Oh, *bother* you, Watson!" She suddenly looked more flustered than I had ever seen her. "All right. You may have noticed that I have been . . . not at my best around Martita. It has taken me a time to ascertain why, but I have now examined the evidence, and I think that there can be only one conclusion: I *like* Martita more than anyone else I have ever met in my life. If you were anyone else, I should tell you that it was just a pash, but it isn't at all. It's much more than that."

"I did guess," I admitted, taking a deep breath. "I've seen you helping her, even when you don't need to. You get tongue-tied around her, and you blush all the time. I *know* you, Daisy!"

"Oh, how frustrating!" said Daisy. "I might have guessed you'd notice. But I do so hate it, Hazel. Love is idiotic, and I despise it, but Martita is simply so *pretty*."

I almost laughed at Daisy's face—it was so furious.

"Now you understand how I feel about Alexander. I can't help it, either!" I said.

"Of course I don't understand about Alexander!" cried Daisy. "That is entirely different. His arms are too long, Hazel, and he's not as intelligent as you are. Whereas Martita's arms are a perfect length."

"She's as old as Bertie!" I said, ignoring the jibe about Alexander. Daisy can be very cruel when she's upset.

"I know!" said Daisy. "I'm not *stupid*, Hazel. I know she's nearly a grown-up and she doesn't care a pin for me, but all the same I can't stop looking at her. It's so unfair!"

I could see her cheeks shining with pinkness, and I knew that this was not an act. It was really true. It ought to be impossible: the Daisy I knew was perfectly scornful about love. But what I had come to realize was that there might be another reason why Daisy disliked romance. I remembered how eager she had been to help the Big Girl Violet with her letter-writing problem last year at Deepdean. I thought of how she spoke about King Henry, our old Head Girl, and held that up against the way she sneered at me for being in love with Alexander. Once I had looked at all the clues properly, there was an obvious solution to the mystery: what Daisy struggled to understand was not simply that I was in *love* but that I was in love with a *boy*.

"Oh, Daisy!" I said.

"Hazel," said Daisy, gulping. "If you—if you leave the

Robin Stevens

Detective Society over this, remember that I am allowed to do horrible things to you. Medieval tortures, Hazel! And I shall, you know I shall!"

My heart thudded in my chest. "Why would I leave the Detective Society?" I asked. "You don't *want* me to, do you?"

"No!" cried Daisy. "But—you might . . . I know pashes are all right at Deepdean, but we're not at Deepdean now and this isn't just a pash and you might— I mean, you would be quite within your rights to be shocked at me."

"I don't understand what you're saying," I said furiously. "Do you think I'm going to stop being your friend because you like Martita? Because you don't like boys? Why, it's not *me* who was horrid about Alexander and thought we should have to stop being friends because of him. I don't care about that sort of thing at all, you *know* I don't. You're my best friend and nothing you do can change that."

"Well, I should think if I murdered someone you might be quite upset with me," said Daisy rather huskily.

"You're a—a *chump*!" I said and I hurled myself at her.

"Sometimes, Watson, I'm not sure I deserve you," said Daisy, hugging me fiercely. "And I will never say that again, so you will simply have to remember it."

I thought that I was not likely to forget it.

"Now," said Daisy, sitting back and clearing her throat, "to business. How are we to clear Martita's name?"

"How do we know we can?" I asked. "Or that we *should?*"

"Hazel Wong, I—" Daisy began. Then she sighed. "I suppose you do have to say that."

"I do!" I protested. "You know we can never trust anyone on a case, and sometimes the people who seem the nicest are the ones to blame."

"I *do*," said Daisy, nodding. "But all the same I know that it wasn't Martita. I know absolutely. And I also know that it looks very much as though it was. Therefore the Detective Society has a new purpose: to defend Martita's honor."

I wanted very much to tell her that this might prove difficult, but I didn't. I could see the light of battle in Daisy's eyes, and I knew that I would be utterly unable to talk her out of this quest.

Part Four
Star-Crossed Lovers

I shall *prove* to you that Martita cannot be the murderer!" cried Daisy. "You see, there is one very important flaw in the Inspector's case. Yes, Martita was the last person we know about who saw Rose alive. Yes, they argued—but they argued in Rose's dressing room, *on the ground floor*. The evidence we saw of a scuffle on the well-room floor proves that Rose was alive and capable of defending herself when she was brought there. So it doesn't make sense that Martita killed her in her dressing room, or lured her out of the dressing room and all the way down to the well without anyone else hearing it.

"Why would Rose have gone with her willingly after that row? And, if not willingly, why wouldn't she have screamed on the way down? The well room may be insulated, but the rest of the Rue isn't. We have plenty of witnesses who heard the argument, and no one who says that they heard her after that. That is important evidence, Hazel!"

She was panting, her eyes glittering and her cheeks flushed. I did see her point, and I *wanted* to believe her, but I was wary.

"We don't *know* any of that for sure, Daisy," I said. "We're only guessing."

"Of course!" she cried. "So we must re-create the crime and time everything thoroughly. Timing is key to this case! Now, what shall we do first?"

I could see Daisy's mind racing, her thoughts speeding up and scattering in her desperation.

"We can't go down to the well room yet," I said calmingly. "We'll have to wait for the police to leave it. But we *can* investigate the dressing rooms, and we can go and speak to Jim. It's all right, Daisy. Follow me!"

"We're not in Hong Kong anymore," Daisy grumbled. "*I* go first, Hazel—I am the Detective Society president!"

But she went where I pointed, up the little side steps out of the stalls and round the edge of the stage, to slip through into the backstage darkness.

And then she paused, holding up her hand, quite frozen in place.

Two people were standing at the bottom of the stairs to the main dressing-room corridor. They could not see us, as we were crammed into the dimly lit doorway and hidden by bits of old props, discarded costumes, and pieces of broken wood; nor could we see them easily. But we could hear.

Robin Stevens

The Rue, as Daisy had said, is quite porous. The speakers' low voices carried, and they belonged to Simon and Inigo.

"My boy," Inigo was saying. "Hold your nerve."

"What'll I do?" asked Simon, and his voice wobbled like a child's. "Everyone knows I hated her, I don't have an alibi and— What if they arrest me, and it all comes out? I'll be deported. I can't go back, please!"

Daisy grasped my hand in excitement and I squeezed back. This sounded terribly damning.

"I won't let that happen," said Inigo. "I swear it. I'm ready to fight for us both. This is a hard business, my boy, and our color gives us an additional mountain to climb. Don't ever let yourself feel comfortable. If you let them, they will take it all away from you. So you mustn't let them, do you hear me?"

"Yes, sir," said Simon. "Sir—you *were* onstage, weren't you? With Miss Crompton? *You've* got an alibi?"

He sounded hopeful and also rather frightened.

"Of course I have!" cried Inigo. "I was onstage, and then I went to the stage door. My movements are *entirely* accounted for."

But my skin prickled at something in his tone. I was not sure I believed him.

"Come," said Inigo. "We should not stand here talking. I have had thoughts on your death in Act Three."

Their footsteps padded away, Simon's echoing Inigo's all the way up the stairs.

I breathed out.

"Well," whispered Daisy. "How very interesting! Come on, Hazel. Now, we find ourselves next to Rose's dressing room. We must go in!"

Its door was closed, and the room was locked—but locks are not much use against the Detective Society these days.

I leaned against it casually to keep a lookout, while Daisy picked the lock with a pin from her hair. It only took a moment, and then we were slipping inside.

The gas jet in this dressing room was off, and so we had to take out our flashlights and play them about the room. It really was large—there was even a sofa in one corner. I could see why Martita had been cross to lose it.

But, in the dark, its size made it creepy. There were wigs on their pedestals, and makeup and cold cream scattered about in front of the mirrors. There was damp in the air too, and I shivered. It suddenly smelled a little like the well room, and my mind pitched back there, down the long drop of the well to the white-clad figure in the dark water below.

I got a fright when we shone our lights on the stand of Rose's Juliet costumes: her ballgowns, her day dresses, and her beautiful funeral dresses from Act Five. For a moment, I thought that they were people—but of course they hung limp and empty. I reached out in the darkness and took Daisy's free hand.

"Oh yes, she was upset and hadn't changed into her day

Robin Stevens

dress yet. She was still wearing the nightie from the balcony scene," said Daisy. "That's where that white thread comes from. I do wish we were allowed to look at the body when it's brought out of the well, so we could match it properly, but grown-ups are so silly. Just because we look sweet, people think we don't have strong stomachs."

"I *don't* have a strong stomach," I said. "This place is horrid, Daisy. I feel like there might be someone lurking somewhere."

"Of course there isn't!" said Daisy briskly. "More's the pity. Now, what can we tell from this room? What is here and what is missing? I can begin. There should be another white nightdress on the rack because we know that Annie makes two of every costume, but there isn't. What's happened to that? Write it down, Hazel."

I did as I was told and then peered around. There was Rose's chair, half pushed back, as though she had gone somewhere in a hurry. I imagined Rose getting up, walking toward the door, reaching for . . . And then I had it. "Her coat and handbag are missing," I said. "Just as though she *did* leave. No, wait!"

I crouched down and peered into the far corner of the room—I had caught sight of a crumpled pile of blue fabric wrapped around something bulky. "Daisy, what's that?"

Daisy threw herself onto her hands and knees and scuttled over, prodding at it with her flashlight.

"It's Rose's coat!" she cried. "And her handbag too. That's interesting. Someone put them out of the way here, presumably so they wouldn't be seen by the people searching for Rose last night. But they're not really that difficult to find, are they? So . . . what does that mean? That the murderer didn't mind if Rose was found later? Otherwise, why wouldn't they have made a better job of getting rid of them?"

I frowned. That did seem odd. "What's in the handbag?" I asked.

"Nothing much," said Daisy, her handkerchief wrapped round her fingers as she poked about inside. "A powder compact and a handkerchief. Dull! All right, let's leave that here. Now, Hazel, what else can we discover from this room? I know one more thing—there's no sign of a struggle here—no furniture overturned or things in disarray. That agrees with our theory that Rose can't have been hurt here. Now, I think that while we're downstairs we ought to go and speak to Jim and take a look at his book. This will require a little espionage. I know our first case seems an awfully long time ago, but some of the techniques we used are still relevant. Hazel, do you remember the gym?"

J im stared at us in alarm as we came rushing toward
   him.

"What's happened to you?" he asked.

"She turned her ankle in the corridor!" I gasped, holding
Daisy up with difficulty. She has grown quite a lot since
the last time we tried this particular ruse, and now she had
to lean down to put her arms round my neck, and I had
to stand uncomfortably half on tiptoe. "I think she might
have broken it!"

"No, I'm sure I haven't!" said Daisy bravely, but her face
was red (from holding her breath) and tear-stained (from
squeezing her eyes shut and yawning until they watered).
"But—oh! It does hurt terribly!"

We hobbled our way over to Jim's seat in his cubbyhole,
and Jim limped out to meet us. He led Daisy to his chair and
fussed over her, getting her settled and propping her foot up
on a low stool. Daisy winced and gasped and whimpered,

managing to take up all Jim's attention. As she did so, I leaned across the cubbyhole shelf, looking as concerned and hopeful as I could—and then, when I was sure that Jim was occupied, glanced down at the signing-in book that sat there.

I had come to know it very well during our time at the Rue. It was large and close-ruled, with a column for the date, another for names, and two for time in and time out. Its rules were simple, and everyone in the company knew them: each morning, we all wrote our name and the time we arrived in blue ink as we came in. Then, when we left, we would all write our name again, in black ink instead of blue.

This, of course, made it extremely useful to the investigation—and, as I looked at it now, I realized something else. Jim did not like to waste paper, so he made everyone cram their names together down the pages. Because of that, it would be impossible for someone to squeeze in an extra entrance or exit between the genuine ones. Whoever had added Rose's name and faked her departure must have used a time that was close to when that person visited Jim, so as not to be caught out by the next person to sign out.

It was possible that the murderer (or murderers) might have also faked the time they had left, but all the innocent members of the company would have been drilled by Jim to write down their exit times correctly, by the big clock on the wall. Witnesses might be lying in their statements, but this was a piece of evidence that could be counted on.

Daisy gave a particularly loud yelp as Jim prodded her ankle, and I knew I was being encouraged to hurry up. I looked carefully at the entries for yesterday evening. There were our names, and Theresa's, at 6:54 p.m. I remembered writing us all down, and checking the time against my wristwatch as well as Jim's clock. They had been synchronized last night, and (I checked my wristwatch again) they were still keeping the same time.

The next name below Theresa's was . . . Rose's. I knew it would be there, but it still gave me a jump. Whoever had forged it had done a perfect job. Her signature matched the one from the morning before, and her time out was supposedly 9:10 p.m.

Next was Lysander at 10:03 p.m., then Annie at 10:35 p.m., and then came Simon at 10:40 p.m. and Martita at 10:45 p.m. Finally Miss Crompton and Inigo left together at 10:48 p.m. Jim had ruled a line below all their names and marked it off at 11 p.m. sharp, when he had locked the doors and gone to his bed in the little room behind his post. He had been back at his desk at 9 a.m. this morning.

I leaned forward and hastily scribbled the times and names onto a scrap of paper I had hidden in my hand.

I straightened up again just as Daisy said, "Oh, do you know, I feel rather better! Why, I think that's cured it! Oh, now, one more thing—what do you do with mail? I gave a friend this address for correspondence and he *promised* to write me a letter, only it hasn't come yet."

"Well, letters all come in to me, and I put them in people's pigeonholes in the post room," said Jim. "But I don't think—"

"Could you just check?" asked Daisy in honeyed tones. "For me?"

"Oh, all right!" said Jim, and he turned away. I looked over and saw Daisy nodding at me. It was time for the second part of our plan. I picked up the black pen and wrote, *Hazel Wong, 1:30 p.m.*

By the time Jim came back, shaking his head, the pen was back in its place on the page and I was standing innocently back from the book—but, if anyone looked later, it would seem as though I had already signed out.

We had proved that someone might have been able to distract Jim long enough to sign the book.

"It's not there, I'm afraid," said Jim.

"Oh—are you sure you didn't put it in the wrong pigeonhole?" asked Daisy.

"I wouldn't do that!" said Jim, shocked. "I have eagle eyes!"

"Of course you have," said Daisy soothingly. "Of course you have. And you're honest too. That's what I told the policeman, anyway."

Robin Stevens

"Honest!" cried Jim, drawing himself up furiously. "Of COURSE I'm honest! Thirty years I've been at this post, man and boy, and I have never had my honesty doubted. As I told the Inspector, I never leave my post, and that's the truth. If I have to go, I go in a bucket. Plenty of people came by, and they'll all tell you that I was here, in my seat, where I should be."

"Miss Crompton did say she saw you during the evening," admitted Daisy.

"But that's not true!" said Jim, still cross, words falling over themselves out of his mouth. It is one of Daisy's cleverest tricks, and it works almost every time—simply tell someone a lie and they can't wait to tell you how wrong you are, even if they catch themselves out doing it.

"I didn't see her at all yesterday evening, not until she came by to make sure that Rose's name really *was* in the book. And I showed her! The only people who came by before the alarm was raised were Mr. Tollington, Mr. Leontes, Mr. Carver, Miss Joy, and Miss Torrera. I remember—I've got an excellent memory. Simon came by quite early in the evening, just before eight. Martita came by four times, three between eight and nine and one just after nine—she was in and out constantly. Annie came by for a cigarette at quarter past nine, and Lysander had his cigarette just before half past. Mr. Leontes stopped to have a chat then as well. They were both there when Martita came back to say that

Rose had gone missing. That was the first time I checked the book, and that was when I saw that someone had put Rose's name in. I thought I was going mad last night, but now I know that someone tricked me. Me!"

His voice was rising.

"It's too dreadful," said Daisy soothingly. "I'm so terribly sorry! I'm sure you did nothing wrong and the police will know that. Now, come along, Hazel. We must go and— rehearse."

She hobbled out of Jim's sight—and then rushed back down the corridor and up the stairs to our dressing room, with me following. We were both breathless with excitement. We had uncovered several very important pieces of information.

III

"Most interesting developments have occurred!" cried Daisy, pushing our dressing-room door closed and locking it. "We now know that it is perfectly possible to trick Jim into not paying attention to the book—you have proved that anyone who visited him might have written in it slyly. And I believe that his evidence means we can come close to ruling Jim out from committing the crime.

"We have yet to confirm timings, but just think! Even if we assume that he met Rose immediately after the argument and after Martita had come by, he would have had to take her down to the well room, kill her, and come all the way back again before quarter past, when he saw Annie. That is less than ten minutes to do an awful lot of things—ten minutes in which he couldn't be sure that he wouldn't be missed at his post. Anyone who arrived and found him absent would raise the alarm at once.

"We know from previous investigations, Hazel, that it is key for a murderer not to do anything obviously suspicious during the execution of a crime, and there is nothing more suspicious at the Rue than not to have Jim in his cubbyhole. I do think, therefore, that we will soon be able to rule him out. And, since his evidence also matches the evidence you collected during everyone's interviews with the Inspector, I think we can believe it."

"Yes!" I said, hurrying to our dressing table and getting out the sandwiches that Bridget had made for us, for it was past our usual lunchtime and my stomach was rumbling. So much had happened in such a short time—I could barely believe it. "And, Daisy, I can't see *why* he'd do it, or even be involved. He didn't like Rose, but she didn't hurt him especially—he was just scornful of her. And he cares so much about his job and his reputation. Why would he ruin it over one actress?"

"Very good, Watson!" said Daisy, taking her ham and cucumber sandwich happily. "Which means that we are left with—"

"*Five* suspects, or groups of them," I said, jumping into her sentence like taking a step into a spinning skipping rope. "Martita, Inigo, Annie, Simon, and Lysander. Miss Crompton might have helped any of them, but she couldn't have done it by herself. They're the only people who had the opportunity to go down to the well room between nine oh six and nine thirty *and* write Rose's name in the sign-out book before nine thirty, and all of them but Annie have proper motives." I took an excited bite out of my fish-paste sandwich.

"Yes, very true," said Daisy, frowning. "And what about the conversation we overheard between Simon and Inigo? Simon has a secret—and Inigo seems willing to do anything to protect him! We must—"

Someone rattled the knob of the door and then kicked it with their foot.

"Hey!" shouted Martita's voice. "Who's in there? Let me in!"

I glanced at Daisy and saw her panic, cheeks red and nose crinkled.

"Go on, Hazel, let her in!" she hissed.

I unlocked the door, and Martita shoved it open and stood glaring around the room, half puzzled and half annoyed.

Her thick dark hair was down around her shoulders and in Juliet's day gown, which had been quickly let out in the bust and hips for her, she looked quite goddess-like—although the sort of goddess who might turn you into a deer and let wolves chase you. I understood, just a little, what Daisy must see when she looked at her. It was an odd moment, rather like stepping out of my head and into Daisy's. I blinked, and then Martita was only Martita again, no different from how she looked on any other day since I had met her.

"What *are* you doing?" said Martita, her voice amused now that she saw it was only us. "I thought something was wrong when you locked the door, but here you are having lunch!"

"Sorry, Martita," said Daisy, standing up, stiff and awkward, color burning on her cheeks. Daisy, who always behaves perfectly, *awkward*! I couldn't decide if I felt amused or sorry for her.

"Everyone has gone off their heads today," said Martita. "I don't blame you. Daisy, will you help me run lines after you've finished eating?"

"Yes!" said Daisy automatically. I prodded her. "I mean, no. Sorry. Hazel and I are really terribly busy."

"Doing what?" asked Martita. "Hazel, even you must have learned your lines by now."

It sounded rather cruel, but she winked at me as she said it. I knew she did not mean it at all, and I remembered how much I liked Martita. But my stomach sank. Whatever Daisy thought of her, she *was* a suspect.

"Oh well," said Martita. "I suppose it doesn't matter, anyway. Rose is dead, and I expect Simon or I will be arrested soon. After all, we're not British, are we? None of the English people could have killed her—that's what the Inspector thinks."

"That's not true! And you didn't do it!" gasped Daisy. "We know you didn't."

Robin Stevens

"But *he* thinks I might have!" cried Martita. "And I can't blame him. After all, I could have taken Rose down to the well room and pushed her in. I *wanted* to."

"I don't believe it!" cried Daisy passionately. "I won't listen to you. Come on, Hazel, eat up. We must be going!"

And, almost before I had finished my last bite, I found myself being dragged by Daisy further into the tangle of the Rue, and further into this strange and confusing case.

IV

ut we had only taken a few steps when we were
stopped in our tracks by Lysander. He must have
heard our voices, for he came out of his dressing
room and blocked the corridor in front of us, standing with
his arms crossed and his thin legs wide apart. In the low-
ceilinged space, with only a dim light behind him, he suddenly looked as enormous as a bogeyman. I remembered
how he had spoken to Rose, and felt a stab of fear.

I stopped short. Daisy, though, kept moving.

"Step aside, *if* you please!" she said in an annoyed voice.
Daisy never does see danger. Nothing is as big as she is in
her own head.

"Now, now," said Lysander smoothly. "What have you
two been doing? You're scuttling about like mice, so I think
you're up to something. And I don't like that."

"None of your business!" said Daisy. "If you must know,
we're playing a game."

"No you aren't," said Lysander. "You're pretending to be little girls, but you're too old for games. Tell me the truth."

And he reached out, seized Daisy's wrists, and pulled her toward him so sharply that she fell against his chest.

I felt dizzy all over. This was such a shockingly inappropriate thing to do that I simply did not know how to respond. I was frozen with horror. But of course Daisy and I are very different, and Daisy never freezes.

She gave a little gasp, and then in one swift movement she twisted out of his grasp and brought her right knee up smartly between his legs.

Lysander went down sideways, swearing (quite rude words that I will not write here, of course), and Daisy bent over his prone body.

"Never underestimate little girls," she hissed. "And never do that again." Then she turned and held out her hand to me.

"Come on, Hazel," she said.

I rushed toward her, and together we walked away from him down the corridor.

I realized then that I was still shaking.

"It's all right, Hazel," Daisy said.

I looked at her and saw that her face was set and pale. "You're all right and so am I. I shall never let any harm come to either of us, you know that. Or, at least, not the physical kind of harm. I can't save you from seeing awful things, for example."

"I know!" I whispered back. "But that was horrid! I think he really wanted to hurt you!"

"He was most certainly rattled," said Daisy. "Which is useful to us, really. We have seen that he's nervous, and behaving foolishly because of it—he is most certainly a good suspect. And I also believe we have seen something else: he doesn't mind hurting women. We know that he and Rose were . . . flirting . . . and we also know that she had begun to go sour on him because he was so upset by all those flowers in her dressing room. He was furious with her—and he really might have done something awful. Men like that can do dreadful things to women they think have wronged them.

"What if he lured her down to the well room last night, pretending he wanted to be romantic, but it was really a trap? Shoving Rose into a well would fit with Lysander's nasty temperament!"

Daisy rubbed at her wrists with a rueful expression.

I shivered worse than ever. "Ugh!" I said. "That's horrid!"

"It's murder, Hazel—it's always horrid!" said Daisy. "But, yes, I do agree that it isn't nice to consider. It's very grown up, isn't it?"

"It's far too grown up!" I said. "I really don't like all the parts of being older, Daisy."

I had realized that at the Rue we were not seen as

children, but as smaller grown-ups—which meant we could not go unnoticed. We had to explain ourselves and prove ourselves, and take part in the grown-up life of the company. And I found I did not like that.

"You're such a chump sometimes, Hazel," said Daisy, rolling her eyes. "Whether you like it or not, you have to grow up. Even if you pretend you aren't older, everyone else notices that you are. Now, take a deep breath—good—and another—and another. All right?"

"Yes," I said. "I'm all right, Daisy. I can detect."

"Of course you can!" she said. "It's the one thing you know absolutely how to do, Watson. Buck up! Let's hunt for more leads in Wardrobe."

I squeezed her hand. Daisy winked at me, reached down, and ripped a long piece of lace from the hem of her costume. Then she pushed at the door to Wardrobe and cried, "Oh dear! Annie! I'm afraid I've done something dreadful to my dress!"

B ut, instead of the door opening, it stuck, and there
was a scream from inside the room that made both
of us start. I clutched at Daisy's arm. Had something
else happened?

"Who is it?" Annie's voice cried out nervously.

"It's us!" Daisy called back. "Daisy and Hazel! I've ripped
my dress—please let us in!"

It was very odd, I thought, that the door was locked.

There was a pause, and then the door rattled and cracked
open a few inches. Annie appeared in the gap.

"It is you!" she said, sounding relieved. "I thought it
might be *the murderer*. Oh, all right, come in!"

Daisy and I went in carefully, and found the room in
dim, warm half-darkness, full of racks of costumes and
dressmaker's dummies—and Annie, hovering in a dark
corner, clutching her hands together and chattering away.

"I'm so pleased that you aren't anyone dangerous!" she

cried, lunging forward to pat at the fluttering piece of lace drooping from Daisy's skirt. "I was so afraid. Now, you're right—you have ripped it. Stand still, Daisy darling. Let me look at it. Oh, that's a nasty tear, just exactly like the time I was working on *Anything Goes* and Amy Snot's skirt got caught in the doorway and almost ripped in two. Hazel, lock the door again, will you? Doors can be very dangerous. I once cut my hand quite badly on one that hadn't been properly sanded. I know a woman who never likes to go through a door if she can help it, although I do think there might have been something else odd about her apart from the doorway issue, really. It isn't normal to be so *very* afraid of them."

She had knelt down in front of Daisy and begun busily pinning up the rip, talking all the while. I drifted away from her toward the racks of costumes, running my fingers through the brocade and velvet and shot silk and fur. They seemed to glow with warmth and beauty, and I could almost feel the rich colors under my hands. I rubbed the tip of a fur collar against my cheek and smiled.

There were dresses draped across three dummies, halfway through being re-hemmed. There is something oddly formal about a dress when it is on a dummy, I think. It suddenly stops looking like clothes and begins to look like a person. You can almost see the character of its wearer, as though they're really there and their arms and head have simply been erased by a piece of India rubber.

One was the Nurse's heavy black-and-white robe—of course, the Nurse would have to be played by someone else in the cast now that Martita was playing Juliet. One was another of Juliet's dresses that was being altered for Martita. I could see where the hem was being taken down and the bust let out, for Rose, like Annie, had been a dainty woman, while Martita was taller and fuller-figured, and the last . . . was Juliet's second nightgown, the one we had been looking for! So this was where it was!

I almost began to search over it for the missing thread that we had found on the well room's ladder, but then I remembered: Rose had gone into the well wearing its double. This gown could tell us nothing. But, all the same, I ran my hand across it. It was a little damp, with a shadowy brownish stain on its skirt.

"Tea," said Annie, and I turned and saw her half looking up at me, stitching away at the lace on Daisy's skirt while she held it in place with her left hand.

"Poor Rose was holding a cup of it when she stepped on that glass last night. She spilled it all over her skirt and we had to change her into her spare while I washed this one. It's a stubborn stain—it's not all out yet. I did say to her how lucky it was that we have two of each costume."

"Isn't that normal?" asked Daisy, wriggling impatiently.

"It is for the shows I dress," said Annie. "I was in a production once where the actresses only had one of each

Robin Stevens

dress, and the leading man spilled wine over the bodice of the leading lady. She simply had to go on for Act One wearing Act Three's dress. I vowed never to let it happen again. Rose was such a beautiful person to dress; such a nice waist and very pretty arms. She looked lovely in capped sleeves—so quaint!"

"So you liked her?" I asked, turning back to Annie.

"Of course I did! She was lovely, always so kind to me. And I felt sorry for her. It's a dreadful thing to lose your family, especially as young as she did. When I think about my own parents, and my sister—it's terrible."

"Oh, do tell us what happened!" said Daisy.

Of course, Annie was delighted to talk about it.

"It was awful!" she cried, blinking her heavily made-up eyes and shaking back her blond curls, which were falling over her face. "She was thirteen—at least, I think she was? She was on holiday with her mother and father at— Oh, I can't recall. I think it was Blackpool, one of those places with a pier and bathing and donkey rides on the beach. I always think they're such terrible value for money, don't you?"

"I don't think I've ever been on a donkey," said Daisy. "Is it anything like a pony?"

"Goodness, I have no idea," said Annie, "but, if pony rides are anywhere near as bony and slow, then I don't know why anyone bothers with them. Anyway, so Rose was there with her parents—she wasn't called Rose Tree then, of course—that's only her very clever stage name—she was little Susan Brown. Whatever her name, the three of them went out boating, only something went wrong. The boat capsized and they were all simply swept out to sea. Her parents couldn't swim, and drowned, but Susan was carried by the current and washed up on a beach a mile away. She was found by a local girl. She went to live with her doddery old aunt, and then, as soon as she turned eighteen, she went to London to go on the stage. Isn't that romantic?"

I thought it sounded utterly awful. Daisy, though, was nodding away.

"So you were here in Wardrobe last night?" she asked.

"Of course," said Annie. "I had that dress to clean. There was tea all over it and I knew Rose might want it today. But I did go to borrow a cigarette off Jim. I don't like to smoke around the costumes—it's a fire risk. I know a wardrobe mistress who fell asleep in her room and her lit cigarette fell onto a pile of lace. She went up like a candle! I've been mortally afraid of that ever since. Oh, poor Rose!"

"So you can't *prove* where you were apart from the time you went to see Jim?" asked Daisy.

"Goodness me, you sound like the police!" said Annie, head bent as she stitched. "No, of course I can't. How was I to know that someone was about to kill poor Rose? If I had, I wouldn't have been alone. Imagine, they might have come in here and killed me too! Really, you never know. I heard about a man in the East End who went on a murder spree. He killed absolutely everyone who got in his way, and the only person who escaped was a poor man who managed to climb out of his bedroom window, absolutely naked!"

"Well, yes, but that was a hundred years ago," said Daisy. "I don't really think this case is like that one."

"How do you *know*?" asked Annie dramatically. "I'm afraid for my life today. I didn't see anything—anything at all—but I keep imagining what might happen if I *had*. If I *did* know something. Oh, the murderer might come for me next! I don't feel safe in my own Wardrobe!"

"The police will catch whoever did it!" I said.

"But they might not!" said Annie. "Until they do, I'll be keeping this door locked behind me, you can guarantee that. I shan't be the next victim!"

"I'm sure you shan't," said Daisy. "After all, you'd have to know something, and you've told us you don't."

I happened to be looking up then, and I saw something flash across Annie's face. She turned her head away again, down to her work, and I almost wondered if I had imagined it. Except I was sure that I had not.

T hat was deeply odd!" Daisy hissed to me as we left
Wardrobe and heard its lock click behind us. "Why
was she *so* afraid? She's not an important actress, is
she? No one wants to kill her! She's just the dresser."

"I don't know," I said, trying to shake the uncomfortable
feeling in my stomach. "I think—I think she might be hiding something."

"She was acting strangely, wasn't she?" Daisy agreed. "I
think she *did* see something, or find something out— Oh
bother, I wish people would simply tell us everything! But
then I suppose our cases wouldn't be half so interesting.
Now, Hazel, I have had another thought. I suspect that
clodhopping policeman with the Inspector will care more
about his stomach than about guarding the well room.
He'll want to go for lunch, and therefore I believe that now
is the perfect moment to record our timings, and re-create
the crime. Are you game?"

"Of course!" I said.

"Excellent," said Daisy. "Now. First measurement: Wardrobe to the top of the stairs. Then do the top of the stairs to Theresa's office."

We walked from Wardrobe back along the dressing-room corridor (Lysander, thankfully, had gone). Standing outside our own dressing room and Theresa's office, I checked my wristwatch carefully.

"Five seconds from Wardrobe to the stairs, and thirty seconds from the stairs to Theresa's office!" I whispered.

"Good," said Daisy. "Now, top of the stairs to the door of Rose's dressing room, and then on to the stage door."

We crept down the stairs again, past Rose's door (fifteen seconds), and then the steps to Jim's cubbyhole. He looked up at us from the newspaper-wrapped fish and chips he was eating.

"Hello, Jim!" Daisy called out. "I'm feeling so much better, thank you!"

"Twenty-five seconds," I whispered to her.

"We must go!" Daisy trilled, ignoring Jim's confused face, and we turned and made our way into the theatre again, facing the stairs with Rose's dressing room at our backs.

Down the stairs we went, once, twice, lower and lower, and then out into the stuffy dark of the theatre's lowest level. We wound past clanging boilers, and found ourselves in the corridor that had the well room at its end.

The policeman, just as Daisy had thought, had gone. It was empty apart from us, and eerily quiet. I glanced at my watch—two and a half minutes.

But this corridor was quite crammed with bits of old scenery that were spiky with broken wood and trailing wire; things that might easily catch a trailing skirt or hook an unsuspecting ankle. It was hard to move quickly and quietly through the Rue, even for someone who knew it well. Just as I thought that, I felt my stocking catch against something. The wool pulled and tore with a small noise, and I yelped.

"Shh!" hissed Daisy. "Hazel, unhook yourself from that nail and hurry along. You're ruining our timings and we shall be late!"

"We're solving a murder, not going to a tea party!" I said—and then I saw from Daisy's rather shocked face that what had come out of my mouth was one of the things that, a few months ago, I might have kept inside my head. "I didn't quite mean that," I stumbled, kneeling and tugging at my stocking, which seemed well and truly entangled. "It's just that there's no need to hurry, is there?"

"Of course there is," said Daisy. "We're pretending to be a murderer! Oh goodness, move aside. *I'll* fix it." With a rush, she dropped to crouch next to me, her face intense and serious as she peered at the caught stocking. Her slim fingers poked at the nail and she sighed.

Robin Stevens

"This is dreadfully stuck, Hazel! I don't know how you managed— Wait! Don't move a muscle!"

"What is it?" I asked, suddenly wobbling, for of course it is the hardest thing in the world to avoid thinking about something as soon as someone has told you not to do it.

"That nail," said Daisy almost dreamily, "is a dangerous one. It has clearly been responsible for more snags in the past. Look, here, beyond the bit of wool from your stocking. There's something else. It's been pushed back—we really wouldn't have seen it if it wasn't for your clumsiness, but I've almost—got—it—THERE!"

And she sat back on her heels, holding up something white.

I had the oddest tug of memory, as if my brain had snagged on a nail of its own. I remembered our very first case, and the nail that had caught the white piece of Miss Bell's lab coat. This, whatever it was, was white too, but it was not tough material. It was thin and soft, drooping against Daisy's fingers.

"It's more from Juliet's nightdress!" cried Daisy. "And since we've just seen the one in Wardrobe, which was stained but not ripped, it stands to reason that the dress that caught on this nail is the one worn by the corpse. I know quite certainly that this piece is from her skirt—the bodice was embroidered and is quite a different kind of material. Now we know for certain that Rose *walked* to the well room quite willingly. If she was carried, her skirt wouldn't have caught on this nail."

"I suppose that's useful," I said thoughtfully, "but it doesn't really give us anything new."

"Isn't it a bother?" Daisy agreed. "All this evidence to do with our victim and none left by our murderer! They were annoyingly careful, weren't they? It's as though they knew they would be up against the formidable might of the Detective Society."

"They knew they'd be up against the police," I pointed out. "They're formidable enough."

"Yes, but everyone expects the police," said Daisy. "And, as I have told you countless times, Hazel, the police make terrible mistakes, even clever policemen like the Inspector. No one expects us, which is why our work is so crucial. Now, I shall put this fabric into my handkerchief for safekeeping. Start your timings again, if you please—we're almost at the scene of the crime!"

Of course, this meant that I had to climb back into the well room. After I had paused at the door to check my watch and scribble down the time (two minutes and forty seconds from Rose's dressing-room door to here), there was nothing for it but to face the horror of the murder scene.

And it was horrid—for many reasons.

As we stood at the bottom of the ladder, shining our flashlights around the room, Daisy tutted crossly and I let out a gasp. The space had already been dirtied by the feet of the other actors, but now it had been truly ruined by the police, and their efforts to get Rose up out of the well.

The floor was wet and sticky. The bare footprint we had seen had been erased by splashes of water and tracks from many other people—there were the coroner's neat brogues, heavy hobnailed police boots, and the Inspector's large, flat shoes. They had run ropes over the lip of the well, scuffing the stones, and there was a messy, wet print where they had lowered the body before they stretchered it away.

"Clodhoppers!" said Daisy, disgust dripping from her voice. She sounded so furious, but she was quite right. Thank goodness we had seen the room before the police arrived. "However are we supposed to work in these conditions? But of course we must. Watson, get out your casebook and let us do our best to re-create the scene."

I turned back in my book to the notes I had made this morning. There was the footprint I had sketched, and the room itself with the clue of the white thread marked in.

"So, the murderer lured Rose into this room," said Daisy. "*How* they did it will depend on *who* it was. Flirtation, if it was Lysander. Simon too, perhaps—Rose might have only been pretending to despise him. Annie might have asked her to come down for a chat or a smoke, because they were friends, and Inigo and Simon might also have invited her down to smoke."

"What if Inigo or Miss Crompton said they wanted to talk about something to do with the theatre?" I suggested. "And they wanted to do it somewhere very secret? They might have made her think she was going to get another role, or something?"

"Very possible indeed!" said Daisy. "Good, Watson. Now, what about Jim?"

I shook my head. "Daisy, now we know the timings, I

Robin Stevens

can't see how Jim could possibly have done this. He walks with a limp and very slowly—you've seen him. It took us almost three minutes to get down here from his cubbyhole, and it would take the same time for us to get back again— so six minutes. Jim was the closest person to this room, but even so, if he moved at his slow pace it would take him more like ten minutes all together. He wasn't away from his desk for more than about nine minutes, we know that—he wouldn't have had time to kill Rose as well! We have to rule him out."

"Hazel, that is brilliant!" cried Daisy. "All right. So we must now work out how long the crime itself would have taken. Rose came down the ladder on her own two feet, unaware that anything nefarious was going on. I think we are agreed on that, aren't we? The door closed behind her and her murderer. Then what?"

"Then—then the next thing we know for certain is that she and the murderer fought," I said. "We saw the scuffed footprints on the floor. They came all the way across the room to *here*, and this is where we found the proper print of Rose's foot. The murderer must have been trying to get her close to the well. And then—"

"They uncovered the well; they pushed her in headfirst; they put back the cover and they rushed out of the room again," said Daisy, nodding briskly. "Simple. Now, Hazel, I have a task for you. Come here and be Rose."

"What?" I asked, taken aback. "I don't want to."

"I don't care whether you *want* to or not," said Daisy. "We must know how much time it took for the murderer to commit the crime. She was a small woman and you're small—let's see how quickly I can force you across the room and then into the well."

I sighed and told myself it was all for the good of the case.

I took up a position a few steps from the ladder. No sooner was I in place than Daisy lunged at me. She got me about the shoulders and began to drag me toward the well.

I yelped and fought back, much more fiercely than I'd been intending to. There was something frightening about this room, and feeling Daisy's hands gripping me. We stumbled and went over into the mud and dust. I was short of breath, my eyes dazzled, and I really did feel panicked. I kicked out and Daisy shrieked.

"Goodness me!" she gasped. "Stop *wriggling*, Hazel! Why don't you let me kill you!"

That broke the spell. I was no longer Rose, struggling with her killer. I was Hazel Wong again, and this was all a play.

"I don't want to!" I puffed back at her. "That wasn't nice. You're not supposed to really hurt me!"

"Good, Hazel, very good!" said Daisy, sitting back on her heels. "Do you know, I think we have proved an interesting

212   *Robin Stevens*

point. You are little, but you are fierce. It was rather hard to get you toward that well! I think our murderer would have done something to stop Rose struggling."

"But—there weren't any hand marks on her body, the coroner said so."

"Indeed," said Daisy, a faraway look in her eyes. "But that really means very little if the murderer used something wide like a scarf. I read about it in one of Uncle Felix's books."

"That is disgusting!" I cried.

"It's a *fact*, Hazel!" said Daisy, hurt. "The book said strangulation usually takes four or five minutes. Once Rose was dead, it would be quite easy to pitch her into the well. Imagine!"

I thought. It was horrible—but it made sense. "It's clever," I said reluctantly. "I think you might be right."

"Good," said Daisy. "I know. So . . . four minutes to kill Rose, and then at least one more to put her down the well and leave the room again. That *does* rule out Jim, doesn't it? And you know who else it rules out?"

"Annie!" I cried. "The argument was at five past nine, and she was seen by Jim at nine fifteen. There wouldn't be enough time, even if she went straight from Wardrobe. But Lysander is still in, and Simon, and Inigo and Miss Crompton—although they have to be in it together, or not at all. And—Martita too."

I saw Daisy flinch.

"Hazel—" she began, but at that moment, the door to the well room was flung open. A square of brightness sprang up on the wall above us, sending light shooting down across us.

We both raised our hands against it, squinting as the light was blocked by two figures.

"I thought I might find you here," said the Inspector's voice in amusement. "You do get into the most interesting places."

It was awful, but not too surprising, that he should have caught us—but the voice that spoke next made me gasp.

"My dear niece," said Uncle Felix. "You told me you were going to stay *out* of trouble."

I put out my hand and seized Daisy's. She did not even squeeze back. She was frozen, like a rabbit in front of a surging car.

"I suppose we ought to have known better," Uncle Felix went on. "At this stage, I should almost be prepared to suggest that you have been *causing* the crimes. How else can you explain being present at so many murders?"

"I—" stammered Daisy. "Uncle Felix, listen—"

"I am not interested in your excuses, Daisy," interrupted Uncle Felix. "Now, come along, if you please. We are going home, and that is where you will be staying for the foreseeable future. Amateur detection hour is *over*."

Robin Stevens

Part Five
Death Lies on Her

I

Uncle Felix rushed us to the stage door, hardly giving us time to collect our things from our dressing room. I felt nervous and upset, and I knew I was feeling those things because Uncle Felix was too. He might be a most interesting grown-up whose job was really quite similar to our detective missions, but he was also Daisy's uncle, and so I knew there was a part of him that couldn't bear the idea of her getting into any trouble at all.

Daisy held her head high and refused to be hurried, but I hung my head as hot shame flooded through me. I felt little and silly—really, what good *could* we do?

Daisy nudged me. "Chin up, Hazel!" she whispered in my ear. "He shan't cow us! He's only playing a part, anyway. He knows he *ought* to be cross."

"I heard that, Daisy," said Uncle Felix. "I assure you I *am* cross with you. I am also cross at the world, which seems determined to turn my niece into a hard-boiled private eye."

"Why shouldn't I be a detective?" asked Daisy. "I'm not a child!"

"You certainly *are* a child; the most annoying sort who thinks she's an adult," said Uncle Felix. "And you've taught Hazel to think the same way."

"I haven't taught Hazel *anything*. Why do you *always* assume it's entirely *my* fault!" cried Daisy.

"It really is my fault just as much as Daisy's," I agreed. "I am sorry, though. We didn't mean to upset you."

"I *know* you didn't," said Uncle Felix, sighing as he nodded to Jim and wrote down all our names in Jim's book in black pen. I hoped he would not see that my name was there twice. "But the fact is that everyone's talking about this crime, which means that everyone will be talking about *you*. Outside are a pack of reporters, just waiting to get our pictures. And we don't need any more of *that*, not after the trial last year. Tip your hats down on your heads and cover your faces with your free arms."

"Why should I?" asked Daisy brazenly.

"*Bertie*," said Uncle Felix.

I saw Daisy flush. Uncle Felix had said the magic word. Apart from her feelings for Martita, there are only four people Daisy truly cares about in this world, and one of them is her brother. She put her arm up to cover her face with her cuffs. I hid my face with no persuading—I do not want to be any more famous than I already am.

218   *Robin Stevens*

Then Uncle Felix bent his head so that his profile was hidden in the collar of his greatcoat and shoved us forward, through the stage door.

My eyes were dazed by sudden brightness, and for a moment it was as though we had stepped out into the Hong Kong noonday sun. But then the light faded and I saw a crowd of cameras with flashbulbs pressing in on us, all held by men and women with hard, eager faces and open mouths.

"Are you connected to the murder of Rose Tree?" they shouted. "Are you suspects? Are you the police? Who *are* you?"

Uncle Felix simply shouldered past them silently, trailing us behind him like the tail of a comet. Then we were out on Shaftesbury Avenue, the traffic flying by us. It was only early afternoon, but fog was already creeping in, turning the lights of the taxis dim and mysterious. A car screeched up to us and I saw Bridget at the wheel, grim-faced. Uncle Felix opened the back door and shoved us in.

I stumbled, my palms against the car's wooden floor, and then dragged myself upright to see Aunt Lucy sitting in the back seat, waiting for us with her arms crossed and a stern expression on her face. Daisy piled in behind me, and Uncle Felix slammed the door on us and leaped into the front seat.

"Bridget, drive!" he cried, and Bridget, in a smart

chauffeur's cap and gloves as well as her usual neat black-and-white maid's dress, pressed her foot down on the pedal and sent us flying away from the herd of reporters.

"You *are* in trouble," said Aunt Lucy to us quietly. "How do you always manage it?"

"We get into trouble because we notice things," said Daisy. "Just like you! Honestly, I don't know what you're both so cross about. You would have done *exactly* the same thing if you'd found a dead body when you were our age."

Aunt Lucy's expression flickered. "That isn't the point, Daisy dear," she said. "Whether I would have or not, I am not your age anymore, and Felix and I have a lot of dreadful knowledge about all the nasty things that might happen to curious little girls."

Robin Stevens

The car was silent all the way home. I felt a little calmer, but I was still rather worried about what our punishment would be. I could see that we had made our position rather worse by trying to hide what had happened at the Rue from Uncle Felix. I wanted to tap out a Morse code message to Daisy, but I knew that there were three grown-ups present who would understand it more quickly than she would.

Just as we were walking through the front door, Aunt Lucy leaned forward and hissed, "Don't say anything about our lessons!" in our ears.

Daisy looked back at her, unblinking, and Aunt Lucy cleared her throat rather uncomfortably.

Uncle Felix settled himself in the living room, and Bridget and Aunt Lucy stationed themselves on each side of him. Daisy and I sat on the sofa, shoulders touching for moral support. It was a little like an interview with a group of terrifying teachers.

"Now," said Uncle Felix, "what are we to do with you? You *persist* in finding dangerous crimes!"

"You don't need to do anything with us!" said Daisy at once. "We're perfect."

"A murder happens, and you choose not to tell us about it!" cried Uncle Felix. "You had ample opportunity. You could have telephoned the moment you found the body, Daisy. Why didn't you?"

"We didn't want to upset you," said Daisy smoothly.

"We knew you'd bring us home," I said in a quiet voice.

"*That's* more like it," said Uncle Felix.

"Now, Felix, the girls made a poor decision today. But none of us could have known this morning that there'd be a murder!" said Aunt Lucy. "This isn't about blame."

"Lucy, while they are in our care, we're supposed to make sure they are safe!" said Uncle Felix rather wildly. "We can't hand them back to their parents chopped up in a bag!"

"No one is chopping anyone up," said Aunt Lucy, at exactly the same moment as Daisy said, "In five years I shall be twenty, and then you'll see!"

"I'm sure we will *all* see. The world is hardly ready. But you *aren't* twenty yet, and I can't treat you as though you are. There have to be consequences. Whether you like it or not, you are not to be allowed back at the Rue until

Robin Stevens

this mess has been cleared up—and I mean cleared up by Inspector Priestley, not by you. You will remain here, in the flat, and Bridget will simply have to look after you, even though it is terribly inconvenient. Do you understand?"

"No!" hissed Daisy. "You're—you're such a *grown-up*! Ugh, come along, Hazel! Let's go to our room."

"And you can have dinner in there too!" Uncle Felix shouted after us.

I think that was supposed to be a punishment—which shows again that Uncle Felix does not have much understanding of children.

"Bother Uncle Felix!" said Daisy, sitting down on her bed with a bump. "Trying to be responsible and sensible! Ugh!"

"I think he did understand," I said, sitting next to her. "I mean, he's not really cross with us, just worried. And he's right that your family . . . have been mixed up with the press quite a lot this last year."

"He's clever," said Daisy gloomily. "He knew that *Bertie* was the only thing he could say to make me play along. And, now that he's banned us from the Rue, he'll stick to his guns like anything. Oh, this is infuriating!"

"Do you think he really won't let us go back?" I asked. "Will we have to drop the case?"

I felt panic rising in my throat. The Detective Society had faced difficulties in the past, but never anything like this. We were far away from the scene of the crime, and the pieces of our puzzle were not yet complete. Could we solve the case with what we already knew? What if something else were to happen at the theatre while we weren't there?

"We certainly will *not* drop the investigation!" said Daisy, setting her chin. "We have plenty of evidence, and we understand the case far better than anyone else. And we have to help Martita, Hazel. She has nothing to do with this, I know it, and we have to prove it."

There was a knock on the door. Bridget came in, carrying a tray piled high with food: a rich stew, with lemon meringue pie for afters. We ate balancing plates and bowls on our knees, talking over everything we knew about the case, and it did feel rather like having a midnight feast at school, not a punishment at all.

We did not know that something truly terrible lay just around the corner.

Robin Stevens

I woke on Monday morning—today—and wrote down everything that had happened. I remember feeling rather more cheerful. I had even begun to think that Daisy might be right about Martita's innocence. The evidence pointing to her seemed too theatrical to be true; something an actor in a play about murder would do, not a real person.

I thought about Lysander, and how frightening he had been yesterday. A man like that really might hurt a woman who had upset him. . . .

And then there was Simon. He seemed friendly on the surface, but I got a sort of double feeling when I thought of him. He was hiding something, I knew it—but what he had not hidden was his hatred of Rose. He had wanted to play Romeo, and had been prevented by Rose's cruelty.

From what we had overheard Inigo and Simon saying, Inigo seemed to be just as angry at Rose, and willing to protect Simon by any means necessary. We also knew that the Rue was struggling after a bad production earlier in the spring. Could Inigo and Miss Crompton be working together to bring publicity to the theatre by getting rid of one annoying actress?

And finally, what about Annie? We had ruled her out as the murderer—but why *had* she been so afraid yesterday? Was she hiding something too? Had she seen something important?

Once Uncle Felix and Aunt Lucy had gone to work, Daisy and I ate breakfast—buttered toast and marmalade, and soft-boiled eggs in little china egg cups. Daisy was already fidgety and restless, and watching Bridget closely for any sign that she might be distracted enough for us to slip away from the flat. Without the Rue to give shape to our day, the hours stretched ahead of us, as cloudy and vague as a London fog.

Although it was May, the day outside was gray and rather raw-looking, with tendrils of last night's fog still lingering at street corners. People rushed past below, shivering in light spring coats.

"Nasty day," said Bridget, hurrying by with her dusting cloth, and I made a polite agreeing noise. Daisy opened *Enter a Murderer* and began pretending to read.

"Good book that," said Bridget, flicking it with her duster. "It took me until page forty to work out who did it."

"I solved it on page *thirty*," said Daisy at once, wrinkling up her nose.

"Well, aren't you a genius, then," said Bridget, winking at me. "You must be related to Mr. M."

Then the telephone rang.

"Hello? Allô? Ni hao?" said Bridget efficiently into it. There was a chattering pause. "Yes, this is the Mountfitchet residence. No, Miss Wells and Miss Wong are not available. You can give any message to me."

Daisy had sat up in her chair like a mongoose seeing a snake. "Who is it?" she mouthed at Bridget, putting down her book. "Is it for us? *Is it?*"

"I assure you, you can trust me with anything," Bridget was saying. "Yes, Dublin. Is that so? Well, I work with Mr. Mountfitchet. He can confirm that if you like."

More chattering on the other end of the line.

I was sitting up too now, and I could feel my heart beating. Who was it? Why did they want to speak to us? *What had happened?*

"No!" said Bridget in a very different tone of voice. "No—really? Yes. Yes, I understand. Thank you. Goodbye."

She put the receiver back in its cradle and turned to us. Daisy was blazing with impatience next to me, and my fists were clenched. I had one of my detective moments then: I knew, very simply, that whatever Bridget was about to say to us would be very terrible indeed.

"Girls," said Bridget. She frowned and twisted her hands together. "That was Inspector Priestley. He was calling about the Rue Theatre case."

"Yes, yes, what did he *say?*" gasped Daisy.

There was a pause that felt long to me, but my wristwatch only counted two ticks.

"There's been a development in the case," said Bridget at last. "He wanted me to tell you. Annie Joy never went home to her room last night. Two witnesses saw her walking toward Westminster Bridge just before midnight, and she hasn't been seen since. Her hat, coat, and handbag were found washed up beside the river, with a note inside the bag. A body has been found in the estuary this morning. The Inspector thinks—well, he thinks *she jumped.*"

Robin Stevens

D aisy dragged me back into our room, her cheeks flushed with excitement.

"Detective Society meeting, Hazel!" she cried. "At once! We have had the most stunning development in the case!"

"Do you really think she did—jump?" I whispered. "Poor Annie!"

"Perhaps she did!" said Daisy, trembling with excitement. "Perhaps she's the murderer and she was feeling guilty. But I don't think that's the most likely explanation. Remember when she let us into Wardrobe? She was afraid *until* she saw who we were, and that tells me that she was worried about someone *else* finding her, not us. Someone specific."

"You think she knew who the murderer was?" I asked. "I was wondering . . . She was behaving so oddly!"

"Yes, exactly, Hazel! She knew something, and that knowledge made her afraid! I believe that her death is likely to be a *second murder—made to look like suicide*. Our killer has struck again! Oh, I wish we were at the Rue. It's so annoying not being properly part of the case!"

"Well, we can still work on our suspect list," I said. "We can rule Annie out, for certain!"

"Very true," said Daisy. "And, now that we know what has happened, our next steps are clear. We must look into the alibis of our remaining suspects for the time of Annie's death, just after midnight, on Westminster Bridge, and to do that we *must* get out of this flat! I say! We could climb out of the window—we've done it before!"

"Of course we could," I said. "But Bridget is here, and I think she'd stop us if we tried."

"I could outwit her!" snapped Daisy, the color still high in her cheeks. "Goodness, it's warm in here. Aunt Lucy and Uncle Felix have turned into old people."

"It isn't warm," I said. "You're just cross."

"I'm not cross, I'm *thinking*!" said Daisy. "You mark my words, Hazel, I will find a way out!"

SUSPECT LIST

1. Miss Crompton. MOTIVE: She was Rose's greatest ally at the Rue Theatre and seems sad that she is

Robin Stevens

dead—but she has also been honest about the fact that Rose's death will be good for business, and will help the Rue's money troubles. She clearly cares most about the Rue, and about her company—might she have been willing to hurt one member of it to help everyone else? OPPORTUNITY: She seems to have an alibi from 9 p.m. until just before Rose was discovered missing at 9:30 p.m.—she was onstage with Inigo—but she did also go to the loo for a few minutes. ~~Could this be enough time for her to have gone to the well room with Rose and killed her there?~~ This is NOT enough time—unless her alibi is a lie! NOTES: She did not visit Jim at the stage door until after Rose's disappearance that evening, meaning that she had no clear opportunity to forge Rose's name in the book. But could she be working with someone else—like Inigo?

2. Simon. MOTIVE: He does not like Rose. He hinted, and Inigo confirmed, that he was supposed to play Romeo until Rose objected to the color of his skin. Was he angry enough with her to do something terrible? OPPORTUNITY: He was with Inigo when they overheard the argument between Martita and Rose, but afterward left him and went upstairs to

his own dressing room until the alarm was raised at 9:30. Could he have left it to murder Rose? From our reenactment of the crime, we know it would have taken him approximately twelve minutes to go down to the well room, murder Rose, and go back to his dressing room. NOTES: Visited Jim's cubbyhole and so could have forged Rose's name in the book.

3. Annie (Wardrobe). ~~MOTIVE: No clear motive. Rose was friendly with her—but she did seem to be uncomfortable with Rose's behavior toward other members of the company. OPPORTUNITY: She was in the loo on the first floor when Martita and Rose had their argument, but was then alone in Wardrobe at the crucial time. It would have taken her approximately twelve minutes to get down to the well room and back again. She has no alibi! NOTES: Visited Jim's cubbyhole and so could have forged Rose's name in the book.~~ RULED OUT! Annie has become the second victim. She was seen walking toward Westminster Bridge just before midnight last night; her handbag, coat, and hat were found beside the river this morning, and a body that we believe to be hers was found in the estuary. The Inspector thinks she committed suicide—there is a note in her handbag—but we are not so sure. Annie

was behaving oddly yesterday, and saying she was afraid. Did she know something about the murder? Has she been shut up by the murderer?

4. Inigo. MOTIVE: He disliked Rose intensely and says that she is the reason why Simon was not able to play Romeo. He also wants to use her death as publicity. OPPORTUNITY: He was with Simon and Miss Crompton when they heard the argument between Rose and Martita, and he says that after this he went back onstage to talk to Miss Crompton until he left to see Jim just before the alarm was raised by Martita at 9:30. If this is true, then he may not have had time—unless he was working with Miss Crompton. He could have gone down to the well room, murdered Rose, and gone back onstage in approximately eleven minutes. NOTES: Visited Jim's cubbyhole and so could have forged Rose's name in the book.

5. Lysander. MOTIVE: He had been flirting with Rose, but Daisy and Hazel noticed that they had been arguing more and more lately. He is a very threatening person, and he was angry with Rose. OPPORTUNITY: He was in his dressing room, alone, during the time Rose must have been murdered—he

does not have an alibi! NOTES: Was at Jim's cubbyhole when the alarm was raised, and so could have forged Rose's name in the book. He behaved threateningly toward Daisy yesterday—he seems capable of violence. It would have only taken him approximately twelve minutes to go down to the well room, murder Rose, and go back to his dressing room.

6. Jim (stage door). MOTIVE: ~~He did not like Rose, and resented her being part of the Rue. But did he feel strongly enough about her to murder her?~~ OPPORTUNITY: ~~He says he was at his post all evening. Is this true?~~ RULED OUT: He has a limp. He would have needed more time to kill Rose than anyone else, but he was not away from his post for more than nine minutes on the evening of the murder. Even the closest of our other suspects could not have murdered Rose in under eleven minutes.

7. Martita. MOTIVE: She hated the fact that Rose was playing Juliet. She felt that the part should have been hers, and was jealous that Rose was allowed to be the star. OPPORTUNITY: She left the stage when Rose refused to come on to rehearse

Scene Five. Inigo, Simon, Miss Crompton, and Annie all say that they heard her arguing with Rose in Rose's dressing room at about 9:05. We do not know where she went after that. Could she have murdered Rose before she raised the alarm at 9:30? NOTES: Visited Jim's cubbyhole and so could have forged Rose's name in the book. It would have only taken her approximately twelve minutes to go down to the well room, murder Rose, and go back to her dressing room. Rose walked to the well room rather than being dragged there—would she have gone with Martita?

PLAN OF ACTION

1. Check Jim's stage-door book and ascertain whether Jim can be trusted.

2. Look at timings and decide which of our suspects had enough opportunity to commit the crime.

3. Go back to the scene of the crime and reenact the murder.

4. Visit Rose's dressing room and look for clues.

5. ~~Talk to suspects~~ decide if any of them could be working together.

6. Find out which of our remaining suspects have alibis for the time of Annie's death.

7. Rule out Martita! (NB Daisy wrote this!)

8. Discover the killer.

Robin Stevens

B
ut Daisy had still not managed to escape when the afternoon post came, and with it two very important things.

The first was a great bundle of newspapers (Uncle Felix and Aunt Lucy like to take them all)—and their evening editions had all heard about Annie's disappearance.

MURDER IN THE THEATRE!
NEW LEADS!
SHOCKING INTERVIEWS!
WOMAN MISSING!
SECOND BODY FOUND IN
RUE MYSTERY!

Daisy and I sat poring over them. Seeing all those headlines made me feel rather sick, and very small. I have never been able to watch how the rest of the world saw one of our cases. I have only lived them, and told the story that Daisy and I saw. These words, none of them from my pencil, turned the real people at the Rue into a story I could not control.

I looked more closely at one.

Missing!

The *Evening Bugle* has discovered that the Mystery of the Rue Theatre has taken a new and dangerous turn. Annie Joy, 25, of Southend, Essex, a member of the ill-fated Rue Theatre Company, is MISSING from her Soho accommodation, Scotland Yard has confirmed. She was last seen walking toward Westminster Bridge just before midnight yesterday, seemingly in great distress, and the police fear that she may have been intent on causing herself harm.

Sorrow at the Rue

Miss Joy's disappearance is the latest in a shocking string of events at London's Rue Theatre. The Rue's most shining new star, Rose Tree, was MURDERED just two days ago. Is the venue cursed? Its owner, Miss Frances Crompton, was not available for comment, but the director, notable thespian Inigo Leontes, gave this tragic statement: "Poor darling Annie was a beloved member of our company, a young woman with marvelous talent. Our production of *Romeo and Juliet*, which opens in just two days, on Wednesday the 27th of May at 7:30 p.m., will sorely miss

Robin Stevens

her. Tickets are still available from our box office, and I hope the public will flock to see the play, as a loving tribute to both Rose Tree and Annie Joy."

Vanished into the Night!

A witness, who asks to remain anonymous, says that Miss Joy bumped into him as she was walking down Charing Cross Road just after 11:30 p.m. "She was wearing a red coat," the witness said. "She stood out in the fog. She was walking fast and she looked afraid. She stumbled into me and I saw that she was crying. I asked if she needed assistance, but she ran away before I could help." She was then seen by another witness at 11:45, near Westminster Bridge. Miss Joy asked this man, who has also requested to remain anonymous, for a cigarette. He says that her hands trembled as she held it up to be lit. . . . This was the last sighting of Miss Joy, before she vanished into the night forever. . . .

Belongings Found!

Miss Joy's hat, coat, and handbag, badly waterlogged, were discovered on the banks of the Thames this morning. There are reports that a NOTE may have been found inside the handbag, but police refuse to confirm this.

Body Found!

The body of a young woman was also found DROWNED in the

Thames Estuary this morning. Did Annie Joy do dreadful violence to herself?

"Our Little Darling"

Miss Joy's parents, Henry and Mavis Joy, wept this afternoon at their modest but tidy family home in Southend, Essex. "She was our little darling," said Mavis, 46. "Our youngest. We are devastated, and so is her brother."

CAN YOU HELP?

Have you seen tragic Annie? She has been described as a slight young woman with curly blond hair and a red coat. She was wearing red patent shoes and a green scarf and hat, and carrying a blue handbag. If you have any information relating to her, call the *Bugle*'s office now.

"What a silly article!" said Daisy scornfully. "*Our little darling.* I'll bet you her parents didn't say any such thing. And look at Inigo turning it on like anything! But at least we have some useful new information. We know Annie's last movements, and we have the timing of her death all but confirmed as just before midnight. Oh, if only we could get out of this idiotic flat. It's so *hot!*"

Daisy kept on turning over newspapers restlessly, her hands smudging the newsprint, while I looked at the second bit of post—a letter addressed to me.

Robin Stevens

Of course, as soon as I picked it up, Daisy pounced.

"Ooh!" she said with relish. "Another letter from *Alexander*."

I could feel my face heat too. "So what if it is?" I asked defiantly. Alexander and I have been writing regularly since our last case together. I tell myself fiercely that everything is all right between us now. We are friends, and nothing more. But I know that there is a deeper truth beneath this. I feel the same way toward Alexander as ever, and I know how he feels about Daisy, and so nothing is all right, and I do not think it will ever be.

"No reason," said Daisy. "What does he say? Has he heard about the murders yet?"

I opened the letter, running my fingers carefully under its seal. I could see Daisy flinching with annoyance—she wanted me to simply rip it open. So I moved more slowly than ever, unfolding it and smoothing it out on my lap like a present.

Dear Hazel,

I hope you and Daisy are well. George and I are in jolly good spirits, though terribly jealous of you gadding about in London. Nothing at Weston can live up to the excitement of what happened when we saw you last.

Our half-term started on Friday, and I'm with

*George at his people's again. They're great, though
I miss Mom and Dad. Sorry, Hazel, I shouldn't
have said that—I know it's even harder for you.*

*Anyway, what I'm writing to say is that we'd
love to see you and Daisy again. Or are you too
busy and famous for us now? Just in case, we'll
call for you at your uncle's apartment on Tuesday
morning. If you could get away, it'd be spiffing.
And we'd love to watch you rehearse your play.
It starts soon, right? We want to see Daisy acting
the star. Say we can. We miss you.*

Alexander

I got the up-and-down, hot-and-cold feeling I have
whenever I read one of Alexander's letters. I could not help
being a detective and poring over every word. *We miss you*
was an encouraging clue (although I wished he had said *I*,
not *we*), but *We want to see Daisy acting the star* was utterly
depressing. It reminded me that, for all I have changed, I
am still not the star. I am not the president of the Detective
Society. I am only Daisy's shadow.

"They want to see us," I managed to say. "But I don't
think Alexander knew about what happened at the Rue
when he wrote."

"Of course they will by now! And of course they want

to see us!" said Daisy, frowning and sighing. "Alexander is quite obsessed with me—it's such a bore. But I admit that I always like to see George, and Alexander does at least slightly improve with age. By the time he's twenty he might be only ordinarily annoying."

"*Stop* saying that he's obsessed with you!" I said, and I could feel my face flushing and my heart pounding.

"But it's true! Goodness, why do people always get so upset when I say things that are true?" asked Daisy.

"Because it's not nice! Imagine if I teased you about Martita. I haven't once, Daisy, not *once*. It's just the same as how I feel about Alexander, and you might understand it now!"

"Oh, lay off, Hazel!" said Daisy furiously. She rubbed at her forehead. "I—I suppose you're right. My brain feels muddled. I'm just so terribly tired of being cooped up inside. Can't we get out at all?"

"Certainly not," said Bridget, passing by with a duster. "Mr. M.'s orders."

"Oh, please!" said Daisy, cheeks pink with hope. "We'll be as good as gold, honor bright!"

"Daisy, stop it," said Bridget. "I've got the kitchen presses to clean, dinner to make, and Mr. M.'s case notes to type up. Be patient and he'll let you out tomorrow, I'm sure."

"Do you really think so?" asked Daisy at once.

"I do," said Bridget. "He's a paper tiger. Be good, Daisy, come on."

"All right!" trilled Daisy. "Hazel, let's go to our room and be as good as *gold*."

She was using her most polite, grown-up-friendly tone. I eyed her suspiciously. I have learned all too well that, when Daisy speaks in that voice, she means absolutely nothing she says.

Robin Stevens

O f course, I was right.

"Hazel, we must ignore Bridget!" hissed Daisy as soon as we had closed the door to our room. Her cheeks were now very red and her eyes were glittering. She slipped her hand over mine and her palm was burning hot.

"We have to escape and investigate Annie's accommodation! We have to get to Soho—or at least one of us does. I'm going to climb out of this window, get down into the street, hail a taxi, and be away before Bridget can stop me. You must cover for me! I am ordering you as your president to help me now."

"Daisy . . . ," I said. "Are you—are you all right?"

"*I have never been better!*" snarled Daisy.

"Daisy," I said again. "You look odd. Are you sure there's nothing wrong?"

"Of course not!" cried Daisy hoarsely, and she ran at our

window and wrestled with the catch, trying to get outside.

At the same moment, the door to our room opened. Bridget came in, took one look at Daisy, and went rushing toward her with a furious cry. She threw herself at Daisy, who was now halfway out of the window, and simply tackled her at the knees. Daisy went down with a shriek, crumpling in Bridget's arms in a way that looked utterly staged.

But then Bridget drew back and knelt beside her, annoyance melting into concern, and I saw that Daisy was not getting up. Her eyes were closed and that dangerous flush was still across her cheeks.

"Daisy, love?" said Bridget. "Are you all right?"

I rushed to Daisy's side and bent down to shake her shoulder. Daisy has done this sort of thing before, and so I was expecting her to flinch against me to show me that she was really only pretending.

But she did not. She stayed limp, and her eyelids fluttered feverishly. I remembered her hot hands, her hoarse voice, her bright cheeks, and her flustered behavior. I had thought they were clues that Daisy was annoyed and excited by the case. But . . . what if the solution was something far more ordinary?

Bridget picked Daisy up and laid her on her bed. Daisy opened her eyes and struggled to sit up as Bridget felt her forehead.

Robin Stevens

"Daisy," she said. "Stop wriggling about! You're burning up. You've got that flu that's going around."

"I do not!" said Daisy. "I am perfectly—all right—really I am—will you *stop* making the room spin about like that! It's really exactly what I'd expect from Uncle Felix, having a secretly spinning room. Hazel, tell him to *stop it*."

"The room isn't spinning, Daisy," said Bridget. "It's your head."

"What nonsense!" cried Daisy. "I'll have you know that there is nothing wrong with me at all. I'm not the weak one—Hazel is. My head does not spin for anything and I—"

Here she broke off in a fit of coughing that made her cheeks redder than ever.

Bridget pushed her back against her pillows.

"Tell her, Hazel!" Daisy cried.

"I won't tell her anything," I said, folding my arms. "Daisy, don't be silly. Look at you! You've got exactly what Theresa had—what half the company have had!"

"Hazel Wong, you absolute traitor!" gasped Daisy. "I shall never talk to you again. This is the end. You'll be sorry when I die; then you'll wish you'd been nicer to me."

"She won't die, Hazel," said Bridget to me. "Go and fetch some blankets, will you? Daisy, if you don't stop struggling, I shall have to dose you with something to make you sleep. It's what I do when Mr. M. is ill, otherwise he *will* get up and go to work."

I thought, not for the first time, how funny it was that Daisy and Uncle Felix ever disagreed. They were so very similar. Or was that the key to their arguments?

"If you try, I shall spit it out!" cried Daisy, struggling in a rage. "And then I shall run away and—" She broke off to cough again. "Oh bother, whatever is the matter with me?"

"You're ill, Daisy," said Bridget calmly. "It happens, even to people like you."

Daisy argued until she was purple in the face, and then, without even stopping to take a breath, she fell asleep.

She slept all the way through Bridget clattering about in the kitchen, making dinner, Uncle Felix coming in, throwing back his head and laughing at her, and Aunt Lucy walking quietly in after him to carefully adjust the pillows behind Daisy's head.

At last, Daisy gave a dainty little snort and fluttered her eyes open. I braced myself for more furious orders.

"Hazel," she said, licking her lips and blinking at me. "You can have my pudding at dinner. I don't feel . . . quite . . . like it."

And, just like that, she was asleep again.

"Bridget!" I shouted. "Aunt Lucy! Help!"

"Good heavens, whatever's the matter?" asked Aunt Lucy, appearing in the doorway with Uncle Felix.

"I think Daisy *is* dying," I said. "She just offered me her pudding!"

"She's not dying," said Aunt Lucy briskly, padding over to Daisy and feeling her forehead and jaw. "The fever's caught up with her, that's all. She'll have a rough night of it, but she's young and strong—she'll be quite all right soon. I shall call the doctor just in case, but it's nothing more than the flu."

Daisy was tucked up in bed, muttering, "*Watson . . . body . . . dead . . . murder . . . Martita!*" under her breath.

"At least she's having exciting dreams," said Aunt Lucy. "Felix, she really *is* your niece."

Uncle Felix groaned. "It's inevitable, isn't it?" he said. "I kept on hoping she'd be ordinary."

"Daisy's much better than ordinary!" I said, rather stung.

"You both are," said Aunt Lucy, winking at me. I beamed back at her quite without meaning to—and thought once again how perfect it would be to grow up into someone as interesting as Aunt Lucy. It would almost make up for not being a child anymore.

"Aunt Lucy, Uncle Felix—George and Alexander might visit tomorrow," I said, remembering. "I mean—they want to see Daisy, but—"

Aunt Lucy and Uncle Felix exchanged a flicker of a glance.

"Yet another problem to solve," said Uncle Felix. "I can't

Robin Stevens

imagine your father would be happy with you seeing boys unchaperoned, would he?"

My face burned.

"The real problem is," said Uncle Felix, screwing in his monocle thoughtfully, "which is more dangerous: men or murder? I can see the case for both, personally. What if we simply sent you both to a nunnery?"

Aunt Lucy cleared her throat.

"I am being denied the nunnery," said Uncle Felix. "So. You may see the boys, I suppose, Hazel. But Bridget will supervise. If you leave the house with them, she must be with you, and you may not leave for anything longer than tea. Do you understand? And don't forget, if you go out I can hold Daisy hostage."

"Yes, Uncle Felix," I said.

"We are *never* having children," said Uncle Felix, turning to glare at Aunt Lucy.

And I *meant* to obey him, I really did. I thought George and Alexander would arrive, and we would simply go to tea and talk about the case. I never expected . . . what happened.

Part Six

In the Bottom
of a Tomb

It is Tuesday evening and I am home again. I am also in a fearful lot of trouble. Daisy, sitting up in her bed in her white nightie with her cheeks a little less pink than they were yesterday, has just said, "I don't know whether to hate you or be fearfully impressed with you, Hazel." I'm not sure I know, either.

Here is what happened.

My sleep was awful and broken on Monday night. I had been put in the guest bedroom, but all the same I could hear Daisy through the wall, having dreadful fever dreams that made her toss about like a cat in a sack and cry out furiously. She kept on saying my name, and every time she did I would wake in a panic in case she was in danger.

At last, I sat up, shivering and sweating both at once, and clicked on the electric light beside my bed. I got out my casebook and a pencil and wrote up the rest of Monday. When Bridget came to bring in breakfast, I was still awake, feeling slightly light-headed and unreal. I went in to see Daisy.

She was awake too, drinking beef tea and complaining.

"Hazel, being ill is dreadful," she said. "I do not recommend it!"

Then she fell asleep again.

All that morning, I drifted about the house, unable to concentrate. I tried on clothes in the costume room, trying to look like someone else, but I kept on looking just like myself. I also kept on turning to my right, to see what Daisy thought, before I remembered that she was not there.

I was waiting and waiting for the doorbell to ring, my nerves stretched like a string, so that when it did I thought for a moment I might be imagining things.

"Hazel!" called Bridget. "It's for you!"

I went rushing into the sitting room—both too fast and too slow, tripping over my own feet—and there were George and Alexander, unbearably real and, as always, much more person-sized than they were in my imagination.

George, looking perfectly turned out as always, in a very elegant new shirt and with his hair Brylcreemed, stuck out a hand and smiled at me. And then I was turning to Alexander, not sure if it was proper to hug or simply shake hands.

But of course Alexander was still Alexander, and he simply swept me up in a large, cheerful hug. I told myself sternly that I ought not to enjoy it, for it meant less than nothing.

Robin Stevens

Alexander likes me—of course he does. That is the problem. He likes me in every way but the way I like him.

Alexander stepped back and looked around in confusion.

"Where's Daisy?" he asked.

"She's ill," said George at once.

Alexander and I both stared at him.

"It's not difficult to work out!" George protested, shrugging his shoulders. "Bridget looks rushed. I can smell beef tea boiling. Hazel looks tired, she doesn't have her handkerchief in her pocket and Daisy isn't here. Daisy can't be dead, otherwise Hazel would be crying with her handkerchief in her hand. But, if Daisy were simply ill, it would explain the beef tea and Bridget—and Hazel would have sat up worrying about Daisy all night, and given Daisy her handkerchief when hers were all used up. See? Elementary."

"Show-off," said Alexander, grinning good-naturedly.

"Who am I showing off to?" asked George. "Hazel's cleverer than I am."

I shot him a glance.

"Is Daisy all right?" Alexander asked, worried. "I mean—will she be?"

"She'll be perfectly all right!" I said. "She only has the flu. It's been going round the Rue."

At the Rue's name, George's and Alexander's eyes lit up.

"Tell us all about it!" said Alexander. "Come on, do! We've

read the papers, but they don't tell us much. It really isn't fair that you girls get all the best mysteries."

"Well, we *are* the best Detective Society," I said, and blushed. That was the sort of thing Daisy would usually say—but, of course, she was not here to say it.

"Hazel!" called Daisy's voice. "Hazel! I can hear George and Alexander! Bring them in at once!"

I paused.

"Don't bother about decency, Hazel!" cried Daisy impatiently. "I've just woken up and I'm *fearfully* bored. I think I'm getting better. Boys! Come here at once!"

I sighed. We had been granted an audience with Daisy.

"Fifteen minutes!" Bridget said warningly as she walked by carrying a tray piled high with broken bits of crockery. "And don't go tiring her out, otherwise you'll be in for it. Stay on the other side of the room and don't let her sneeze on you. Oh, and Hazel—stop giving her your hankies."

Daisy was sitting up in bed, a new nightie on and her hair brushed around her shoulders in a golden cloud. I saw Alexander look at her and then look anywhere else but her, and it made my heart hurt.

"George!" said Daisy regally. "Alexander! Thank you, Hazel. Now, I imagine you want to hear about the Rue. Well! I suppose we can tell you some things. Not everything, of course."

Robin Stevens

We all protested.

"SOME things," Daisy went on. "Hazel, I think you ought to explain. I could, of course, but I don't want to."

I stared at her, and she turned ever so slightly pink.

"Also, I may not be entirely mentally acute," she added. "Hazel, TELL!"

So I told. I put some things in that I knew Daisy didn't want me to—but it was my story and I was telling it. I felt once again how much power there was in that.

"Golly!" said George, when I had finished.

"Spiffing!" said Alexander.

"It isn't bad, is it?" said Daisy.

"So, what do we do now?" asked Alexander, staring from George to Daisy to me. "How can we help?"

"You can't—" Daisy began. Then she took a deep, composing breath. "Well," she said, "there is one thing. We were going to do it yesterday, but then I was struck down by this infuriating sickness."

"You want to go to Annie's boardinghouse," said George at once.

Daisy eyed him rather crossly. "Let me finish!" she said. "But yes, as it happens. We have investigated the Rue, and we know our suspects. The only part of this case that is quite unknown to us at the moment is the Soho accommodation from the newspaper reports. It also seems important to me that someone looks at the scene of the second crime—Westminster Bridge. I am glad that you agree."

"But we can't get there!" I protested. "We have to have Bridget with us, even if we go out for tea!"

"Hazel," said Daisy, "really. We have been in London for almost a month. I should think you know how to get lost in it by now."

Robin Stevens

lexander, George, and I stepped out of the building, into the late spring London air. The day was cloudy, pale and slightly chilly, and we were buffeted by the people hurrying by. Everyone seems to move so very fast in London—as fast as in Hong Kong, but grayer and crosser. Bridget was just behind us, and I could feel her sharp attention on us.

We walked demurely down the road, turning left and right until we came out onto the wide cluttered expanse of Theobalds Road. There was a Lyons tea shop in front of us, looking most inviting with trays of brightly colored cakes in the window. At that moment, I dearly wanted to go in, but my mission was clear. A red London omnibus trundled by in front of us. I swallowed, and glanced carefully at George and Alexander beside me. George cleared his throat, and that was the signal.

We had all agreed what was about to happen. I had seen

it in my head ten times over. But all the same my heart raced and my hands tingled and my throat felt thick with nerves.

Alexander's hat fell off his head.

"Oh heck!" he said loudly, and bent to pick it up, blocking Bridget's path. She knelt too, to help him, and that was my chance.

"Go, Hazel, go!" hissed George, and he gave me a sharp but not unfriendly shove. I stumbled and tripped over my own feet, and went running after the bus. If I stepped on, I would be disobeying Bridget and Uncle Felix. I would be doing something more obviously bad than I ever had before. I would be running away, just as surely as my friend Lavinia had once run away from Deepdean.

I took a deep breath and jumped up onto the bus.

The back was open, like all London buses, and the conductor took a penny from my (only slightly shaking) hand and gave me a half fare. I tucked it into my glove and went winding down the rocking, petrol-smelling bus, passengers clinging to its rails and jouncing on its seats.

Behind me I heard a shout. I turned and saw that George and Alexander had also made their break—they were fleeing in opposite directions down the street. Bridget had begun to dash after Alexander, but then she turned and saw my bus chugging away from her. She picked up her skirts and pounded after me.

Robin Stevens

We had known this would happen, of course, and that was why I was on the bus. Bridget could outrun me if I was on foot, but she could not catch up with a bus so easily. Keeping low down in my seat, I held my breath, took off my beret, and held it in my hands, squeezing the soft felt between my fingers.

The bus picked up speed and Bridget began to fall behind. I rang the bell, its noise silvering out around me, and then I stood up, clapping my hat back on my head. We had selected the beret very carefully from the costume room—it could be turned inside out to reveal a quite differ-ent color. If Bridget was looking for a green head, she would not be expecting a blue one.

I leaped down from the bus, into a press of people. Everyone was hurrying—shopping bags and attaché cases buffeted me—and I almost knocked into a suited man who glared at me furiously. I wove through the crowd, keeping low, and leaped on the next bus I saw. Then I got off again almost immediately and ducked into a telephone box at the side of the road.

Off came my coat—my hands trembling and my arms feeling twice as large as they ordinarily did—and I turned it inside out, to reveal its purple lining. It, too, had been pilfered from the costume room. I took out a pair of lensless glasses from my pocket and jammed them on my nose, and then stepped out of the telephone box and jumped up onto a number 17 bus going the opposite way. At every moment I was expecting Bridget's hand to fall onto my shoulder—but it did not.

The bus wove through the streets, and I kept low down in my seat once again and tried not to look out of the window. At last the bus pulled up in a squeal of tires beside Tottenham Court Road station. I stepped out once again into the brisk spring afternoon air, the wind blowing back my hat, and car horns and shouts and bicycle bells dinning in my ears.

I was trying to recall all the things Daisy had told me about throwing off a pursuit. I could hear her voice in my head, cuttingly pointing out that I was moving too slowly, that I ought to take off my hat to renew my disguise, that the man there—yes, there—might be suspicious, that I was being far too Hazel and not enough Daisy—but then I took one more breath and felt, from the tips of my ears to my heels in their rather new, rather pinching shoes, that I was quite alone, in the rush of London, and I had thrown off my pursuit as well as even Daisy could.

It was odd, walking with glasses, like having shadows at the corners of my eyes. They kept on sliding down my nose and almost off my face. Somehow they made me see the world quite new, the colors brighter—or perhaps that was only my nerves. All my detective senses were working, watching the patterns of the crowd, the policeman next to

Tottenham Court Road station, the man selling nuts from a stall, the young women who pushed past me, arm in arm, chattering and laughing.

I turned down Charing Cross Road, toward the Rue Theatre, and ducked into the first tea shop I saw. I bought a penny bun and ate it in the street. It was warm in my hand and sweet on my tongue, and I felt extremely daring. I stopped outside Foyles and stared at the display of books in the window, trying to keep my breathing calm and my heartbeat slow and look at everything while not seeming to look at anything at all.

I caught sight of George, a borrowed red scarf wrapped round his neck, browsing rather casually outside our appointed meeting place, one of the secondhand bookshops dotted down the street. They all have small, faded, green-and-blue awnings outside, with rows of dusty green and blue and red leather books stacked beneath, and collectors go up and down the road looking for paper treasures.

George was reading so intently, his dark eyebrows furrowed with concentration and his shoulders hunched, that he did not notice me. I crept up behind him, holding my breath and thinking that I was about to get one over on him. I stepped forward—and without looking up from his book, George said, "I see you, Hazel."

I couldn't help it. I let out a small shriek, and then clapped a hand over my mouth guiltily.

"I saw you there half a minute ago," said George. "That hat suits you."

"Thanks," I said, still feeling rather cross with myself.

And then suddenly I was seized from behind. A body thudded into mine and hands caught my arms and squeezed them against my sides. I screamed and dug my elbow firmly backward into my assailant's chest.

Robin Stevens

O of!" said a voice above my ear. "Ow, Hazel! It's me!"

"Alexander!" I cried, furious at myself for being caught, and for being so distracted now by the waft of clean boy smell coming off him, and his hands on my arms, and the slight warmth of him I could feel even through my coat. I struggled away, red-faced and upset, and turned on Alexander. He backed away from me, blushing in horror. He was wearing a swapped hat and a blue scarf that matched his eyes.

"I thought you were a murderer!" I cried. "Or Bridget!"

"I'm—I'm so sorry, Hazel," said Alexander and he rubbed his hand through his hair awkwardly. "I didn't mean to upset you! I thought it would be funny."

"Alex!" said George, putting a calming arm round me. "You idiot—"

"Hey!" called a voice. "Hey, you! Boys! What are you doing? Unhand that girl!"

We all turned to see an old man in a threadbare jacket, his whiskers slightly untrimmed, coming down the street toward us. He was shaking his fists and he looked quite furious.

"Unhand her, I say!" he cried. "Dirty ruffians!"

Then he caught sight of George properly. "You—!" he cried, and he called George a word that I will not repeat here, for it was shocking and not at all nice. "What do you think you're doing? Coming over here and attacking our—"

He put out a hand toward me and then froze as he took in *my* face. I had frozen too. I wanted to back away, to simply stop existing on this street in front of this horrid person. But George drew himself up and crossed his arms elegantly.

"My good sir," he said, "do you know to whom you are speaking? *I* am the Prince of Bengal and these are my friends, the Princess of Kowloon and the Duke of Massachusetts. We are waiting for my father, the Maharajah, to come out of this bookshop so he can take us to the Ritz for tea. Do you intend to prevent us from going about our business?"

The man quailed. George certainly knows how to behave like a prince, and not just because his father really *is* a knight. I tried to look like royalty and pretend that my knees were not knocking together.

"Well?" said George sharply.

The man glared at the three of us. "London," he said bitterly, half to himself. "It's not like it was in the good old days."

Robin Stevens

Suddenly I knew exactly what Daisy would say. "No, it isn't," I said, taking off my glasses. "It's better."

"Didn't we do well?" asked George, once the old man had stormed away. "Hazel, you were brilliant!"

"You really were!" agreed Alexander, beaming at me so warmly that I had to duck my head.

"George was too!" I said, to distract myself. "Oh, hurry— let's go and find Annie's accommodation before Bridget catches up with us!"

IV

But Soho, when we turned right onto Old Compton
Street, turned out to be rather different from the
cheerful, if dusty, Charing Cross Road, where
tradesmen's vans clattered and housewives hurried by, carrying parcels done up with string. This road was damp and
cobbled, and slipped under our feet unsteadily. Houses rose
up around us, narrow and dingy, with pinched people peering out of them as they hung limp clothing out to dry.

Poky little shops clustered together, neon signs hanging
above them with words that would light up in the evening,
but in the day looked simply empty and sad. Some of the
signs were quite rude, and some of the people walking about
in the streets looked rude too. I wasn't quite sure what to
do with my eyes, so I kept them cast down at my feet, at
the peelings and slops and rinds and worse that clotted the
spaces between the cobbles.

This place reminded me very much of Wan Chai in

Hong Kong, but an older, odder version, without the glitter and excitement of Hong Kong streets. Alexander and George tucked their arms through mine and we walked three abreast—and, although I knew that they were pretending to be worldly, they were just as embarrassed and awkward as I was.

The boardinghouse was just off Greek Street, a tall, thin building with cracked windows. There was a woman standing outside it, brushing away at the pavement and looking tired and cross. "What d'you want?" she asked us roughly. "You're not press, are you? You look too young to be press, but I wouldn't know these days. They just keep on getting younger and younger, seems to me."

"No, no, we're not press," said George quickly. "We're— well, this is Mr. Joy. *Annie's brother.*"

We had planned this out with Daisy beforehand, after consulting the newspapers. There had been no pictures of the Joys, but we knew that Annie had a brother, and so we thought our best hope was for Alexander to pretend to be him.

Alexander stared hopefully at the woman, trying to look as sad as possible. She widened her eyes, and then leaned forward to peer into Alexander's face. "You don't look much like her," she said. "Annie was a little thing and you're a beanpole."

"People always said that about us," said Alexander, in a

most extraordinary accent that was half Essex and half RP, with a small American twang still threading through his words. "They thought we couldn't be brother and sister. We used to joke about it. Poor Annie!"

I passed him my handkerchief, as I saw he was about to wipe his eyes on his sleeve. Somehow he had managed to conjure up real tears. George and I glanced at each other in amazement, and then quickly looked away again.

"Mum sent me—she couldn't manage it," Alexander went on. "If I could just have a quick look in her room, with my friends—there are some keepsakes that Mum and Dad want."

Tears came into his eyes once again. I could see that the woman was touched, and I had a burst of sudden, horrid guilt. Where was Annie's real brother? Was Alexander hurting him, acting this part? But there was no way of stopping this play now that we had begun.

"Well," the woman said, "you oughtn't, but—if you promise to be in and out in five minutes . . . And don't touch anything else, all right? It's top left."

"Oh, thank you awfully!" cried Alexander, his American accent slipping through in his excitement. "Come on, er, chums, let's go!"

Through the peeling doorway we rushed and into a dingy hall. There were no electrics here, only a small, unlit oil

Robin Stevens

lamp, a broken chair, and dark, narrow stairs leading away upward. Fearing every moment that Bridget might appear behind us, we went clattering up the stairs, which creaked and complained underneath our hurrying feet. We wound upward through the house, past closed doors with people snoring behind them, past the sound of dancing feet and voices rehearsing lines, past all the odd debris of a boarding-house: a single shoe with a hole in its sole, a pair of cami-knickers hanging off a newel post (embarrassing—we all looked away), an apple core rotting quietly in a corner of the stairs.

At last we came to the top floor, dizzyingly high and with a peculiar smell to it like dead flowers or stale breath, and there was the door to Annie's room. George pushed it open and we all stepped inside.

In front of us was a narrow bed, and a wardrobe and chest of drawers of thin wood. It looked very lived-in: shoes were shoved into a corner, there was a ewer and basin half full of mucky water, and several stockings were drying on the radiator.

"All right, Pinkertons and Detective Society member!" said George. "We must search this room—and quickly. I shall take the floor. Hazel, you look at anything below the level of the windowsill, and Alexander, you look at every-thing above it. Understood?"

We all nodded at each other, and (although it was odd

to be ordered around by a detective who was not Daisy, and odder still to see how the Pinkertons managed their investigations) I was glad to have a purpose.

What would we find? Had Annie done herself mischief, or had she instead been hurt by someone else, someone she had agreed to meet on the night she died? If so, who was it? Who had hurt her? Were there clues in this room that would lead us to the end of her life, and Rose's?

Robin Stevens

V

I went first to the bed. I could tell it was Annie's—I could see pale, fine hairs and smears of makeup on the pillow, and when I lifted it up I found a rather limp pair of pajamas smelling of Annie's perfume. The linen had not been changed for ages, but the bed was made quite carefully. If Annie had lain down last night, she had tidied up before she left the room. That gave me a shiver—the person who had tucked in these sheets had been alive just a few days before, and now she was not.

I quickly put back the bedcovers and turned to the chest of drawers. I pulled open the top drawer, and inside, beneath a layer of underthings, something rattled. I brushed a pair of stockings aside and found myself staring at a pile of books. Each was the size of my hand, in cheap imitation leather with a year embossed on the front in peeling gilt. I saw 1936, 1932, 1927 . . . the older the date, the more worn the book appeared. I opened 1936 and saw what I had suspected: that it was a diary, with a week laid out on every page. Every inch was filled with Annie's looping script, smudged where her hand had rubbed across the page as she wrote.

> *February 10th: First day of a new show at the Criterion! Dishy lead. Must find out how he takes his tea. Had a lovely idea on the Underground about a shot silk dress. Remember: buy liver.*

It was exactly as vague and wandering as one of Annie's conversations. I flicked through the pages, but, where May 1936 should be, there was a great gouge out of the book. Ten pages were missing—the whole of the month. The last entry was at the end of April:

> *April 25th: Went to see Happy Families at the Lyric this evening. The eau de Nil bathrobe in the final scene was divine. The play made me feel like a child again—it's funny how easy it is to remember everything from when I was sixteen, when now I can hardly remember a person I met last week. I'm sure she won't remember me, but I mean to find out . . . Ripped my stocking getting out of the station on the way home, heard someone mentioning Mussolini and thought they were talking about mussels. Perhaps I'll have mussels for tea tomorrow.*

I put 1936's diary down and dug through the drawer again, piling books in my arms and laying them out on the floor in a row. George and Alexander both stopped what they were doing to watch.

"Golly!" said Alexander. "What have you found?"

"Diaries," I said, pulling out the last two books. "The pages for the latest entries are missing—she must have taken them with her, the last time she left this room! But everything else is here."

"If the police didn't take what's left of that diary, they really must think it was a suicide," said George, frowning. "Otherwise they'd be hunting through it now. I suppose all we can do is read everything else she's written, in case it gives us a clue. If she saw something, she'd have noted it down there. And she *must* have seen something, or heard something—you're sure you don't remember anything particular?"

"She was behaving oddly the last time we saw her, but she didn't say anything then. And before that . . . I don't know!" I said, feeling rather hopeless. "She said so *many* things, it was hard to pay attention."

"Exactly the sort of person likely to become the second victim in a case like this," said George knowledgeably. "The type who doesn't know what they know, and is liable to babble it out to the wrong person."

"That's the great thing about talking," said Alexander.

"The more you do it, the less people actually listen to you."

That was true, I thought. Annie chattered so much that my brain had refused to take in much of what she said.

I had been ordering the diaries by date as Alexander spoke, and now I sat back and stared at the line of them. There was one for each year, beginning in 1918 and ending in 1936. The 1918 book was on very thin paper, and when I opened it the frontispiece read *ANNIE'S DIRY, AGE 7, 139 SEVEW STRET, SOWTHND, ESSIX.*

"You've missed one," said George, pointing.

"I haven't!" I protested—then realized he was quite correct: 1926 was next to 1928—1927 was missing. Puzzled, I went digging through the drawer again, and then through the rest of the clothes. George stuck his head underneath the wardrobe, and Alexander lifted up the mattress of the bed—but the diary could not be found.

I looked around the room again and peered into the wardrobe. I had another moment of knowing exactly what Daisy would say.

"The diary is missing," I said. "But look what else is here. Her good coat and hat, her nicest handbag. The red coat she was seen with—that's her everyday one."

"So?" asked George.

"So she didn't dress up," I said. "Annie was dramatic—she loved clothes. Why would she wear her ordinary clothes if she planned to throw herself off a bridge? She'd want to

278 *Robin Stevens*

look as nice as possible. But if she was only going to meet someone, she'd wear her usual things."

"Hazel, you're right!" said Alexander, grinning. "That's clever of you. I didn't see a telephone downstairs, so she must have arranged the meeting on the day she died. And that makes it likely that it was someone she saw at the Rue—otherwise how would they have contacted her?"

"We can't say that yet!" George told him. "But I admit it does make sense. Can we find any more clues here, before we move on?"

But there was nothing—just bits of cotton wool clotted with makeup in the wastepaper bin, smeary fingermarks on the ewer and basin, fair hairs wrapped round a curling iron.

"Come on," said Alexander excitedly. "We've found everything we can in here. Annie left here on the night of her death. Where did she go next?"

She was seen on Charing Cross Road, and again near Westminster Bridge," said George as we hurried away from the boardinghouse. I had slipped Annie's 1936 diary into my pocket as we left. It burned a guilty hole in my thoughts. The police hadn't thought it important, and so really it was not stealing . . . but still it felt wrong.

"So, down this road and then here . . ."

George led us through narrow London streets, ducking and dodging round carts and taking unexpected right and left turns. He belonged here, I saw—this city was part of him, the way Hong Kong is part of me. We hurried down an echoing little street with buildings leaning close overhead—and there in front of us again was the open stretch of Charing Cross Road and Leicester Square, horses and cars jostling and hawkers and newspaper sellers shouting. The Rue was just away behind us.

"So, she would have turned right here," said George.

"This is where she bumped into the first witness. Now, if she kept walking toward the river . . . Come on, this way. There's really nowhere else to go—"

And we followed him all the way down the road until, in a shocking instant, it opened out into the wide glory of Trafalgar Square. Soho was forgotten behind us. Here was nothing but air and light. Pigeons whirled and settled, the British flag snapped to my left and right over St. Martin-in-the-Fields church and the National Gallery, and in front of me the fountains splashed and glittered in the sun as it pushed its way at last through puffy little spring clouds. Above everything, high above the hats and coats of the people hurrying through the square, Nelson soared on his column. He was guarded down on the earth by four magnificent lions, their mouths a little open as if to warn the people in the red London buses crawling by not to go near.

I sighed, because it was all so beautiful, and clean, and bright.

"Isn't the British Empire awful?" said George. "This whole place was built on slave labor, you know."

"George!" said Alexander, elbowing him.

"I'm not being rude, I'm being truthful," said George, drawing his eyebrows together crossly. "Lots of beautiful things have awful histories."

"All right, let's not fight," said Alexander. "Come on. So Annie walks down the road and arrives here. Where would she go next? Down on the Embankment, beside the river?"

"No," I said. "I don't think she would go that way. It was almost midnight, and it was foggy. If *I* was trying to get to Westminster Bridge, I'd go the most brightly lit way."

"But, Hazel—" Alexander began.

"No, I think Hazel's right," said George, stopping him with a hand on his arm. "*We'd* go that way, Alex. But imagine being Annie. The witnesses said she was nervous—bumping into them, asking for a cigarette to steady herself. So, she walks under lamps—let's see, that would be down Whitehall, all the way to the Houses of Parliament. Then she turns left, onto the bridge. Come on!"

Off we went again, crossing Trafalgar Square and moving down the long, wide road beyond it, the buildings on each side of us becoming larger and more white, until I really could feel the full force of the British Empire bearing down upon me.

Then Big Ben rose up in front of us like a cathedral, its gold stone glowing. The round yellow faces with their heavy black hands glowered down at us, and I imagined being Annie, coming here at night, the cold fog swirling around her coat, the light from the lamps just firefly specks in the darkness. I shuddered.

"This is where the second witness saw her," said George. "Just here, it must have been. She asks for a cigarette, then she walks away . . . and is never seen alive again."

282   *Robin Stevens*

We stepped onto the long stone span of Westminster Bridge, following Annie's invisible
path. In the dark, in the mist, it would have
felt lost and lonely, but today we could see the gray buildings of London stretching far away on either side of us,
under the cloudy gray and blue sky. I looked at the dome of
St. Paul's, like something from a fairy tale, at the spires and
rickety buildings of the East End. Beyond that, I knew, was
Tower Bridge, and then the Thames Estuary, where Annie's
body had been found.

Then I tilted my head downward. Below me was
the Thames, muscular brown water churning away against
the pillars of the bridge. It looked terribly far. I shuddered
and stepped backward, almost knocking into a man in a
suit who was striding down the pavement. He shouted at
me and hurried on.

George was leaning against the nearest wrought-iron

lamppost, one of the many that were measured out across the bridge, staring out into space.

"It looks like it ought to be safe here," he said thoughtfully, without turning to me. "All these lamps, lit every night. All these people crossing the bridge every hour. Omnibuses and carts and taxis and cars. But that's not true, not when you think about it. A city's the loneliest place, really. People might see you, but no one will notice you unless you do something like, well, bump into them. Imagine Annie standing here after dark."

"She was wearing that red coat!" said Alexander. "She'd glow under the lamp."

"She might," said George. "But only if she was beneath it. And, Hazel, you said it was foggy that night, didn't you?"

"Yes!" I said. "When we left the Rue, it wasn't dark yet, but the fog was already coming in. In the end, it was a proper pea-souper."

"Exactly," said George. "Thick yellow fog curling around everyone. Imagine Annie walking through it. Even in the brightest coat, she'd only be properly visible if you were very close to her, like both those witnesses were. She arrives on the bridge, she's standing near here, and then . . ."

"She jumps?" asked Alexander.

"No, I *don't* think so," said George. "All right, so the police found a note in her handbag—but we didn't see any evidence in her room that she'd written one. It might have been one of those ripped-out diary pages, of course, but it's an odd thing to choose for your last letter, a bit of scrap paper. And then there's her clothes. Hazel's right—she wouldn't choose to wear her everyday coat and hat. *I* should want to wear my Sunday best, if I was her, and I care about clothes like she did. I don't think that Annie ever meant to die. I think Daisy's right: someone else pushed her off the bridge."

"Ugh!" I said. "But how did they manage it? Annie was afraid of the murderer, we know that, so why would she come to meet them here?"

"What if she just got a note?" said Alexander, frowning so his dimple showed. "Something pretending to be from another member of the company. So, she's waiting for that person when the murderer comes up to her, disguised so she won't recognize them at first."

"Good, Alex! Once they were standing at the railing with her, it wouldn't be at all hard to do away with her," said George. "I say, Alex! You be the murderer. Go and stand behind Hazel. Closer than that! Closer!"

"Why do I have to be Annie?" I asked, flustered.

"You're the smallest," said George. "And you're a girl. You've already proved that you know more about how Annie would think than we do."

As Alexander stood behind me, so close that his hand touched my elbow, I took a deep breath and imagined as hard as I could that I was not Hazel but Annie Joy. I was expecting to meet someone I knew from the Rue, where everyone was always putting their arms about each other and calling each other "darling."

"I don't think I'd be worried if they came up behind me like this," I said with difficulty. "I'd be more surprised if they were standoffish."

"So, it'd be easy for the murderer to get close if Annie believed she was meeting a friend. All right, Alex, what would you do now?" asked George.

"I'd—er—I'd put my hand over her mouth so she couldn't scream," said Alexander. "Hazel, I mean Annie, I'm sorry about this."

He raised his arm and very gently put his left hand over my mouth. His right hand was on the small of my back. It was absolutely the most embarrassing thing that had ever happened to me in all my life. I was going to murder George, I told myself. I was going to murder him just as soon as— I turned my head and saw Alexander staring straight back at me. He was so close that I could count the freckles on his nose, and I could have *sworn* that he was looking at me the way he sometimes looks at Daisy.

"And then you'd push her in!" said George cheerfully. "There, see, it's quite easy."

I spun round and glared at him. He stared back at me quite innocently, but I was sure I saw the ghost of a smirk on his lips.

Robin Stevens

"I don't know," said Alexander, stepping away from me very quickly and shifting from foot to foot. "Wouldn't it be easier if I bent down, picked her up in my arms, and threw her over? All our suspects are bigger than Annie, right? If she was little like Hazel, it wouldn't take much. It'd be over before anyone noticed."

"I am *not* reenacting that," I said, trying not to sound breathless.

"Oh, but—" said George, and he was certainly smirking now. Then his eyes caught something behind me. "Oh. Oh *no.*"

I had never heard George speak in that tone of voice before. Alarmed, I turned my head to see a group of four people rushing toward us. Two of them were blue-coated, high-hatted policemen, but the man in front was wearing a greatcoat and a most impressive scowl.

It was Inspector Priestley, and behind him was Bridget. I felt the full, sickening force of what I had done.

At least Uncle Felix would be able to see that it was not just Daisy who could get into trouble, I thought.

A nd that, of course, is how I got back here, in disgrace, which in this case means bed without supper.

I would be all right with it if I couldn't smell shepherd's pie cooking.

Daisy (who is well enough to sit up in bed, newspaper articles fanned out all around her, and tease me) said she is not surprised that all I care about is my stomach. What she means is, she is rather jealous that I got to have an adventure without her. I told her that there are plenty of things I care about other than food, and I meant I was sorry about the adventuring.

Anyway.

When Inspector Priestley found us on the bridge, he looked the most ruffled I have ever seen him.

"Miss Wong," he said. "I spent two hours this afternoon fearing that you might have become the next victim in this case. You have forced me to divert resources away from my murder investigation to look for you, and you have made it obvious to Miss Wells's uncle that you are still investigating this case. If he chooses to report this to my superiors, I will be in a very difficult position. I am disappointed in you. I was lenient with you before, but now I have to be firm. You must stop your work, and leave it to my men and me. Do you understand?"

I nodded miserably. I couldn't speak. I felt shame to the tips of my toes. I *had* been silly. I had tricked Bridget and let the Inspector down. By becoming a runaway, I had broken our promise to him to keep our involvement in the case secret from the rest of the police force. I hated the very thought of stopping our work, but if continuing our investigation meant the end of the Inspector's career—I could not be so cruel.

"What about us?" asked George. "It wasn't just Hazel who ran away!"

"Be quiet, Mr. Mukherjee," said the Inspector. "You know perfectly well that you did so because of Miss Wong and Miss Wells."

"That's not true!" said Alexander. "It was our idea too!"

The Inspector turned his gaze on him, and he gulped and stopped talking.

George and Alexander were dispatched back to George's house in a taxi with one of the police officers, and the

Inspector and Bridget traveled with me in ominous silence. When we arrived back at the flat, Aunt Lucy was waiting for us at the door. She simply said, in her best governess voice, "Bed. Now. Felix is *not* happy."

I went to bed.

Daisy has just been brought more beef tea. She dabbed at it with her spoon, sighed, and said, "You have it, Hazel. I simply can't face another sip. It tastes *brown*."

I drank her beef tea, even though she was quite right.

"Now," said Daisy. "Will you stop feeling upset so we can solve the case?"

"We can't, Daisy," I said. "Really, we can't anymore! If we do, Uncle Felix will complain officially about Inspector Priestley letting us be detectives, and his career will be over."

Daisy looked mulish. "But we can't stop!" she cried. "We're too far on! Hazel, we must have a Detective Society meeting to discuss what we have uncovered. Once we've done that, we can work out our next move. I agree with you that we mustn't harm the Inspector's position. He is one of the better grown-ups we know, after all. But there must be something else we can do."

"I suppose so," I said unhappily.

"Excellent! Now, Hazel, you have made several very important strides forward, and I have not been idle, either.

Robin Stevens

Get out your casebook, if you please, and then reach under my bed and bring me the box you will find there."

I did so, curiously. The box was a sturdy tin that said PINS on its top—but, when I opened it, it was not full of pins at all. It was a treasure trove of sweet things. There were fat pads of Turkish delight scattered with icing sugar and studded with nuts. There were gleaming dark twists of licorice, sherbet lemons spilling out their fizzy insides, and penny chews still in their paper wrappers.

A card poked out from under the Turkish delight. I dusted off the sugar and opened it to read:

HAPPY 15TH BIRTHDAY, MISS DAISY. REMEMBER US ALWAYS.
    YOUR LOVING FRIENDS AT FALLINGFORD

There were Chapman's, Mrs. Doherty's, and Hetty's signatures—Chapman's as old and wandering as he is, Mrs. Doherty's speckled about with grease from some recipe, and Hetty's in her familiar scrawl.

"It's my birthday present," said Daisy. "A little late. It came a few days ago."

"You didn't show me!" I protested. "And—should you be eating sweets?"

"It wasn't the right time. And of *course* I should be eating sweets!" said Daisy, shocked. "I am nearly recovered from my illness, and I find I want bunbreak again. The next time I refuse will be the day I am dead and buried. And even then I shall want you all to eat plenty at my funeral."

"Oh, please don't die!" I said.

"Goodness, you sound like Beanie," said Daisy with a sigh that turned into a sneeze. "I won't. Haven't I promised you that before? No dying and no murdering anyone. I was perfectly clear, and you know I never go back on my promises. Pass me some Turkish delight and then let's discuss the case."

We munched happily. I sucked on a sherbet lemon and felt the lemon fizz rush up my nose.

"Now," said Daisy, rather stickily, "you have told me all about your daring exploits. Really, Hazel, you *are* getting bold! Rushing about London with boys, visiting seedy locations, almost falling off a bridge—"

"I didn't almost fall off anywhere!" I protested. "And anyway it was you who told me to do both those first things."

"Yes, but I didn't quite believe you would," said Daisy. "Hong Kong Hazel has followed us home and no mistake. Anyway, while you were off being disreputable with George and Alexander and proving that Annie really *was* murdered, I was also working. I know I am ill, but really there's no point resting *too* much. I already did that all yesterday, and I found I'd quite lost patience with it. So.

Robin Stevens

Bridget was out, hunting for you with the Inspector. Aunt Lucy and Uncle Felix were out doing . . . well, whatever it is they do at work all day. Saving Britain, I assume. I managed to get into the hall—one of my most difficult adventures to date. I hardly imagined that it would be so difficult to move when you are unwell. I'm quite sure the floor was lurching, and I had to order myself forward in the sternest way.

"But I arrived at the telephone in the end, and I set about persuading the operator to connect me to the people who could tell me where all our suspects were on the night of Annie's death."

"And where were they?" I asked eagerly.

"Well," said Daisy, savoring her information, "they weren't *in*. Lysander was out with some fellows from a rival company, and only got back to his accommodation after two on Monday morning. Apparently, he was reeling from drink, and had to be escorted home by a policeman. Of course, I checked this by calling the police station, pretending to be Lysander's sister. It seems he was outside a pub in Charing Cross at one a.m.—which is close enough to Westminster Bridge for him to have been able to slip out, keep the appointment with Annie, and return again. So, that was Lysander. We can't rule him out.

"Next I tried Simon. He was at a jazz club in Soho with *his* friends, watching a new band perform, and didn't come back to his accommodation until two, either. But the bother is that the band didn't begin their session until midnight, and Simon was late to meet his party. He only arrived at half past twelve, so he could have met Annie, killed her, and then walked to the club in that time. Isn't London exciting, Hazel? I can't wait until I'm twenty. I shall go dancing all night and not bother with sleep at all."

"*I* will," I said. "Even when I'm twenty."

"Well then, I shall come and wake you up in the morning so we can have breakfast together. So, both Simon and Lysander are washouts in terms of their alibis. But there was one person who *wasn't*: Inigo. He went to dinner at Rules in Covent Garden. He had a big table with ten guests, and they stayed from eleven until half past one. Inigo was there the whole time—I asked the waiters and they confirmed it. So he's *got* to be ruled out."

"But what if he's working with Miss Crompton?" I asked. "He might have killed Rose, and she might have killed Annie."

Daisy shook her head. "No, listen," she said. "Miss C. has an alibi too. I called her flat in Lambeth and Theresa answered. Miss C. came home at half past eleven. She'd insisted on one of their friends who's a lady doctor coming round to see how Theresa was getting on, and this doctor friend stayed until half past twelve. So she can't have done it, either."

Robin Stevens

"Does that mean Martita's out too?!" I cried. "Was she at the flat with them?"

Daisy flinched.

"Not . . . exactly," she said. "When I called, Theresa was very prickly. She thought I was calling about Martita. You see, after the end of the rehearsal that day, Theresa and Martita seem to have had an argument. I think it was about Rose—Theresa wouldn't say exactly, but I think she accused Martita of committing the crime, and Martita was furious. Martita ended up piling some things back into her bag and storming out, saying she wasn't going to stay there anymore if they thought she was a murderer. Apparently, Miss Crompton went out looking for her as soon as the doctor had gone, and finally found Martita in an all-night café on the Embankment at four in the morning. It's just like Martita—so pigheaded! And it means that she was wandering around London at the crucial time, with *no* alibi at all. She might easily have caught a bus from Lambeth to Westminster Bridge in time for the meeting with Annie. We can't rule her out at all!"

Daisy threw herself back on her pillows, coughing furiously. "But she still didn't do it," she said between sniffs. "I *know* it."

"*How* do you know? Daisy, we can't just guess!"

"I'm NOT guessing!" cried Daisy. "Wait! Hazel! GOODNESS!"

"What is it?" I asked. "Are you all right?"

"It is true that I was practically at death's door yesterday," said Daisy. "But I am quite healed now, and at any rate I am still a simply brilliant detective, no matter how ill I am. And I've had a MOST exciting thought about the case!"

"You aren't quite all right yet," I said. "You're getting better, but you're not healed. What have you thought of?"

"Don't *spoil* it, Hazel. I'm trying to say something important!" snapped Daisy, proving my point. "Listen. After I did my telephoning, I was bored again, and I don't like being bored. So I began to read the newspapers. I read everything from the last few days about the Rue, including—*this*!"

She brandished a torn-up bit of newspaper, very closely set, at me.

Miss Tree's life had already been marked by tragedy. She lost her parents, the Reverend and Mrs. Hamish Brown, in a boating accident during a family holiday in Southend, Essex, in 1927, when she was thirteen. Miss Tree (her stage name) debuted on the London stage only last season, and seemed likely to become one of its most shining stars. Her untimely death is a tragedy in more ways than one.

"But we already knew that about her parents. How does this help us?" I asked curiously, for I did not see what Daisy was getting at.

"Well, I kept it because it gives one fact that none of the other papers have bothered with: Rose's father was a reverend. I thought it was funny because she ended up on the stage, which is really the sort of profession that the church despises. But, now that you've told me about Annie's diaries, something else occurs to me. What was the date of the one that was missing?"

I gasped. "Nineteen twenty-seven!" I said. "And—"

"And where was Annie from?" asked Daisy, eyes shining with detective excitement.

"Southend, in Essex!" I cried. "The missing diary in Annie's accommodation. *That* was for 1927, the same year Rose's parents died. What if Annie knew Rose when they were younger? We thought it was odd that they were friends, didn't we? This would explain it!"

"Yes! What if Annie was afraid not because of something she saw on the night of Rose's death, but because of something she knew about her past?" Daisy asked.

"You think it's connected to Rose's parents' death!" I said. "It could be! It's such a strange coincidence. Look, Daisy,

Robin Stevens

there was something from Annie's latest diary that I couldn't make sense of before but would fit with what you're saying."

I took out the stolen diary and opened it at the last few entries.

"*Went to see* Happy Families *at the Lyric this evening,*" I read. "Daisy, remember—that was the last production Rose was in! Annie must have seen her! *It's funny how easy it is to remember everyone from when I was sixteen, when now I can hardly remember a person I met last week . . . I'm sure she won't remember me, but I mean to find out . . .*

"DAISY! I think Annie did know Rose from when she was younger! And I think she was trying to hide it. Remember, she was being so odd about where Rose's parents died yesterday. She said she didn't know, but if it was the town she grew up in, she ought to have done. I think she was lying to us. What if . . . she was hiding the truth of the story because Rose's murder is connected to the deaths of her parents in 1927?"

"*Yes!*" hissed Daisy. "Hazel, you are . . . not a genius, because only I am that, but very close to it. And if Annie *did* know something about the deaths of Rose's parents, and she's died herself now—what if that accident in 1927 wasn't an accident? What if *they* were murdered too!

"So—Rose's parents are murdered by person or persons unknown. Rose manages to escape that day—the papers said she was found washed up on the shore. What if that local girl who found her was *Annie*? All right, so Rose confides something to Annie about what just happened, swearing her to secrecy, for not everyone is as brave as you and me, Hazel. The two girls part ways and both stay quiet . . . until years later, when they both become part of the London theatrical scene, and find themselves in the same production of *Romeo and Juliet!*"

"But why should that change anything?" I asked.

"BECAUSE!" cried Daisy, clearly enjoying herself. "I think someone *else* at the Rue was part of the events of that day. Every murder needs a murderer, does it not? And that person would have to shut Rose and Annie up once they realized they both knew what had really happened. The murderer must think that they've succeeded. But they've reckoned without us!"

"But why would someone want to murder Rose's parents?" I asked.

"Well, we shall just have to work that part out," said Daisy. "But, really, don't you think it's possible? It would make everything fit in the most marvelous way!"

"It could be," I said. "It could!"

We had made important strides forward in the case. But, since we were forbidden from continuing the investigation, what were we to do with what we had discovered?

Robin Stevens

SUSPECT LIST

1. Miss Crompton. MOTIVE: She was Rose's greatest ally at the Rue Theatre and seems sad that she is dead—but she has also been honest about the fact that Rose's death will be good for business, and will help the Rue's money troubles. She clearly cares most about the Rue, and about her company—might she have been willing to hurt one member of it to help everyone else? OPPORTUNITY: She seems to have an alibi from 9 p.m. until just before Rose was discovered missing at 9:30 p.m.—she was onstage with Inigo—but she did also go to the loo for a few minutes. Could this be enough time for her to have gone to the well room with Rose and killed her there? This is NOT enough time—unless her alibi is a lie! NOTES: She did not visit Jim at the stage door until after Rose's disappearance that evening, meaning that she had no clear opportunity to forge Rose's name in the book. But could she be working with someone else—like Inigo? RULED OUT: She has an alibi for the night of the second murder—and, since Inigo has one too, she certainly can't be involved.

2. Simon. MOTIVE: He does not like Rose. He hinted, and Inigo confirmed, that he was supposed to play Romeo until Rose objected to the color of his skin. Was he angry enough with her to do something terrible? OPPORTUNITY: He was with Inigo when they overheard the argument between Martita and Rose, but afterward left him and went upstairs to his own dressing room until the alarm was raised at 9:30. Could he have left it to murder Rose? From our reenactment of the crime, we know it would have taken him approximately twelve minutes to go down to the well room, murder Rose, and go back to his dressing room. NOTES: Visited Jim's cubbyhole and so could have forged Rose's name in the book. ANNIE's MURDER: He was at a jazz club in Soho, but he only arrived there at 12:30 a.m. on the morning after Annie's murder. He could have gone to meet her on the bridge and killed her, and then gone on to the club.

3. Annie (Wardrobe). MOTIVE: No clear motive. Rose was friendly with her—but she did seem to be uncomfortable with Rose's behavior toward other members of the company. OPPORTUNITY: She was in the loo on the first floor when Martita and Rose had their argument, but was then alone in Wardrobe

at the crucial time. It would have taken her approximately twelve minutes to get down to the well room and back again. She has no alibi! NOTES: ~~Visited Jim's cubbyhole and so could have forged Rose's name in the book.~~ RULED OUT: Annie has become the second victim. She was seen walking toward Westminster Bridge just before midnight last night; her handbag, coat, and hat were found beside the river this morning, and a body which we believe to be hers was found in the estuary. The Inspector thinks she committed suicide—there was a note in her handbag—but we are not so sure. Annie was behaving oddly yesterday, and saying she was afraid. Did she know something about the murder? Has she been shut up by the murderer? We now think that she did know something—about a murder nine years ago! We suspect that Rose's parents were killed, and Annie witnessed some part of it!

4. Inigo. ~~MOTIVE: He disliked Rose intensely and~~ says that she is the reason why Simon was not able to play Romeo. He also wants to use her death as publicity. ~~OPPORTUNITY: He was with Simon~~ and Miss Crompton when they heard the argument between Rose and Martita, and he says that after this he went back onstage to talk to Miss

Crompton until he left to see Jim just before the alarm was raised by Martita at 9:30. If this is true, then he may not have had time—unless he was working with Miss Crompton. He could have gone down to the well room, murdered Rose, and gone back onstage in approximately eleven minutes. NOTES: Visited Jim's cubbyhole and so could have forged Rose's name in the book. RULED OUT: He has an alibi for the second murder! He was at a dinner at midnight, and so could not have left to kill Annie.

5. Lysander. MOTIVE: He had been flirting with Rose, but Daisy and Hazel noticed that they had been arguing more and more lately. He is a very threatening person, and he was angry with Rose. OPPORTUNITY: He was in his dressing room, alone, during the time Rose must have been murdered—he does not have an alibi! NOTES: Was at Jim's cubbyhole when the alarm was raised, and so could have forged Rose's name in the book. He behaved threateningly toward Daisy yesterday—he seems capable of violence. It would have only taken him approximately twelve minutes to go down to the well room, murder Rose, and go back to his dressing room. ANNIE's MURDER: He does not have an alibi for the time of Annie's death. He was at a pub near Westminster Bridge.

6. Jim (stage door). MOTIVE: ~~He did not like Rose,~~ ~~and resented her being part of the Rue. But did~~ ~~he feel strongly enough about her to murder her?~~ ~~OPPORTUNITY: He says he was at his post all~~ ~~evening. Is this true?~~ RULED OUT: He has a limp. He would have needed more time to kill Rose than anyone else, but he was not away from his post for more than nine minutes on the evening of the murder. Even the closest of our other suspects could not have murdered Rose in under eleven minutes.

7. Martita. MOTIVE: She hated the fact that Rose was playing Juliet. She felt that the part should have been hers, and was jealous that Rose was allowed to be the star. OPPORTUNITY: She left the stage when Rose refused to come on to rehearse Scene Five. Inigo, Simon, Miss Crompton, and Annie all say that they heard her arguing with Rose in Rose's dressing room at about 9:05. We do not know where she went after that. Could she have murdered Rose before she raised the alarm at 9:30? NOTES: Visited Jim's cubbyhole and so could have forged Rose's name in the book. It would have only taken her approximately twelve minutes to go down to the well room, murder Rose, and go back to her dressing room. Rose walked to the

well room rather than being dragged there—would she have gone with Martita? ANNIE'S MURDER: Martita stormed out of Miss Crompton's Lambeth flat late that evening, and was alone, on the streets of London, all night, until Miss Crompton found her in a cafe at 4 a.m. the next morning. She could have gone to Westminster Bridge to meet Annie—she has no alibi. Once again, she cannot yet be ruled out.

PLAN OF ACTION

1. ~~Check Jim's stage-door book and ascertain whether Jim can be trusted.~~

2. ~~Look at timings and decide which of our suspects had enough opportunity to commit the crime.~~

3. ~~Go back to the scene of the crime and reenact the murder.~~

4. Visit Rose's dressing room and look for clues.

5. ~~Talk to suspects—~~decide if any of them could be working together.

Robin Stevens

6. Find out which of our remaining suspects have alibis for the time of Annie's death.

7. Rule out Martita! (NB Daisy wrote this!)

8. Discover the killer.

9. Find out the truth of what happened to Rose's parents. Are they the key to this mystery?

10. Get back to the Rue Theatre!

Part Seven

These Violent Delights Have Violent Ends

I can tell that Daisy is still sick—but not with flu. She is quite ill with worry about the case, and she is trying very hard to hide it from me. She has spent a really un-Daisyish amount of time staring into space. She has covered the newspapers around her bed with anxious scribbles. Some of them are plans of London and of the Rue Theatre (which I have taken and copied out nicely in this casebook), some of them are disjointed odd notes (*What about the white thread? WHAT IS THE MOTIVE??*), and some of them are simply Martita's name, traced again and again in pencil and pen until the word almost goes through the paper.

"I am not obsessed!" said Daisy when I picked up one particularly intricate page and stared at it. "I do not do that sort of thing. That is Hazelish behavior. I am merely thinking carefully."

We had managed to get a letter to Alexander and George

in with the Tuesday evening mail, asking them to investigate our last three suspects more carefully. Conveniently, Daisy was being dosed with hot lemon and honey drinks, so it was not particularly difficult for me to make up a batch of invisible ink, or for Daisy to slip my completed letter in with all the other mail.

Find out all you can about the backgrounds of Lysander Tollington, Simon Carver, and Martita Torrera, real name Marta Pao! Write back as soon as you can!

We had been trying to keep away from Uncle Felix, but on Wednesday morning Daisy could bear it no longer. She went striding into the dining room as he was eating breakfast, her hands on her hips and her cheeks pink with resolution.

"Uncle Felix!" she cried. "I am perfectly healthy. I have not coughed for three hours and I can do five jumping jacks without getting tired. Look!"

As the three of us watched, she flung herself into the air five times.

"As you will observe, I am absolutely better!" she said triumphantly, panting.

"You are not absolutely better," said Uncle Felix. "What do you want?"

Robin Stevens

"I want you to stop pretending you need to protect us," said Daisy. "Uncle Felix, the first performance of *Romeo and Juliet* is tonight, and we *have* to be there. We're in the middle of solving the case! We know that you've threatened Inspector Priestley to make sure that he doesn't let us go back to the Rue and it simply isn't fair of you. He's an excellent policeman—in as far as there *are* excellent policemen—and he is good at his job. But we are better."

Uncle Felix sat frozen, his cup of tea halfway to his lips.

"It's not *fair!*" Daisy went on passionately. "You never have to tell our parents and I *promise* Hazel and I won't get hurt and we'll really do our *best* from now on to stay out of trouble if you'll only let us do this one thing. This case *needs* us, and I promise to never, *ever* ask you for anything again! *Please!*"

"Daisy, you are exhausting," said Uncle Felix. "You are a child, and Hazel is a child, and even very clever children cannot be detectives in murders. *Nice* child detectives stick to smuggling cases, haven't you heard? Hazel's exploits yesterday proved to me that you are danger to both yourselves and others. The *only* place you will be going today is your room."

"But I said *please!*" cried Daisy, incensed. "And anyway, when you were my age you would have done exactly the same thing!"

"Not *exactly* the same," said Uncle Felix. "When I was fifteen, I was climbing out of windows in my boardinghouse every night. When your mother was fifteen, she tried to run off to France with her dance instructor—but of course they went the wrong way and ended up in Lisgard. However, just because we did foolish things ourselves doesn't mean that *you* can."

"That is absolutely unfair!" howled Daisy. "I SAID PLEASE!"

I looked at Aunt Lucy, who had ducked her head and was making marks on the ordnance survey map she had spread out in front of her.

```
W    I    L    T
A    W    S    I
I    I    O    T
T    L    R    X
```

I blinked. I read it down the lines, left to right, twice, and it still said the same thing. WAIT. I WILL SORT IT.

Aunt Lucy scrubbed it all out, and then she stood up and said, "Excuse me, Daisy, Hazel. Felix my love, will you come into the other room with me for a moment?"

There was toast in front of us, but for once I could not bear to eat a bite. Daisy and I sat in hushed silence, glancing nervously at each other. What was Aunt Lucy doing?

Robin Stevens

Bridget came in and dropped the mail in front of us, and I snatched up the letter addressed to me in Alexander's handwriting.

"I shall read it later," I said, stuffing it into the waistband of my skirt. Daisy nodded stiffly.

Then Aunt Lucy and Uncle Felix came back into the dining room.

Uncle Felix was scowling and Aunt Lucy was smiling gently to herself. I stared at her, hardly daring to hope, but Aunt Lucy gave nothing away.

"Felix, dear?" she said.

Uncle Felix cleared his throat.

"You are my niece," he said to Daisy.

"Ugh, more's the pity!" hissed Daisy, narrowing her eyes at him.

"By which I mean, although you are not precisely *my* child, you are related to me. And I have been made to see that there are—certain familial similarities between us."

I glanced at Aunt Lucy then, and I saw her smiling into her hand. I swallowed down a giggle.

"It has been brought to my attention," Uncle Felix went on, "that if a dead body had landed at my feet when I was fifteen years old, I should have stopped at nothing to uncover the truth of what had happened to it. My youth would not have concerned me, and—I can understand that you do not see in quite the same way I do how very young you are."

"I'm *not* young!" howled Daisy. "I'm older than EVER!"

"Quiet!" said Uncle Felix, so sharply that Daisy and I both jumped. "I am trying to see the matter from your point of view—the point of view I would have had at your age. I am trying to remember that you have already had certain detective successes. I am *trying* to tell myself to care about your safety a little less fiercely than I do. But don't you see, Daisy—you are my beloved and only niece. I can't go to Selfridges and buy another one of you if something goes wrong."

"*Beloved!*" said Daisy, gaping.

"*Only,*" said Uncle Felix, clearing his throat and looking away.

I held my breath. Daisy had gone a funny color.

"And?" prompted Aunt Lucy, looking up at last.

"And I *suppose* I see that allowing you back to the Rue for tonight's performance—under the supervision of Inspector Priestley, with myself and Lucy watching over you from the stalls—might be acceptable. *If* you promise in the strongest terms not to put yourself in any more danger than you have to, and to tell us the *moment* you've uncovered the truth in the case . . . it looks very much as though you will be making your stage debuts tonight, after all."

"YES!" cried Daisy, leaping out of her seat with a most

unladylike shriek. "Oh, Uncle Felix, you BRICK!" She flung herself on him, and Uncle Felix went slightly pink.

I could feel my heart pounding with my breath. Were we truly being allowed to finish the case?

I turned to Aunt Lucy.

"Thank you so much!" I whispered. "Will it really be all right?"

"I will make sure it is. You're good girls, and good detectives," said Aunt Lucy quietly. "You deserve one more chance. Now—promise me not to die?"

B ack at the Rue!" cried Daisy, spinning round and
round and round on the empty stage. "Marvelous!"
I simply stood and breathed in its lovely
greasepaint-and-powder-and-wood smell, something a little hot and a little dry, something wide and huge, as though
my nose could tell that beyond the lowered curtain in front
of us was echoing space, rows of waiting seats all the way up
to the gilded rafters.

I heard someone step through the stage door behind us,
and turned to see Martita.

For once, she was smiling at us, and she looked so *nice*
that I struggled to believe she was really one of our last
three suspects.

"Welcome back," she said. "Do you know, the dressing
room felt too big without you."

"I told you it would," said Daisy rather giddily, leaning toward Martita very slightly like a plant to the sun, and

then she looked embarrassed at her own boldness.

"Are you better?" asked Martita, still smiling. "Truly? I don't need germs around me, you know."

"I am *entirely* recovered," said Daisy.

"She really is," I agreed.

"Well, come on then!" cried Martita. "Let's go and get you ready!"

As we rushed through the backstage corridors, past the props room where people were making last-minute changes to sets and swords and candles, past Miss Crompton, who strode by, barking, "Welcome back, girls," everything seemed almost unchanged—but there was an eerie, missing feeling to the Rue, for Rose was gone, and so was Annie.

Wardrobe on the first floor was very quiet when we went in to get our costumes. Everything was rather disarranged, for the new dresser had just started, and she did not know the theatre yet. Half the wig stands were empty, the dresses pulled off their racks, pins and needles dropped across the floor in careless haste. Only Juliet's other nightgown still stood on its mannequin, creepily upright, like a reproach to us. We hadn't solved Rose's case, and now Annie was dead too.

"Someone else's been at it," said Daisy, peering. "Martita, have you been trying to let it out? Look, these stitches are a bit clumsy."

I got another funny feeling in my stomach at that. Daisy

shouldn't be asking Martita a question like this, not when she was under suspicion.

"Of course I haven't," said Martita. "Simon! Come in here! Have you been altering my dresses?"

"What's wrong?" asked Simon, poking his head round Wardrobe's door. "Where is that new dresser? I can't find her and she has my doublet. Hey, Daisy, Hazel! Welcome back!"

"Did you sew this dress?" asked Martita.

Simon laughed. "No way!" he said. "Why, does it look like I did?" He grinned at us—but again, I got the same feeling: that underneath his jollity Simon was really not cheerful at all.

"Is Simon all right?" I asked quietly, once he had gone.

"None of us are all right, Hazel darling," said Martita. "But—no. He's been . . . well, he's got a problem. You see, he's got an alibi for Annie's death, but he can't use it."

"What do you mean? Why ever not?" cried Daisy. "Why hasn't he told the police?"

Martita frowned. "Promise you won't tell anyone?" she asked.

"All right!" said Daisy. "What is it? What is it?"

Martita gave her a funny look.

"He was with his friend," she said. "Mark Tull. He's got a Soho flat not far from Simon's, and that's where Simon went after rehearsal was over. He was there until he went to the Flamingo Club at half past twelve."

Robin Stevens

"But why shouldn't—" Daisy began. Then her face went very red and she stopped speaking.

"Oh!" I said, for I suddenly knew what Martita meant. Simon had been *with* Mark Tull, in a grown-up way. "But why can't he tell the police?"

"Because Mark's been in trouble with the police before. Two men together—it's a crime," said Martita simply, shrugging. "It's a stupid law, but it's true: if you're a man, and the police find out you like men, they have to arrest you. And, if Simon was arrested, he'd be sent back to America. His London stage career would be over."

"But that's not *fair*!" said Daisy, speaking very quickly. "That's idiotic—why, people like that aren't hurting anyone!" I knew she was thinking of Bertie, and I was too. It was awful.

"Oh, I know! It's wicked and wrong of the law," said Martita. "Which is why you must *swear* not to tell anyone. Do you promise? Simon's one of the best people in this company. He didn't commit either of the murders, and he can prove it—but only to you."

"I promise," Daisy said.

"I promise too," I agreed. I had finally understood something. If Simon *did* like men, then the conversation we had overheard between him and Inigo at last made sense. He had been afraid that the police would find out about him and Mark; it was nothing to do with Rose's murder at all.

Then I had a horrid thought. "It isn't—what about girls who like girls?"

Martita gave me a sharp, serious look. "It's quite different," she said. "The police don't bother about that at all."

"Oh!" I said. "Why not?"

Martita shrugged again. "Don't ask me," she said. "It's all stupid. But people are stupid everywhere."

"I don't know why we're talking about this," said Daisy breathlessly.

"Neither do I, of course," said Martita, deadpan. "Look, I've got to get back to rehearsals. You'll be all right here?"

I nodded. And I thought to myself that although that conversation had cost Daisy something, we had discovered a very important truth: that we could rule Simon out.

Robin Stevens

As soon as Martita had gone, Daisy sprang back to life.

"Did you hear that, Hazel!" she cried in a rather high-pitched voice. "Simon has an alibi! He didn't kill Annie, and that rules him out from killing Rose!"

"We have two suspects left," I said. "Lysander and Martita. Daisy, I think you ought . . . to be ready. Just in case."

"Do be *quiet*, Hazel!" said Daisy. "You're talking pure nonsense, and you *will* be proved wrong. Look, get out that letter of Alexander's you've been stowing in your waistband. Let's see what he and George have uncovered, shall we?"

I unfolded Alexander's letter, which had some polite nonsense apology written in ordinary ink, and turned it over so that the blank back was facing us. Then I went up on tiptoe to hold it against the gas jets around the dressing-room mirror.

Words began to flare and form as the paper heated, running together into close-written sentences. Alexander had squeezed in an awful lot of information.

"What does it say?" asked Daisy, for of course she cannot read Alexander's shorthand as easily as I can. It's almost our own private language, and that thought always gives me a glow.

"All right. Simon first. *Simon Carver, born September 1908 in New York to Mason and Eugenia Williams. Began his professional career as a singer, but then Inigo Leontes discovered him during Inigo's 1927 tour of America—he sponsored Simon to come over to England in 1934 and trained him up as an actor.* Daisy, if Inigo and Simon were in America all through 1927, he really *can* be ruled out. He can't have had anything to do with what happened to Rose's parents!"

Daisy nodded. "What about Lysander?" she asked.

"*Lysander Tollington. Born April 1906 in Rochester, Kent, to Admiral Manfred Tollington and his wife, Marguerite. Here's the exciting thing—the birth certificate is signed by a Reverend Brown. We've checked and he's Rose's father—his parish at that time was in Rochester. He conducted the marriage ceremony too, in July 1905. George says that's exactly nine months before Lysander was born—he thinks that's suspicious, and so do I. It might have been a setup!*"

"Oh!" said Daisy. "I see what George is getting at! Hazel, think about it—this is *exactly* the evidence we were hoping for. What if Lysander's parents . . . weren't really married when he was born? They might have paid off Reverend Brown to fake their marriage certificate, to make everything look respectable and aboveboard—and that would give them the *perfect* motive to murder him years later!"

"But why should they bother so much?" I asked.

"That's perfectly obvious," said Daisy, waving her hands in the air. "Grown-ups are idiots, especially important ones like admirals. All they care about is their reputation. It would be considered terribly shocking to have a baby with someone you weren't married to, and it might truly have ended the admiral's military career. I don't know *why*, mind you. People are the same whether or not they have the proper piece of paper. But that's how it is. It happens all the time in books, you know—reverends marrying people even though they're already married, or being paid to enter a marriage that never happened in their parish records."

"It makes sense!" I said, excited. "But how do we prove it?"

"Bother, I don't know!" said Daisy. "Make Lysander confess to it, perhaps? Needle him about it? You know how fearfully upset he gets when anyone talks about his parents. Hazel, I really do think we've solved the case!"

"Perhaps," I said doubtfully. "But, Daisy, there's something here about Martita. *Her father is Portuguese, but her mother's name is Martha. She's English, and Martita lived with her in Essex for a few years when she was a child—not far from Southend. Her parents might have known the Browns. Perhaps there's a secret they wanted to keep as well?"*

I gulped, and looked up at Daisy. It was not what she wanted to hear, not at all. But sometimes detection is a very unpleasant business. I hated to admit it, but although the evidence was stacking up against Lysander, it was also pointing to Martita. She had motive and opportunity. She did not have an alibi for either of the murders. Her family history fitted with our theory that the 1927 deaths of Rose's parents were the causes of the two more recent murders. What if the answer Daisy couldn't bear was the true one? What if we had been deceived, yet again, by kindness?

I stood in the wings, Daisy trembling resentfully next to me, and watched the final whirl of last-minute rehearsals. The actors playing Peter and Benvolio were back, and so was Theresa. But everything felt subtly out of true, and everyone was brittle with panic. The actress now playing the Nurse was only half sure of her lines, and Theresa (still a little pale) was constantly hissing at her from the prompt corner next to us.

"She'll be the death of me, girls," Theresa said to us, winking—and then her face dropped as she realized what she'd said.

Martita, though, despite the fact that she was shaking with high-pitched nerves, was word-perfect. Even her balcony scene was excellent. She might have been preparing for this for months, I thought, and shuddered.

Miss Crompton and Inigo watched her, smiling like proud parents. I saw them glance at each other, and knew that although they must be innocent, what had happened here at the Rue would only help them and the theatre. That was a strange and uncomfortable thought.

I looked at Lysander next. He was grandstanding, making his Romeo center stage no matter who else surrounded him. He didn't act *with* Martita but *at* her—he was aggressive, teasing, and rather horrid. I saw again that he was a person who really might cause harm and not care about it.

Martita or Lysander? I wondered. *Lysander or Martita?* I knew which of them I wanted it to be, and I knew which of them I thought it was.

And then, almost as quick as breathing, it was only a few minutes to curtain up.

Daisy sat in our dressing room, pink and pale by turns. "It isn't nerves," she said to me. "It's something different. Can't you feel it, Hazel? Can't you?"

I could. There was a low, stinging buzz in the air, something dangerous and wrong. It was there in every face, in every voice.

I took a sip from a glass in our dressing room and accidentally dropped it. "Just like Rose!" I said with a shudder.

"Don't be a chump, Hazel!" cried Daisy, but she clenched her fists as she stepped round the fragments on the floor.

It did rather feel as though we were moving along the

Robin Stevens

same path as we had on the night of Rose's death, those few short days ago—or as though we were tied to a railway track while a train hurtled, whistling eerily, ever closer.

There was a thump from out in the dressing-room corridor. We stuck our heads round the door to find that Simon had somehow managed to fall headlong over a bucket that someone had left there. He was nursing his left hand and wincing.

"This production is cursed!" cried Martita behind us.

"It isn't cursed!" said Miss Crompton. "Don't be ridiculous. And don't say that *here*, for goodness' sake, or you'll start a riot. Theresa, fetch the bandages. Simon darling, can you stand to wait to have it bound up until after you're killed in Act Three?"

"It's not cursed," said Lysander, coming out of his dressing room with a slam. "There's just a murderer in the theatre."

"Will you stop!" said Miss Crompton. "That's enough!"

"*All the world's a stage*," said Lysander, smirking, "*And all the men and women merely players . . . And one man in his time plays many parts*. That's true, isn't it? *Very* true in this case."

"It's from the wrong play," said Miss Crompton. "And you know it. If you make any mistakes this evening, I shall have you replaced. We've got full houses for a month thanks to all this business. For once I can afford it."

"Isn't murder useful?" asked Lysander. "The first two have gone down so well—I wonder if there'll be a third, to get you full houses all year?"

And I felt absolutely terrified.

Robin Stevens

D ownstairs, in the pit, the orchestra started up, and the Rue was suddenly full of the shuffle and chatter of hundreds of people. It filtered through from front of house to the backstage corridors. I still felt nervous almost to weeping. We were missing the final pieces of the puzzle. We did not yet know enough to point the finger at the murderer. All we had were suspicions.

I peeped outside our dressing room to see the new dresser Miss Crompton had hired hurrying away, a basket of props in her arms . . . and then I noticed Theresa leading four people down the corridor toward us: Uncle Felix, Aunt Lucy, Alexander, and George.

"Daisy!" I cried. "Uncle Felix and Aunt Lucy are here— and *Alexander and George* are with them!"

Daisy, carefully painted to be Rosaline, looked up at me in the mirror, her face surrounded by the glow of the gas jets. "Let them come in," she said rather grandly. "Uncle Felix knows everything, after all."

"Daisy and Hazel!" called Theresa. "Your family's here!"

And I had an odd moment of realizing that this was true.

"I want to come in to congratulate my niece, the famous actress Daisy Wells!" shouted Uncle Felix.

"And Hazel Wong too," I heard Alexander add.

"AND HAZEL WONG TOO!" boomed Uncle Felix, and my heart did another strange flip in my chest. Alexander had remembered me. *Me*. Not Daisy, me.

I had to turn away as they entered.

"Goodness!" said Aunt Lucy. "Look at you. Don't you look grown up!"

"You don't look anything like yourself," said George.

"Dear niece, your friend is right. You have on the most excellent disguises," said Uncle Felix, beaming at us both. "I should hardly have recognized you. It's such a useful skill to be able to conceal one's appearance. In fact, I should almost think you'd been taught. . . ." He glanced with sudden suspicion at Aunt Lucy, who gazed back at him blandly.

And, at that moment, something clicked in my head.

I wasn't sure what it meant. But . . . but . . .

"Overture and beginners!" cried Theresa, out in the corridor. "Overture and beginners, please! Five minutes!"

Daisy *looked* at me and I knew that the same key had turned in her mind. She did not show it outwardly—she

Robin Stevens

was absolutely delightful with Uncle Felix, Aunt Lucy, George, and Alexander. She took the flowers Uncle Felix had brought us both and smiled and said thank you. But, as soon as they had gone out of the room, she whirled round to me, her eyes blazing.

"Hazel, you see it too!" she cried. "Costumes! Disguises! *Acting!* We haven't been thinking about this mystery in the right way at *all*!"

"I know," I agreed, feeling light-headed with shock. "Being an actor isn't just about speaking lines. It's about—"

"It's about *being someone else entirely*," said Daisy. "Goodness, what a clever murder!"

"If we're right . . . ," I began.

"Of course we're right!" Daisy butted in. "Oh, Hazel, all the facts we think we know about the murders are wrong. We have to go back and look at everything again, from the very moment you and I left the Rue on the evening Rose disappeared."

"We have to tell the Inspector," I said.

"Not yet!" said Daisy. "Oh, not yet, not until we can prove it! It's so fantastical, isn't it? If only we had some bits of paper to wave at the grown-ups!"

"There's the white thread and the footprint," I said. "And the murderer must have slipped up somewhere, I know it. It *has* to be in my notes!"

"Yes, Watson! I have great faith in you. Even at the Rue,

the perfect place for deception, you can't fake everything perfectly. Oh, how were we taken in for so long? There was another play backstage and we never noticed it!"

We were sparking off one another again, working together in the way we do sometimes, when it feels as though we are really two halves of one person. In these moods, it feels as though I do not need to speak, only think, and Daisy will catch my meaning.

Through the walls came the muffled clatter of applause and the swelling hum of the orchestra.

"Daisy!" I said. "We have to go on soon!"

"I *know*," said Daisy. "But, while we do, we must keep thinking about the case. What else can we use to prove it?"

I closed my eyes and covered my ears with my hands. I blocked out the music, the smell of makeup . . . and then I opened my eyes again.

"The coat," I said, my heart racing. "Everything we read in the newspapers!"

"WATSON!" said Daisy. "You genius! All right. We're getting somewhere. Every moment you have, read through your case notes. There must be something in them that's useful!"

"Of course," I said. "What'll you do?"

"I need to check timings, now that our old ones are all wrong. I shall go and stare at the prompt book over Theresa's shoulder. I know the opportunity is there, during Act Two, but I need to prove it."

"You don't think anything else will happen?" I asked nervously.

"I think it almost certainly *will*. We know that the murderer loves to act and be in the spotlight. Think what'll happen when they see someone else in that spotlight tonight!"

My breath caught. Daisy was right, and we had to move as quickly as we could.

We did the Detective Society handshake and then nodded at each other.

"Detective Society forever," whispered Daisy. "Go and do me proud, Watson!"

"Only if you do me proud as well," I said, grinning at her despite my nerves.

My mind was full of detection—but first I would have to overcome a much more difficult ordeal: stepping onto the stage in front of a real audience. I told myself I had rehearsed. I told myself I only had to say a few lines. I told myself that it didn't matter if I botched them.

But all the same, as I waited to go on, my legs were trembling and my hands were slippery and I could feel perspiration rising up on my forehead.

I was sure that I could not do it, that I was going to have to turn and run—and then Daisy gave me a sharp shove and I was tumbling onto the stage with the other servants, into the beam of the lights and the roaring emptiness of air between us and the audience.

I wobbled to my mark and turned to the First Servingman just as he shouted, ". . . in the great chamber!"

"WE CANNOT BE HERE AND THERE TOO!" I shouted back at him, as loudly as I could, as loudly as I'd practiced with Martita.

I felt all the breath rush out of my body and my knees went limp. *I had done it.*

I retreated back across the stage, and as I did so I could have sworn I heard someone clapping, from far away in the stalls.

I hovered in the wings, stage right, flicking frantically through my notes, listening to Romeo and Benvolio making their speeches before the party scene and waiting for Daisy to dance as part of the revels and then float across to where I was standing. There is an awful lot of murder in *Romeo and Juliet*—although I had been hearing the play for weeks, somehow it had never seemed so obvious to me as it did tonight. That is the funny thing about becoming familiar with something: it begins to wash over you. You do not really hear or see what is there, only what you are expecting.

That is where we had gone wrong with this case, where we had almost tripped up for good. We had been expecting certain things. We had become *too* familiar with the Rue, and with the people in it—we had allowed ourselves to be dazzled by the front-of-house glamour, and not looked beyond that, to the paste and paint and hollow spaces that make up a theatre.

Daisy sailed offstage in a cloud of glory. She seemed to hold her head even higher than usual—she really did look like quite a different person. I should never have thought that this beautiful girl, with huge dark eyes and red lips, was my Daisy—not until she wrinkled up her nose at me and hissed, "Don't stare, Hazel! When you do, I'm convinced something's wrong with me!"

People never really change, I thought. *Not in how they act, not in the way they move without thinking.* I drew in my breath and flicked to two particular pages in my notes.

"*Hands!*" I whispered to Daisy. "The wrong hand! Here, look!"

"You *star!*" cried Daisy. "And I have new evidence as well. I managed to look at Theresa's book before I went on and the good news is"—she lowered her voice and drew closer to me as Lysander came striding by—"there *is* enough time! Quite ages. As soon as we stopped thinking that the murder had to have been committed *after* a certain moment, everything makes perfect sense. It's all about entrances and exits! *One* character is offstage in Act Two long enough for the person playing that part to commit murder, and *only* one character. Our hypothesis is not just a hypothesis anymore."

Robin Stevens

My heart was pounding. It was so impossible. It felt like one of Daisy's wilder stories. But it was the one solution that made sense of everything that had happened. We had to stop assuming, and think only of the absolute facts.

"Think of those white threads, Hazel, and the footprint! Think of the dress! Really, the answer was staring us in the face all along. Now, my idea from earlier still holds. I think the murderer will try to strike tonight, during the play, and that will give us the final piece of evidence we need to give to the Inspector and solve the case."

"But what if—what if we can't stop the next crime?" I asked.

"Well, then I shall never forgive myself," said Daisy briskly. "But I should *always* forgive you. I know you think that every dreadful thing that happens in the world is because you didn't stop it, but the truth is that dreadful things would happen anyway, even if you had never been born. The excellent fact is that you *were* born, and that means that you have the chance to make the world a slightly less horrid place. You mustn't think of all the people who've died. Remember all the people who never got murdered because you caught their killers. Well—you and me. Mostly me, really. But, of course, also you."

"Why do you always ruin the nice things you say?" I cried.

"Because I'm English," said Daisy. "I should think you'd understand that by now. Come on, Watson. There's a murderer to reveal, and the play must go on until that moment. Are you ready?"

I gulped. "Ready," I said. "I think so, anyway."

"Excellent," said Daisy. "If you're not sure, then you're ready. Constant vigilance, and Detective Society forever!"

The play spooled on—and I remember it now less like theatre and more like a talking picture. Everything seemed rather distant, or perhaps that was just my brain. I was trying to see everywhere at once, with the sick, horrible fear that if I closed my eyes and turned away, for even a moment, the blow would fall.

But Act Two passed (I saw what Daisy meant about timings), then Act Three. Martita was acting with all her might. I really believed she *was* Juliet, clever, determined, isolated Juliet, planning the most daring trick to escape her fate (I thought Juliet would have been an excellent Detective Society member). I realized then that, truly, the answer had been in front of us all along, in the lines I spoke, and in the character of Juliet and in her clever plan. Romeo ruins it, of course, in the play—but, in real life, our murderer had almost got away with their trick.

Lysander was a handsome Romeo, but for all that I could

not imagine being swept off my feet by him. I remembered how he had grabbed hold of Daisy in the corridor and knew that the true side of him was far nastier than his play-self.

Daisy nudged me. "That's my sensible Hazel," she whispered. For a moment I wondered whether I had said what I was thinking out loud, but then I knew I did not need to.

Of course, I knew that Daisy was imagining running away to Mantua just like the star-crossed lovers do—but with Juliet, not Romeo. It was a different sort of story to think about, and I could not see how it could end happily. But then I realized that I knew the answer, after all. Miss Crompton and Theresa might look old and rather dumpy, and not at all romantic, but I supposed that once they had been young and perhaps even as pretty as Daisy and Martita. Theirs could not be quite the same as Uncle Felix and Aunt Lucy's life together, for they had to keep putting on a polite pretense of only being partners in business, but all the same they had not managed badly.

I supposed that was what this case should have shown me: that sometimes the story really being told is not the one you think you are watching.

Act Four, and Juliet was about to fake her own death. Inigo as Friar Lawrence was striding about on the stage, declaiming mightily. He held up his little vial, so that the lights of the stage sparked off it and threw out green dazzles into the audience.

Robin Stevens

Arsenic green, I thought . . . and I suddenly had a sort of detective premonition. I remembered the basket of props I had seen, and suddenly I realized that I knew what we had been waiting for. *This* was the final act of the murderer's plan.

"Daisy!" I cried. "*The props!*"

"Martita!" gasped Daisy, spinning round. "Martita. *Martita!*"

"What is it, Daisy?" asked Martita. She was waiting in the wings, adjusting her skirts and composing her face before she stepped onstage.

"Don't drink the vial of sleeping potion," babbled Daisy. "Just pretend! And, er, don't kiss Lysander, either."

"Daisy, are you all right?" asked Martita curiously. "You know I have to drink the potion. And Lysander kisses *me*. It's part of the play."

"Um, I know, but please don't!" said Daisy. "We think— we think some of the props have been tampered with!"

"Please listen to her!" I agreed. "Honestly! I saw some-one with them who shouldn't have had them—I think it was *the murderer!*"

Martita stared at us both. I could tell she did not know whether or not to laugh. "But—" she began. "I—"

"Juliet!" hissed Theresa. "Get on, silly girl, it's you!"

And Martita rushed onto the stage.

Daisy and I stared at each other. Juliet was speaking with

Friar Lawrence. She was taking the bottle. Would she listen to us? What could we do?"

"I know what I told you earlier, but we have to stop the play," said Daisy.

"We can't!" I said. "We won't be able to prove who did it!"

"Yes, but if we don't, Martita will actually *die*!" said Daisy. "That's far worse."

Onstage, Martita held up the bottle, lifted it to her lips—and I saw that she had kept the stopper firmly in place. Not a drop of liquid went into her mouth. Daisy sagged with relief, and Martita slumped onto her bed in Juliet's play-sleep. Her parents and Nurse gathered round her, weeping, and then it was Romeo's scene.

Daisy clutched at me as Lysander went striding past us.

"Lysander!" she cried. "Excuse me—Lysander! Don't drink the poison!"

"Don't be an idiot," said Lysander calmly, and pushed by her onto the stage.

Juliet was taken to her tomb. Paris and his Page followed her, grieving (Daisy freshly made up and in her Page's jerkin, posing for the audience), and Paris fought with Romeo in the churchyard. In her tomb Juliet lay as still as marble, and Romeo knelt over her. He held out his own bottle—and, once again, glass flashed in the stage lights.

"Daisy!" I cried. "Quick! He's not going to listen!"

Robin Stevens

And, of course, Daisy acted. She threw herself forward onto the stage.

"STOP THE PLAY!" she shrieked. "DON'T DRINK A DROP!"—just as Lysander threw back his head and drank down the liquid in the little bottle.

There was a moment of awed hush. Then, somewhere in the audience, a seat thumped back as someone leaped to their feet.

"CALL AN AMBULANCE!" screamed Daisy. "He's been poisoned! And STOP THAT WOMAN! Don't let her leave! SHE'S THE MURDERER!"

VIII

I have never before heard such a noise. It was louder than the roar of hundreds of Deepdean girls rushing out of Prayers, louder even than the hum and buzz of a Hong Kong or London street.

The roar of two thousand throats drawing breath together, the hammer blow of two thousand seats closing in unison—and Daisy's shout, seemingly echoing through the air as it was taken up by hundreds of voices.

"Stop her! Stop her! Murderer!"

And, threading through it all, a woman was screaming, far away in the darkness, screaming and screaming in fury. The sound gave me chills all up and down my spine—and so did the scene on the stage.

Martita had sat up from her play-sleep and was kneeling over Lysander, her long dark hair hanging down around him as she shook him and slapped his face. Lysander's cheeks had gone a strange gray color and his whole body twitched.

I remembered Miss Bell's body, the way I had touched it and simply known she was dead. I remembered the horror of seeing Mr. Curtis convulsing—and I knew then that even though Lysander, like Mr. Curtis, was an utterly nasty person, he did not deserve to die. I knew too that there might still be time to save him. So I opened my mouth, stared out into the thick, panicked, heaving darkness, and then shouted out a new line, one I had not practiced.

"WE NEED A DOCTOR! PLEASE! HELP!"

It turns out that there are an awful lot of doctors in a London theatre. Five men and one woman came rushing up onto the stage and made a dramatic circle around Lysander, feeling his pulse and paddling their hands over him. Lysander groaned and convulsed.

"Belladonna!" cried one of them, sniffing the empty vial. "It's belladonna poisoning! This man needs pilocarpine at once!"

Daisy had run off the stage into the stalls, as had Martita. I turned and raced after them, coming upon them halfway down the aisle, in a crush of people all staring at the woman who had been screaming. She was now quiet, lying on the ground in the grip of none other than a rather flustered, rather annoyed-looking Inspector Priestley.

"Hello!" said Daisy. "How do you always manage to know exactly where you need to be?"

"It's a skill," said the Inspector shortly.

Inspector Priestley has been at the close of so many of our cases, ready to lay his hands on the murderer and take them safely away. Perhaps that is why he gives me such a calming feeling. Now, even though everyone was shouting and upset, I knew that things would be quite all right in the end.

I had to look twice at the woman he was holding. She was dark-haired and staidly dressed, with a round, powdered face. I got a shock, because this was the new dresser, the one I had seen hurrying away with the basket of props. How had she managed to appear here? But her pale face was contorted with rage, her mouth open to show cheeks packed with cotton wool. Her dark hair was slipping slightly to one side, its pins losing their grip in her struggle. I could see blond hair underneath and I knew that furious expression.

"A wig!" I cried. "It's Rose Tree in disguise!"

Daisy was glaring at her. "An actress by her very nature is a mistress of disguise," she said. "It's like Lysander said. Rose has played two parts already, and this is her third."

"I'm not Rose Tree!" cried the woman in a Cockney accent. "Rose is dead!"

"You aren't!" cried Daisy. "You're Susan Brown, also known as Rose Tree, and you have been impersonating Annie Joy. We didn't see what you were doing *at first*, but in the end we did. You reckoned without the Detective Society, Rose, and that was your greatest mistake!"

Robin Stevens

"What's the Detective Society?" a woman in the crowd whispered to her husband.

"That's what the police are calling themselves these days, I should think," her husband replied.

"They wish!" cried Daisy heatedly. "Remember that name! One day it will be very famous indeed!"

And, over the chaos and shouting and shoving, Daisy and I smiled at each other.

"All right," said the Inspector. "Let us unravel this knot."

We were all crammed into Miss Crompton's office. When I say crammed, I am not exaggerating—there was Miss Crompton herself, Theresa, Martita, Inigo, Simon, Daisy, Uncle Felix, George, Alexander, Aunt Lucy, the Inspector, and me. In Miss Crompton's big mahogany chair sat Rose Tree—in handcuffs.

She glared around at us, and I could see now that it was Rose. Although her charm was dimmed and her face was rather bedraggled, I recognized the tilt of her little nose, the dimple in her cheek, the curl of her ear.

I wondered how on earth we had ever been fooled— but then I remembered how Daisy's costumes had almost tricked me when she practiced at the flat, and I realized that it was not so surprising. If Daisy, who I know as well as I know myself, could seem to be a different person, then

Rose would have little difficulty pretending to be Annie, a dresser everyone in the company had known for only a few weeks.

People see what they expect to see, and someone's personality is as much in the clothes they wear, how they walk and sit and stand, as in their actual features. And when the person Rose had been impersonating was as exaggerated as Annie, with her dark, kohl-rimmed eyes and bright clothes and curly hair, it would have been easy. All Rose needed to do was curl her own fair hair like Annie's (I ought to have realized from the curling iron that we found in Annie's accommodation that Annie's curls were not natural), and paint her face, and make sure she stood out of bright light. All we had seen was the character of Annie, not Annie herself.

"Is this appropriate for children?" asked Inigo.

"I should think they ought to be allowed to stay in this case," said Miss Crompton. "They uncovered the truth, after all."

"But what about those ones?" said Inigo, gesturing at Alexander and George. "I'm sure I haven't seen them before."

"They're our friends!" I said quickly. "Oh, please let them stay!"

"I certainly have no issue with it, as long as it does not get out to the press," said Inspector Priestley. "They have all done important detective work."

Uncle Felix sighed and screwed his monocle into his eye forcefully. "I suppose this is my fault," he said. "I let them come back here, at great cost, and, although I dislike saying it, they have done me proud."

"Now," said Inspector Priestley, "I gather from what you have said that Miss Tree murdered Miss Joy sometime during the evening she faked her own disappearance, and assumed her identity. Miss Tree then apparently faked Miss Joy's fall from Westminster Bridge the next night. I know from speaking to Jim and Theresa that she was hired from an agency yesterday as the new dresser under the name of Nicole Patton. I have made enquiries and discovered that she has been living in a boardinghouse south of the river for the last few days. But I don't know exactly how she managed the whole performance, and I would not have put together Rose, Annie, and Nicole without Hazel and Daisy's help."

"I know how she did it!" said Daisy. "We do, don't we, Hazel? Oh, isn't this fun! We've got a captive audience and we can finally tell them exactly what happened at the Rue!"

Robin Stevens

T he one mistake we all made was to assume that nothing could have happened until *after* the argument between Rose and Martita," I said, before Daisy could rush in. "We thought that was the last time Rose was seen and heard alive by anyone but her killer— but that wasn't true at all, because *Rose was never killed.* After all, how did we *know* that the body down the well was Rose's? We all thought it was, because it was wearing a white nightdress and had a cut and bound foot, and because Rose had gone missing. But we heard the coroner say that her face and hands were swollen and unrecognizable because of the way she had been stuck upside down in the well. He identified her by her costume, and her general height and weight. He *assumed*, and so did everyone else."

"But!" cried Daisy. "What if it wasn't Rose down the well? What if it was someone else entirely? Annie Joy, the dresser, was similar in build to Rose, and they both had similar-colored hair. Annie's was curly—but her curls were ironed in with curlers. Annie wore heavy makeup and gorgeous, colorful clothes—a good actress like Rose could make herself up like her, put on her clothes, and fake her way of speaking and moving. Likewise, in one of Rose's costumes, with her makeup done like Rose's and her curls waterlogged, she wouldn't look like Annie Joy anymore. She might even be mistaken for Rose Tree.

"But why should Rose need to play such an elaborate trick? Why did she want Annie Joy dead, and why would she fake her own death to do it? Well, we all know that she has a tragic past. Her parents died when Rose was thirteen, in 1927. They died in a boating accident on holiday in Southend, and Rose was discovered by a local girl washed up in a nearby bay, barely alive. Now, this story is supposed to be a very sad one, and for a while we believed that's what it really was. But again, we realized that there might be another side to the story. What if the tragedy was actually a case of foul play? What if Rose's parents had been murdered? We found out that Rose's father had been a reverend, and we assumed that someone must have killed him to cover up some past sin. We knew from the papers that Annie's family was from Southend, and from Annie's diary, and from the things she said, we began to wonder whether Annie had been mixed up in what

Robin Stevens

happened. What if she was the girl who had found Rose that day, and what if she knew crucial details about this past crime?

"We were right about that part—but we kept on thinking that someone else was involved in the accident, someone who now wanted Rose and Annie dead. Again we were assuming. We were making things far too complicated. Because what if . . . oh, tell them, Hazel."

"What if there *was* no other person involved in the accident?" I asked. I saw Alexander's mouth open in amazement and grinned at him without even meaning to. "What if we weren't looking for *another* suspect at all? What if the killer was the only survivor?"

"What if," Daisy pressed on, "*Rose* shoved her parents off their boat and then swam safely to shore, where she was found by Annie—who was sitting on the beach that day? Remember, Annie told us how she never liked to go swimming because she didn't want to get her bathing costume wet. Annie was a nice person—she would have helped Rose without suspecting foul play. But, even so, there might have been something in Rose's story that didn't seem quite right. Annie kept a diary religiously. She would have written her questions down there, and thought about it again and again over the years.

"We know from a more recent diary that Annie saw Rose

again, as an adult, in the production of *Happy Families*, and spoke to her to remind her of their connection. She probably did it innocently, but it must have been dreadful for Rose, just as her career was taking off, to see the one person who might guess the truth about that day. I suspect she suggested that Annie apply for the *Romeo and Juliet* job to keep an eye on her. But when rehearsals started, she realized that it wasn't enough.

"You see, Annie was a talker. She chattered all the time about everything—and she was beginning to talk more and more about dangerous memories. She mentioned childhood and summer holidays quite a lot. Of course, we all generally ignored her—but would that have gone on forever? What if someone had listened? What if someone else began to ask questions?

"Rose must have been terrified. She was now stuck in a play with someone who knew, or at least suspected, her darkest secret—someone who could end her career. And we saw that Annie was becoming uncomfortable with Rose's behavior. So Rose hatched a plan: she was going to murder Annie and then pretend to be her. She used the fact that Martita and Simon hated her to send herself threats, and organize those awful posters. She wanted to get the idea into everyone's heads that Rose was in danger and was going to be shoved down

Robin Stevens

a well—so that when it really happened people would be expecting the body to be Rose. Then she went about planning the murder."

"It wasn't hard for her to look like Annie," I put in. "Daisy's already talked about that. But how to get Annie into the well, looking just like Rose?"

"Hah!" said Daisy, in great excitement. "Well, the key to that was the fact that Annie created *two* copies of each outfit in the play. There were *two* nightdresses in the Rue Theatre, not one—and the only way the murder, and the evidence we found, would make sense would be if *both* Rose and Annie wore white nightdresses when they went into the well room that evening. Perhaps Rose suggested to Annie that they play a trick. They would both put on a nightdress and make their faces up like Juliet, and go down to the well room, to see if they could give someone—Lysander, probably—a fright. That's why we found white threads from a Juliet dress on the way to the well room, and again on the well-room ladder. We couldn't understand why we only found white fibers and the print of a bare foot, and nothing left by the murderer—but, if the murderer was dressed in the same clothes as the victim, it makes sense!"

"Rose set up her dressing room to look as though she was gone, then asked Annie to meet her down in the well room while everyone else was onstage," I put in. "During Act Two, Scenes Three and Four, there's a long stretch where Juliet doesn't appear, and that's what Rose used. She had already made sure to have trouble with her dress onstage in the balcony scene, so everyone would see her and Annie together and be reminded that they were two very different people. Annie was beginning to worry about Rose, but she was still so trusting that she would have gone along with it. Rose could have said that Lysander had asked to meet her in the well room at the beginning of Scene Four, when Romeo has time offstage.

"Once Rose and Annie were in the well room, Rose attacked. She was little, like Annie, but she could have choked her with the gauze from her foot. Then she cut Annie's foot, bound it up with the gauze, opened the well, and shoved her straight down.

"She managed it all quite neatly, but she did get her dress a little dirty as she did so. That's why the dress in Wardrobe was wet and stained when we saw it the next day, because Rose had to wash it. After she was done, she rushed away upstairs to tidy herself before she arrived onstage for her tantrum at the beginning of Scene Five. Then she flounced off to her dressing room. That's where she had the argument with Martita that everyone else heard—seeming to prove that Rose was still alive at five past nine. After that was over, she waited until the

Robin Stevens

noises outside had died down before she crept upstairs to Wardrobe.

"She got changed there into Annie's outfit, wearing a curly blond wig for that evening, and made her face up to look like Annie too. That was when she went down to see Jim, to put Rose's name in the sign-out book and help establish Annie's alibi."

"Then, of course, when the alarm was raised, she helped hunt for Rose, before giving up with everyone else and going home to Annie's accommodation," said Daisy. "She came back in the next day, continuing to make everyone think that Annie was alive and Rose dead. She was hoping that the body would be found fairly quickly, so she could move on to the next part of her plan—we thought it odd that Rose's coat and handbag had been hidden so badly, but it makes sense if Rose was *hoping* they would be discovered, along with the body. Those were her most dangerous hours, because anyone might have looked at her closely enough to notice. But she kept in corners and away from direct light, pretending she was afraid of the murderer, and chattering in exactly the same way as Annie did—and no one was any the wiser. What we ought to have noticed was that Annie had suddenly switched hands, from left to right—but of course we didn't think of it at the time. She didn't quite manage to remember Annie's background perfectly, either. She said she had a sister, but Annie had a brother, and she pretended that she didn't know the details of Rose's trag-edy, which Annie certainly would have done."

"That night, she had to fake her own death—again!" I went on. "She left the theatre at the usual time, went back to Annie's accommodation and then out again, wearing Annie's brightest clothes and carrying her incriminating diary entries from 1927 and the last month. Annie must have written about Rose, and how she was starting to sus-pect Rose really did kill her parents. She made sure she was seen several times—bumping into someone, asking for a light—and then when she walked onto Westminster Bridge she threw the hat, coat, and handbag, with a con-venient note inside it, over the side. We really ought to have thought about that coat—after all, coats don't fall off dead bodies! Finding it on its own would only make sense if someone had thrown it in. She must have tossed the diary entries into a bin, perhaps burning them with that cigarette.

"Rose came out on the other side of the bridge an entirely different and much less noticeable person. She must have been hoping that another body of a similar height and build would be found in the estuary soon—it does happen quite often—and this time she was luckier than she could have expected."

"And that's it!" Daisy finished triumphantly, turning to Rose. "Well, apart from one thing. The birthmark."

Robin Stevens

"This is all nonsense," said Rose, who had been listening to our speech with a very sour, angry expression. "All of it!"

"What do you mean, the birthmark?" asked the Inspector.

"Well, I think you should ask your coroner to look at the body from the well again," said Daisy. "Because I *think* there should be a birthmark on the foot, just underneath the rather large cut. Rose, you had to cut yourself, and the body, because Annie had a birthmark on her right foot. If the coroner had seen it, he might have marked it down as an identifying feature, helping to prove that the body wasn't Rose Tree's. Am I right?"

"Oh—BLAST!" cried Rose. "Blast you! You've thought of everything. I told Annie that Lysander was frightening me. I told her that I wanted her to help me give him a scare, and if she did we could be proper friends. That's all she wanted: someone to talk to. Of all the people who could have found me that day in Southend, it was her. She was so kind, and I was so tired. I said some stupid things; things that didn't fit with the story I told the police.

"I thought she must have forgotten, since I never heard anything—but then she came to see me after *Happy Families* one night, and I realized that she remembered all of it. When I landed Juliet, I made sure that she was given the dresser's job, so I could keep an eye on her. But she kept on *talking*! I couldn't shut her up. I got cross with her once, and she was so upset, but that made her talk even more. So

I decided that there was nothing for it. She'd have to die."

It gave me chills, how matter-of-fact she was about it.

"Your *parents*," I said. "Your *friend*!"

"My *parents*!" said Rose. "Why should I have cared about them for a moment? My father might have seemed respectable, but he was the opposite. He never let me do anything I wanted, and he hit me. He wouldn't let me act, or dance. He told me I was wicked for loving those things. And my mother just—watched. She never helped me because she loved *him*. When I shoved her over the side of the boat, he went in after her, even though neither of them could swim. It was easy.

"And Annie *wasn't* my friend. She was a stupid woman who didn't mean anything. I'd have gone away for a year and then come back onto the London stage with a new name. I could have started a new career. Lysander was beginning to suspect, so he had to go too, and Martita couldn't be allowed to steal my spotlight. None of them mattered. It was all supposed to be *EASY*!"

She made a lunge at me, out of her chair. Daisy and Alexander both stepped in front of me, and Uncle Felix stepped in front of Daisy. Inspector Priestley let his hand drop heavily on Rose's shoulder.

"I think we need to be getting you down to the station, don't we?" he said conversationally.

Robin Stevens

"Just you wait for the trial," said Rose, glaring at all of us. "I shall give the performance of my life."

"Indeed," said the Inspector. "You'll need to. Daisy, Hazel—I salute you. This was a fiendish case."

"It was, wasn't it?" said Daisy happily. "Just look how we're improving!"

We are back at Uncle Felix and Aunt Lucy's flat. I think Uncle Felix is really quite proud of us. He took us out for a bang-up dinner last night, and he even told us about one of his cases at work. He did it in a very general way, but it is the most he has ever trusted us, and Daisy is still shining with joy about it.

Aunt Lucy was rather quiet at dinner, but after we arrived back home she came into our room as we were preparing for bed.

"Girls," she said, sitting down on my bed and gesturing for us to sit down opposite her. "I want to congratulate you. I must say that you continue to impress me. You are far more resourceful than I was at your age, and I am very proud of you. I have spoken to Felix, and we agree that the details of this business do not need to be shared with either of your parents, or with your school—"

"Oh, *thank* you!" I said, for I had been feeling anxious about that.

"Now," said Aunt Lucy, "even my husband has come to understand that you are not likely to give up this detection business of yours. I think that is perfectly sensible, for you are clearly very good at it. But I do want to say one thing: solving mysteries will only get harder, the older you are. You are looking less and less like little girls, and that will make detection difficult in future. Everyone has opinions about how women should behave, and who they should be."

"I shall be so glamorous that no one will have time to worry about anything else," said Daisy haughtily. "That's what Rose showed us, didn't she? That the disguise is all that matters."

"I am not *sure* that's what you ought to take away from this case," said Aunt Lucy. "But I suppose that is true."

"I don't think I can be glamorous," I said nervously.

"You'd be surprised," said Aunt Lucy. "But you do not have to be anything you don't want to be. All I can do is help you to prepare for all the challenges you will face. Daisy, some more work on disguise is in order. And, Hazel, if you would prefer to blend in, then we shall just have to work on making you appear as dull as possible. Codes are fearfully dull. Let's keep training you in that. You never know when it may come in useful."

• • •

That night, Daisy and I could not sleep with excitement. Instead, we got into our beds, took out the remains of Daisy's birthday tuck box as a midnight feast, and talked through the case. We talked for so long that I fell asleep and woke up to find Daisy still chattering, as birds began to sing in the spindly trees outside the flat, and the sky turned gray and faded at the edges.

We talked until breakfast, and after breakfast (heaps of buttered eggs and hot cocoa, served by a very cheerful-looking Bridget) I sat down to write all that last part up while the details were still fresh in my mind.

I was still writing when a procession of visitors began to arrive.

Miss Crompton, Inigo, and Simon came first, just after ten o'clock, to thank us on behalf of the Rue. They made the flat's living room seem very small suddenly—I think that was mostly because of Inigo's cloak, which today was sky blue.

"Congratulations," he said in his sonorous boom. "Excellent work. Who would have thought that Miss Tree would become . . . so enamored of her role that she would copy Juliet and fake her own death?"

"I gravely misunderstood her," said Miss Crompton. "I thought she was dramatic, but not murderous. And to think she killed that poor girl Annie, and tried to kill Martita and Lysander out of sheer spite! It's dreadful. Luckily, Lysander seems to have a strong constitution. He's recovering already, and claiming that he knew all along who the murderer was, which I don't entirely believe."

I thought about Lysander's words, and wondered.

"Will the play close?" I asked anxiously.

"Certainly not," said Miss Crompton. "All this death has been wonderful for our box office. We shall probably run for six months after the press we've had. Everyone wants to see it. In fact . . ." She looked at Inigo.

"We have decided to cast Romeo as we had originally intended," said Inigo, beaming enormously. "Simon will act opposite Martita—let the critics say what they will. The public will still come—it's more than time."

Simon, who had been rather subdued, suddenly beamed. He stood up straighter, and he nodded at Inigo, who clapped him on the shoulder.

"It is indeed," said Miss Crompton. "And, of course, you are both welcome to continue your roles until you return to school next week. It's the least we can offer."

"Very gracious of you," said Daisy, beaming. "We accept. Don't we, Hazel?"

I thought. "Yes please," I said. "We do."

And I realized that I meant it. Acting was not so bad, after all. It was only playing someone else, instead of playing myself.

Simon hung back as Miss Crompton and Inigo left the room.

"Martita's told me that you two ... *know*," he whispered to us after they had gone. "I just want to thank you— for not saying anything. It means *a lot*."

"We never would," I said fervently. "Never!"

"Honor bright," agreed Daisy, blushing.

"I kept on wanting to come out with it," said Simon. "But I was so scared that they'd get the wrong idea and arrest me for murder. I couldn't decide which was worse—I mean, both would have gotten me thrown in prison and then sent back to America. I'm just so grateful that I never had to choose. I'm in your debt, kids, forevermore."

Martita arrived next, and Daisy, who had been bubbling over with pride before, suddenly went very shy and rather pale. She hung back next to the armchair, so I had to be the one to speak to Martita.

"I really am grateful to the two of you," said Martita. "I couldn't understand why I seemed so guilty. It was as though everyone was pointing a finger at me."

"It was all Daisy," I said firmly. "I mean—I *hoped* it wasn't you, but it was Daisy who was sure. She's believed in you all the way through the case. It's because of her that everything turned out all right."

"Did you really?" asked Martita, her hair swinging round as she turned to Daisy. "Always?"

"Er," said Daisy. "I really don't— Hazel, really—"

Robin Stevens

"It was *absolutely* Daisy," I said. "And she was *absolutely* sure. She's the one you ought to thank."

"Well then," said Martita, sparkling, "I thank you, Daisy Wells." And she bowed low, like a courtly Shakespearean gentleman, took Daisy's unresisting hand in hers, and kissed it.

Once she had left the room, Daisy sat down very suddenly on the side of the armchair.

"Hazel," she said in a low voice. "My life will *never* get better than this precise moment. Never. Not if I live to a hundred!"

"Of course it will," I said, nudging her. "We haven't even set up our detective agency yet."

But Daisy shook her head.

We really are to go back to Deepdean next week. We had a telephone conversation with Kitty, with Beanie and Lavinia jostling behind her on the telephone in Matron's office.

"Come home!" cried Kitty.

"Please!" shrilled Beanie.

"Don't hurry!" growled Lavinia.

"Ignore that idiot—we miss you!" Kitty went on. "It hasn't been the same without the two of you. Why, school is awfully dull! Not a murder, or a kidnap, or anything! Lavinia hasn't even run away once."

"We'll be back for the second half of term," said Daisy. "Worse luck!"

"It isn't worse luck!" I called down the line. "We miss you too!"

"I suppose we do," Daisy conceded. "But do try to have something interesting for us, will you? Could you arrange a nice murder?"

"We'll do our best," said Kitty. "Oh bother! Matron wants us to go. See you soon! *Detective Society forever!*"

"Half a term!" said Daisy to me. "What could possibly happen in half a term? It's just exams and Speech Day!"

"You never know!" I said.

The doorbell has just rung again.

Alexander and George are here, bubbling over with excitement about the case. We are to be allowed to go out with them for ices to talk it through—and we have not even had to promise not to detect any crimes while we are gone. Bridget winked at us as she said this. I think she has forgiven me—or at least I hope so.

George offered his arm to Daisy, and she took it, beaming at him. They really do seem to understand each other in the most mysterious way. If this was a story, they would be in love with each other.

And, if this was a story, Alexander—well.

He smiled down at me, his dimple showing. "You were

Robin Stevens

jolly good in the play," he said. "I clapped for you—did you hear? I'll miss you when we all go back to school. Promise you won't stop writing?"

Then he held out his hand, and I took it, and . . . I am beginning to think that even if Alexander has not quite stopped loving Daisy, I might have begun to step out of the shadow she casts in his mind.

"Come on!" cried Daisy. "Teatime!"

And off the four of us went together, into the bright spring day.

Daisy's
Guide to the Rue
Theatre

My Detective Society vice president and secretary Hazel has done a most excellent job writing up our new case—and I do not say that lightly. She is most definitely improving. But it has come to my attention that some of the words she uses may not be obvious to those people who are not actresses like Hazel and me. Below is my list of words that you ought to learn if you want to go on the stage.

Aesthetic—a man who is the very opposite of Athletic, fond of nice clothes and beautiful art. Aesthetes wear their hair long and sometimes put green carnations in their button holes. Bertie and his friend Harold are excellent examples of Aesthetes.

Avant-garde—something dazzlingly new and exciting.

The Bard—a theatrical word for Shakespeare, the man who wrote *Romeo and Juliet.* He has been dead for ages.

Blocking—something actors and actresses do when rehearsing a play. It means learning their movements on the stage.

Boardinghouse—rather like the boardinghouse Hazel and I live in at Deepdean School for Girls, but this sort is for grown-ups who are actors, and who can't afford their own London flats yet.

Bourgeois—a word that means posh.

Brick—a good sort of person, one who can always be depended on in a crisis.

Cadge—this word means to borrow or steal.

Camiknickers—a word for the undergarments that some grown-up ladies wear.

Cow us—this phrase is another way of saying frighten us. It has nothing to do with cows.

Cravat—a sort of loose tie that artistic men droop around their necks.

Eau de Nil—a sort of light green color.

Ewer—a pitcher used to keep water in.

Exeat—a word for a special weekend when pupils at boarding schools are allowed to go and stay with their parents or their friends.

Fish paste—a sort of spreadable puree of very strong-tasting fish, like sardines or anchovies. I think it's delicious!

Flies—the rigging and pulley system above a stage in a theatre, where the lights and things hang.

Flat—a painted bit of set that can be pulled on- and offstage.

Gadding about—being silly.

Iron curtain—a metal safety screen that unrolls behind an ordinary theatre curtain to keep fire from spreading through a theatre.

Jerkin—a sort of old-fashioned waistcoat.

Newel post—the posts at the top and bottom and turns of staircases, sometimes with knobbly bits on top.

Off book—when actors have learned their lines and don't need to look at their scripts anymore in rehearsal.

On book—when actors are still learning lines and holding scripts as they rehearse.

Paper tiger—something that seems frightening but is really all just show, like a tiger made out of drawing paper.

Pash—a sort of love that one schoolgirl has for another. It is not meant to mean anything or be real, but I think that is silly, because the truth is that sometimes it is.

Pea-souper—a very heavy London fog that feels as thick as soup to walk through.

People—sometimes "people" means "parents." So when you say "I am going to my friend's people," you mean that you are staying with their parents.

Prompt—someone whispering lines to an actor who has forgotten what to say next.

Proscenium arch—the big arch that frames the stage in theatres.

RADA—a school for actors in London.

RP—this means "received pronunciation" and is the way that everyone on the BBC speaks.

Shrimps—the smallest Deepdean pupils.

Spiffing—marvelous or fantastic.

Squash—a sweet concentrated juice that you dilute with water and drink in a tall glass.

Stage-door Johnny—a man who likes to wait outside stage doors for actresses they are in love with. I think this is very odd behavior.

Stalls—the stalls are the seats in the main part of the theatre, the ones just in front of the stage.

Tuck—sweets and cakes, kept in a tuck box under your bed. You can keep anything in your tuck box, but make sure never to keep illegal things in there because Matron will find them straight away. It is a very stupid hiding place.

AUTHOR'S NOTE AND ACKNOWLEDGMENTS

This book began when I toured the Palace Theatre in London in 2016. I saw the under-stage corridors, the props department, the wardrobe rooms . . . and, at the very bottom of the building, I saw the well. I took one look at it and I knew I had to use it in a story.

I love going to the theatre, and I love theatrical murder mysteries, but all the same I'm not a theatrical expert. Every correct detail in this story comes from Ngaio Marsh's *Enter a Murderer*, and from my theatrical consultants Kriss Buddle, Anne Miller, and Sam Cable. Every mistake is mine.

Doing historical research is always exciting, but during my research for this book I discovered three people who particularly informed this story, and reminded me once again of how diverse British history really is. Lilian Baylis was a no-nonsense London woman who pretty much single-handedly turned the Old Vic Theatre into *the* place to see Shakespeare in the UK in the 1920s and 1930s, Ira Aldridge was a Black actor who became one of the first true stars of the Victorian stage, and Paul Robeson was a Black actor and singer who traveled from America to light up the London theatre scene in the 1930s. I love basing my fictional characters on real historical figures, and you'll recognize parts of all three in Frances, Inigo, and Simon, though of course they are my own fictional creations. I also read about a 1930s performance of *Romeo and Juliet* where a young woman was chosen for the part of the Nurse. I liked that idea so much that I decided to use it in this story—I know that Martita is rather young, even to play a young Nurse, but stranger casting choices have been made in real life.

In this book I also wanted to write about one of the less-nice parts of British history: the fact that, until 1967, it was a crime for two men to be in love with each other. You would literally be thrown in jail if you were caught. Lots of clever, good, kind people, including the mathematician Alan Turing, had their lives ruined just for being who they were. (Oddly, there was never an actual law against two women being in love, although it was frowned upon in the same way.) Although the sixties seem like a long time ago, it's important to remember that horrible, prejudiced laws are also much more recent. When I was growing up in the 1990s, I never read about characters like Simon or Daisy in a book—there was a law called Section 28 in the UK that banned anyone from telling children about LGBTQ+ people or relationships. I am so happy that this law was repealed in 2003 so that I can write the books I do, and I am so happy that now there are laws in both the UK and the US that say that couples like Frances and Theresa can get married. There is still far to go—it is easy to be frightened and intolerant, and hard to overcome prejudice—but we can each help get there by remembering that we are all just the same, despite our apparent differences. All any of us want is to be loved.

I chose *Romeo and Juliet* as the play in this story for three reasons. First, because I went to school in the UK, and Shakespeare is for some reason about a third of the English curriculum. By the end of high school I could recite pretty much the entire play, and I thought that I might as well put that knowledge to use. Second, because there is lots of murder in it. I think Shakespeare would have been a murder mystery writer if he'd been alive today. And third, because when I was beginning to plan this book, a girl called Poppy asked me to set a mystery during a production of *Romeo and Juliet*. I don't usually take your story ideas, because they are yours, not mine, and so you own them—but Poppy's email was exactly the prompt I needed at that moment. Thank you, Poppy. If you want to find out more about *Romeo and Juliet*, you should watch the Baz Luhrmann film, which is very old now but still good. But please remember: I do not endorse either Romeo's OR Juliet's actions at the end of the play, and I don't think Shakespeare did either. It is not really a romance, it is a cautionary tale.

Finally, this book is a love letter to my favorite parts of London: Charing Cross Road, Soho, Trafalgar Square, the Thames, Covent Garden, Bloomsbury, and the West End.

I love this bright, hectic, bewildering city—every time I leave, I can't wait to go back.

And now, on to the thank-yous.

Thank you to Tim Thompson, Julie Cradock, and the Cheshire Police, for helping me with questions of forensics; to Derrick Pounder, who spent an hour talking to me in great detail through nasty ways in which someone might die; and to Carol Rutter, for helping me with questions about Shakespeare. Huge thank-you to Kriss Buddle, for giving up his time to patiently talk me through theatrical maps and explain to me how a theatre works. I'm pretty sure this book would not exist without him.

Thanks to my readers Kathie Booth Stevens, Anne Miller, Sam Cable, Wei Ming Kam, Charlie Morris, Gráinne Clear, Ana Brígida Paiva, Joelyn Rolston-Esdele, and Eden McKenzie-Goddard for giving me invaluable insights, and to Mariana Mouzinho and Aimée Felone for connecting me with them.

Thanks to the audience at my Imagine Festival event in spring 2018, and to my Twitter followers, for crowd-sourcing this title and strapline. You're better at titles than I am. And thanks, more broadly, to my Detective Society across the world. You really do make me proud to write my books.

Thanks to my author friends, the closest thing I have to colleagues in this strange job of ours, especially to Non Pratt, Maz Evans, Lisa Thompson, Nick Ostler, Mark Huckerby,

AUTHOR'S NOTE AND ACKNOWLEDGMENTS

and the wonderful Team Cooper collective. Thanks to my lovely non-author friends, who remind me that I am actually a real person, and to my family, especially my beloved and only niece, who came to visit and showed me exactly how Uncle Felix feels in this book.

Thanks to my brilliant Team Bunbreak, who have shown so much care and love for this series throughout the years. I was lucky enough to have two editors working on this book in the UK, Naomi Colthurst and Natalie Doherty, and I'm so grateful for both of their insights. Thanks also to my US team at Simon Kids, especially my wonderful editor, Alexa Pastor; my proofreader, Gary Sunshine; and my illustrator, Elizabeth Baddeley, who has created yet another fantastic cover. Thanks to my fiercely brilliant agent, Gemma Cooper, who always knows the right thing to do.

And finally, thanks to my partner, Dee Stevens, who makes me want to be a better person every day.

September 2022